Murder at
Bound Brook

Cape Cod Mystery

An Old-Fashioned Mystery Set on Old Cape Cod

Rick Cochran

Richard Cochran

Bound Brook Isle Publishing

Hull, Massachusetts

2017

wellfleethigh@outlook.com

Cover Design

By

Rick Cochran

ISBN-13: 978-1979134408

ISBN-10: 1979134405

Also by Rick Cochran

Wellfleet Tales

&

Wellfleet Tales II- Confessions of a Wash-Ashore

&

Bound Brook Pond: Cape Cod Mystery II

Dedication

To Ellen, my most honest critic and my greatest support.

And

My parents, Miriam & Dick, who brought us to Cape Cod. You can take the boy from the Cape, but you can't take the Cape from the boy.

Chapter 1 – February 1952

Cape Codders couldn't remember a worse month. February 16, 1952, a nor'easter blizzard stalled off the coast of New England right over the outer arm of Cape Cod. The strong winds roiled the ocean and giant waves pounded any ships unfortunate enough to be at sea. Two days later, as the storm raged and the waters seethed, two giant tankers broke in half in sixty-foot swells. Off the coast of Chatham, the surviving crewmembers of the tanker Pendleton said their prayers, hoped for the best, but expected the worst. Four brave, or crazy, young Coast Guardsmen set out from Chatham Station in a thirty-six-foot boat. Crossing the infamous Chatham Bar, the four "Coasties" doubted they would survive, let alone rescue the tanker's crew. Sometimes miracles happen, and this was one of those times. When word spread, newspapers and radio flocked to cover the dramatic rescue.

Just over a week later, a massive snowstorm hit the Cape and on February 27th in neighboring Orleans, Snow Library, a town institution, burned to the ground. This storm dumped even more snow, upwards of two feet, on the still recovering Cape Cod. Despite the library being in the center of town, the heavy snow prevented fire volunteers and equipment from getting to the rampant blaze. Only one engine could get to the inferno, but in an effort to help, snowplows accidentally cut the fire hose.

Eventually the fire department ran hoses from the salt water of the Town Cove, but by then it was too late to save the historic building. The two storms, the dramatic rescue and the library fire overpowered any other news for weeks. Wedged between the two blizzards, it was no surprise that another event was overlooked.

At dawn of February 19th in the village of Bound Brook there were no miracles or rescues. A lone figure stood on the edge of the pine woods watching another fire spread. The ancient Sea Captain's house was already fully engulfed. Sparks and ashes shot into the air, only to be extinguished by the heavy, wind-blown snow.

The towering widow's walk was the last to catch fire, finally bursting into flames like the wick on top of a giant candle. The figure raised a gloved hand to block the blowing snow, and with a last look, stepped into the woods and down the snowy path. The fire blazed red against the gray sky, but with the blizzard still at the height of its powers, it was hours before anyone noticed. It wouldn't have mattered, because Proctor was already dead.

****

As the winter blast rattled the little shack by Cape Cod Bay, Robert Caldwell, wrapped in an old quilt, huddled beside the wood stove and glanced at the dwindling stack of firewood. It was Tuesday, and the third day of this Nor'easter had almost wiped out Rob's indoor woodpile. Soon he'd have to brave the weather and make his way to the woodshed. He forced himself out of the old wooden rocker and, still wrapped in the quilt, shuffled to the south side window, the only one not encrusted with snow. He wiped the inside condensation from the sand-pocked pane of glass.

The remnants of gale force winds blew the snow in swirls. It was hard to tell whether it was falling or blowing. Rob sensed that the winds had lessened, or at least he hoped so. It was wild enough in the cottage by the shore, but he could only imagine how bad it was out on the water. The old timers said Nor'easters lasted three days, and they were usually right. Folks in the small, isolated fishing community lived and died with the weather and this February was the worst he could remember.

Rob looked around his two-room cottage. One room served as kitchen, dining room and living area. A tiny bedroom extended off the back. He had closed the knotty-pine bedroom door to save heat from the cabin's only source, the woodstove. On the coldest winter nights, like this, he slept on the combination sofa and day bed in the living area. Unlike most of the houses in Bound Brook, his tiny home had no modern conveniences: no electricity, no running water, an old fashion ice box, and only the outhouse in the back as a toilet.

The cottage sat by itself on the edge of the bay and neither power nor telephone lines had been extended that far. In this storm he was making do with the bedpan and chamber pot he kept in the bedroom, which was another good reason to keep the door closed.

He moved to the kitchen area and grabbed the handle of the water pump over the sink. He gave it a plunge, to check that it was still primed, and was rewarded with a spurt of water. Rob pumped the water every few hours to keep the pipe from freezing. It was not usually a problem, but the temperatures in this storm had plunged to the single digits, and he was taking no chances.

Standing by the sink, he surveyed his small domain. Two years before he had insulated the cabin walls, his only concession to modernizing the only home Rob had known. His mother, Roberta, had made the cabin cheerful, filled with her paintings and craft work. She was a caring mother, a blithe spirit, and a fiercely independent woman who made a meager living as a bookkeeper for several of the small businesses in the little town of Bound Brook. Her artwork and needle crafts supplemented her income, but mostly she preferred to keep her creations, or gift them to her extended Tyler family.

Rob shuffled across the hand-hooked rug to the couch that his mother had reupholstered twenty years before. Bundling up on the cozy couch, he looked at the floor. It was hard to see any of the pine flooring because Roberta's hooked rugs covered almost every inch. The beautiful floral patterns and wool material brought warmth to the cabin.

Rob remembered the labor involved in making the rugs: his mother cutting long strips from old wool clothing and scraps, then dyeing the strips with vibrant colors. He remembered the large wooden frame that had taken up most of the dining area. Stretched on the frame was an 8' x 6' burlap backing on which Roberta had traced intricate floral patterns, each flower in its own square, like the stained-glass panes in the Bound Brook Congregational Church.

He remembered watching his mother working the wool strips through the burlap with her rug hook. Gradually a beautiful blossom had emerged, then Roberta would take her shears and trim the wool flat and even. The result was a work of art, a stunning and durable rug that warmed the floor and cheered the soul.

Over a dozen of Roberta's oil paintings, seascapes, and dune scenes, hung from nails on the knotty-pine paneled walls. He was thankful his cousins had stored everything for him during the years he was away in the war.

He eyed the wool rugs and the gorgeous oil paintings. Was this why he had returned to Bound Brook four years ago? After college, the Navy, and a world war, was this what his restless soul had needed? Sure, it was partly the town of Bound Brook that had called him back. He knew almost every one of its eight hundred residents and many of its summer folk. He was still regarded with a degree of reverence as the star athlete and student who had earned a scholarship to a prestigious Ivy League school.

But it wasn't admiration he sought, Lord knows that was a tricky and fickle thing. There were a few residents of Bound Brook he loved and missed—one in particular, but most he could care less about, and some he flat out didn't like. What he sought was a connection, a link to his mother and the life they had lived together for thirteen years, until she was ripped from his life by the sea, in the same bay that she loved to paint, leaving him both a bastard and an orphan.

****

It was the same dream. He was back in Marseille, France near the end of the war. Like most dreams it made sense, and didn't make any sense at all. Rob alternated between being in uniform doing his

Navy Shore Patrol duties and dressed in a business suit being shown a palatial home. He ran through the streets of Marseille breaking up fights between drunken sailors, but he never seemed to be able to keep up with the mayhem. Before he settled one fight a new one would break out. Meanwhile, a woman's voice called his name begging for his help. Even the voice kept changing, one moment speaking French and the next calling his name with the American accent of an all too familiar voice.

Then, interspersed, he was dressed in a suit and tie, and a suave Frenchman had his arm around his shoulder, speaking words of advice in a calm and soothing tone. Then the man grew larger and the voice grew louder, until only the man's face was projected onto a movie screen. Like the Wizard of Oz, the voice boomed and threatened, "Never try to see her again!" A woman's face appeared, brunette and beautiful with pleading eyes, she begged him, "Why did you leave me?" Then the face changed, creamy skin and auburn hair, but still the same refrain, "Why did you leave me?" Then ... a different voice yelled, "Robbie."

****

He snapped awake! A moment of disorientation and then he realized he had dozed off on the couch wrapped in the quilt. His breath produced a chill fog and he knew the stove needed more wood. Stumbling to his feet he grabbed the poker and opened it. Hot embers glowed brightly, but the logs had burned away. He grabbed a handful of bark and wood chips, tossed them in and watched a flame rise, then selected three of the thickest logs left in the small pile and stacked them in the hearth.

A voice outside the cottage called, "Robbie," and he realized it was the voice that had jerked him out of his dream-filled stupor. He went to the sturdy door, probably the strongest part of the little home, unlatched it, and gave it a shove. Despite the best efforts of his six-foot-three frame, the door only opened a few inches before the snow stopped his push.

Damn! He should have opened it regularly to push back the drifting snow. He gave a chuckle. If he had said that cussword aloud in his mother's presence, she would've washed his mouth out with soap.

"Robbie!" Closer and louder, the voice called again.

"I've got a shovel, if I can get to the door, I'll get you out," called the voice.

Rob put his mouth to the door's opening and yelled, "Who says I want to come out?"

"OK, good point, but I sure want to come in," came the voice of his cousin's husband, Ben Brown.

"Give me a minute, then give it a shove. Meanwhile, pull it closed till I tell you when," said Ben.

Rob closed the heavy oak door, made from the planks of an old shipwreck. In fact, most of the shack was made of similarly salvaged wood. The sound of a shovel clanged against the door and in a few minutes, Ben knocked and called again. "OK, give it a try."

Rob threw his shoulder against the door and got it open about three feet before it stuck.

"Good, got it," came Ben's voice as a white, snow-covered being crawled into the cabin pulling a snow shovel.

"Look what the cat dragged in," said Rob, "what on earth made you come out here? I'm doing fine."

"Storm's about blown out anyway, but I came with a message from Chief Foster. With the wind blowing so hard I never heard the fire siren, but Skip Parker stuck his head in and said the Chief wanted both of us if I could get to you." Like most of the adult males in Bound Brook, Ben was on the volunteer fire department, in fact, one of the two deputy chiefs.

Rob reacted to the name of Bill Foster, the local police chief. He was occasionally Rob's boss, at least when Rob was serving in his part-time duties as a special police officer, mostly in the summer. "So, there's a fire and a snowstorm, so fire department and road crew should be busy, but what's he need me for?" he asked.

"Oh, Moose, Bunky and the road crew been out plowing, though I think it will be days before they finish. Must be well over a foot of snow out there and the drifts are over my head. No, Foster needs us all cause it's a fire, a storm … and a death." He took off his wool coat and hung it on the hook by the door before continuing.

"Old man Proctor got himself burned to death when his old fire-trap finally went up in flames. Fire burned itself out. We couldn't've gotten to it anyway, but funny, all those years he didn't have electricity, and he finally gets modernized and then the house burns down. Who knows, with the power out, maybe his old lanterns or a candle did him in? Not many people even saw the flames cause of the storm."

Rob needed a second to take in the news. Cecil Proctor was the biggest "pain-in-the-ass" in town, and while there were several competing for the title, it wasn't even a close contest. He was the oldest of the large Proctor brood. The Proctors had settled the town of Bound Brook in 1600-something and Cecil had acted like he owned it ever since. "Old man Proctor dead? Thought he was too cussed mean to ever die."

"I'm not in a rush to go back out there." Ben was mostly free of his coating of snow. "If you've got any coffee, I wouldn't mind warming up a bit."

"Sure, I'll put some on fresh. We can have a toast to the old S.O.B."

"No disrespect to the dead, but will that toast be to mourn or celebrate?" Ben added with a wink.

"Well, I guess most of the town won't miss him and not sure any of his Proctor kin will either. When it comes to mean old cusses, I hope that God broke the mold after he made Cecil."

Chapter II - The Fire Next Time

After some coffee they tromped through the snow to Ben's house on the edge of what was called "Tyler's Tangle." Rob was dressed in his winter long johns, dungaree overalls, flannel shirt, thick wool sweater, mackinaw jacket, wool Navy watch cap, wool socks, rubber waders, and heavy mittens. It was still cold, but the snow had stopped, and the wind was a strong breeze, not a howling gale. They followed Ben's route over the back path through the pine forest and cedar hollow that separated Rob's cottage on the water from Ben's house in the woods. The trees had caught much of the snow in their branches and the snow in the forest wasn't as deep. The old timers didn't care about pretty views, they cared about shelter from persistent winter winds, so the old houses were built behind hills or down in the numerous hollows that dotted Bound Brook. Rob's house near the shore had been a summer cottage, never intended to withstand the ravages of Cape Cod winters.

Tyler's Tangle consisted of more than a dozen homes, grouped closely together, and all inhabited by members of the extended Tyler clan. Ben's wife, Phyllis Tyler Brown, greeted Rob with a hug. Phyllis was a cousin, and she and Ben had taken Rob in after his mother died. They had become his foster parents, even though they were only a dozen years older, and more like a big brother and sister.

"I'm going with you two," she said, putting on her heavy coat, "The boys are with their cousins next door."

Ben glanced at Rob who nodded. You didn't argue with Phyllis.

The three of them squeezed into Ben's 1940 Ford truck, with the faded lettering, "Brown's Plumbing & Heating" on the doors. Ben drove slowly down a barely plowed road, until the cousins arrived at the fire scene just over a mile away. Proctor had lived on a large lot in Proctor's Hollow, off Proctor's Hollow Road at the end of Proctor's Point. Some people in town claimed that Bound Brook could have been renamed Proctorville. Rob suspected that Cecil would have felt he deserved it.

What had once been a stately three-story home with a widow's walk was now a smoldering pile of rubble. A small stubby portion of the inner first floor stuck out of the ashes. The brick chimney stack was the only remnant left fully intact. Cecil's home had been a late convert to electricity and plumbing. Only three or four years ago, soon after he had returned to Bound Brook, Rob had helped with the project. Ben handled the plumbing and oil heating system, while Corey Proctor did his uncle's electrical work. Rob provided the heavy lifting, light carpentry and a lot of "go-fer" work. On such a big job, at an old historic house, they had to coordinate their efforts.

Proctor was a pain. He was picky, nosy, crabby and impossible to please. His presence had slowed the work considerably, and he'd never expressed any satisfaction with the results. They were all relieved when he wasn't home, no words needed to be passed, but everyone busted their humps to get as much done as possible during his absence. He nickel and dimed every expense, refusing to pay for unseen obstacles. Rob got paid a base wage, but Corey and Ben barely broke even, and would have better off letting someone else take the job. Proctor had selected them, by-passing Bound Brook's other tradesmen, and if they had refused Cecil Proctor it would've had consequences.

Rob stared at the debris and had a sharp vision of the towns he had seen in Europe during the war. Sometimes scenes from the war flashed through his mind, scenes he didn't want to remember, but couldn't stop. (His best friend, Horace "Hoopy" Hooper, had once told him he had the same flashes, but mostly it wasn't anything they talked about.) In this case, the intensity of the flames had driven the deep snow yards away from the ashes and turned the area black with soot. The town's two fire trucks stood nearby, but there was nothing for them to do. A dozen fire volunteers, and a few on-lookers stood and gawked at the devastation of the blaze.

Phyllis headed over to a group of women, while Ben and Rob walked toward the imposing figure of Chief Bill Foster, the only full-time police officer in the tiny town. The Chief was even taller than Rob, with broad shoulders and powerful arms. Even in his early fifties, the retired state trooper and former Boston College football lineman was in good shape, with only a hint of a belly on a frame that must have packed two hundred and fifty pounds. His square jaw and deep voice reminded everyone of John Wayne. The previous year a very drunk Tricky Tyler had not only surrendered to the Chief, but convinced he was in the presence of a movie star, insisted on getting an autograph.

"Well if it isn't the terrible twosome. I was starting to wonder if you were going to make it." Foster said it with a look and voice that made Rob feel like he was part of a western movie.

"Well, wonder-boy here doesn't exactly live in the center of town," Ben reminded the Chief, "I should've used a dog sled to get him out."

"Maybe if he had a phone and electricity, like the rest of the modern world, we could have called."

"Well, Chief, how many people in town have working electricity and telephones right now?" asked Rob.

The Chief just gave him that look police reserve for wise guys and changed the subject, "I need the two of you and Buddy to take a look at this and tell me what you think. Something about this doesn't seem right to me." The Chief waved in the direction of the demolished house where Fire Chief Tommy "Buddy" Barrows was crouching in the snow, looking at something.

The three joined Barrows, "What've you got, Buddy?" asked Ben.

"Well, Chief Foster has asked me to try to figure out where the fire started."

"So what do you think?" asked Foster. "Did you find anything?"

"OK, look," Barrows replied, "I'm no arson investigator, just a carpenter and part-time fire chief. I had a weekend class a couple years ago, but that don't make me no expert. However, I see some things. Before I say anything, I want to know if you guys see it too. Take a look for yourselves."

Rob took in the area where Buddy was standing, and then started walking around the perimeter of what had been the Proctor house. He wasn't sure what he was looking for, but obviously Buddy saw something. Slowly he started to get an impression of the fire. The former Navy Shore Patrolman opened his eyes to what might have happened. The Nor'easter would have pushed the flames and fire from northeast to southwest with powerful winds driving the wet snow into the pyre. He turned to his cousin. "What do you see?"

Ben paused, "Well, the outside walls, especially on the north side, are gone, but some of the inside walls are still partially there. If the fire started inside from a candle or lantern, I'm not sure all the outside walls would have burned to the ground, but I think the inside would have nothing left."

"I think I see what Buddy spotted," remarked Rob. "Over on the north perimeter the ground is bare and the burn mark is intense. It reminds me of a shell crater from the war: the damage spreads out, but the landing spot is clear. What's interesting is that the spot is on the outside edge of the north side of the house."

"Exactly what I saw," chimed in Buddy, "I don't think this fire started inside, it looks to me like it started outside on the north wall. The wind drove the flames up the north side and toward the south and it devoured the place. The snow and moisture must have finally put out the fire before it finished burning some of the interior. Instead of burning inside out, it looks like the fire burned from the outside in."

Chief Foster gave the three of them a stern stare, "So you three are telling me the fire started outside in the middle of a blizzard. If old man Proctor had been out checking the shutters, he might have dropped a lantern, but then he could have run away, and we would have found the lantern. Unless he ran back inside for some reason, he wouldn't end up dead inside the house. We found his body on the first floor, in what was probably the living room. It seems he would have been awake and could have escaped, not like he was in bed. Your explanation about the fire starting outside at least might explain why his body is badly burned, but it isn't charred to a crisp."

No one spoke while the implications sunk in.

"Chief, I think you need to see something." Skip Parker, Bound Brook's other special police officer, walked up and broke the silence.

"What've you got?" asked Foster.

"Come take a look. I was just poking around over by the tool shed and I found something," Skip pointed to the tool shed at the end of what, under all the snow, was a driveway. Beside the shed was the snow-covered outline of a sedan.

The four men followed Skip to the ancient shack, and he held the door open. Inside was a clutter of rakes, hoes and shovels. An assortment of tools hung from the walls, and an old dory stood propped against the back wall. A large hole in its flat bottom indicated it was not currently seaworthy. What caught their attention was on the dirt floor, just inside the door. A large jerry jug, a can used for gasoline or kerosene, was tipped on its side. Foster gave it a slight nudge with the toe of his boot. The can moved easily. Rob bent down to take a closer look. The can was uncapped and empty. A sniff gave Rob the familiar scent of kerosene.

"Nobody touch that," said the Chief. "We'll save it for the Troopers, might get lucky and find some prints."

Outside the shed, the men gathered around the towering bulk of Foster, "So what've we got here, gentlemen?"

Buddy Barrows looked at the Police Chief. "What I think we're saying, in our non-expert opinion, is that this fire was probably arson."

Rob saw the look on Foster's face and the set of his chiseled jaw, "Well, Buddy, I don't think that's the only thing we're saying."

Barrows turned toward Rob with a look of confusion. "What I don't get is, you just said you agreed it started outside."

Chief Foster's deep voice interrupted the exchange, "No, gentleman, Rob is right, if this fire was arson, then it's also probably murder!"

The five representatives of Bound Brook's Police and Fire Departments looked at the aftermath of the fire in silence. The gravity of Foster's statement was just sinking in when a shrill voice broke the mood.

"I knew it, I knew it!" it shrieked, almost in a cackle. "I told Proctor the Lord would have his vengeance. *Vengeance is mine, I will repay, sayeth the Lord.*"

Rob cringed at the sound of the all too familiar voice of the Reverend Joseph Duggan. Duggan had been the minister of the Bound Brook Methodist Church. He had been hired in the thirties, back when Rob was a teenager. Duggan's style of preaching was "hell, fire and brimstone," a throwback to Puritan times. At first the Methodists had flocked to hear his sermons. Duggan's dramatic style could be very entertaining. For a few years, membership flourished, and services were packed. When Duggan kept his message general the congregation could take the weekly scourging of their souls, and then go home to Sunday dinner.

But over the years, Duggan had started to get more pointed and specific. His orations now called out certain members of the community for their sins. While he had never named names, he was specific enough that community speculation was pretty unanimous in figuring out the sinners. Rob knew his unmarried mother had been a target, but the chief sinner was Cecil Proctor, who didn't even attend that church. Proctor attended the Congregational Church, like Rob and his mother. However, Roberta's attendance was like a declaration of war against the church elders, most notably her father, Rob's estranged grandfather, Richard Caldwell.

Under pressure from Proctor and other town elders, the Methodists had removed Duggan sometime during the war. There were rumors about some sort of scandal, and his furious rants had grown tiring as attendance started to slip. Rob had been away and never heard all the details. However, Duggan hadn't given up. With a small but passionate following he had started his own church. At first they had met in homes, then rented the old Elks hall for Sunday services, and now they supposedly had plans to build their own church near the border of the neighboring town of East Brook.

The zealous preacher continued to spout scripture while he shook his finger at the blackened area. "In the words of the spiritual, *God gave Noah the rainbow sign, no more water, the fire next time,"* screeched the skinny minister. "This was no ordinary fire, this was *Hell Fire*, the wrath of the Lord has smote Bound Brook's greatest sinner. I warned him to repent, but he was too proud, too vain, and too pompous. *Pride goeth before destruction, and a haughty spirit before a fall, so sayeth the Lord!"*

"OK, Parson, we get the idea." Chief Foster placed his considerable size directly in front of the wraith-like minister. "Now I'll give you thirty seconds to get your scrawny butt out of here, or I'll charge you with impeding an investigation, minister or not. Now move it!"

When Bill Foster told you to move, you moved. The minister broke his rapturous rant and slinked back into the circle of spectators.

"Can't say I disagree with his message about Proctor, but never did care much for Duggan as the messenger," said Buddy a Methodist Church regular. His comment brought silent nods from Rob and Ben, a chuckle from Skip and a shrug from Foster.

"The Lord works in mysterious ways, but that minister is definitely one of his most mysterious," commented Rob.

"He pisses me off!" said Ben.

"Amen!" added Skip.

Bill Foster grunted. "Right now I could care less about self-righteous Reverend Duggan. We'll take some pictures for the State Police to review, but mostly I'm interested in what Doc Carter says when he examines the body."

Chapter III – Digging Out

The day after Proctor's fire, the road crew finally made it down Neck Road past Rob's cottage. Rob was finishing breakfast when he heard a blaring horn and stepped out the door to the sight of Arnold "Moose" Parker waving from the window of the town truck, now converted to the town plow.

"OK, hot shot, no excuses. We got the road clear, time to dig out."

Rob waved to his former teammate. "Hey, Moose, a pal would plow me out."

Moose backed the truck and then aimed it into Rob's long driveway. Then Moose turned the plow blade from angled to straight and gave the truck some gas. The plow pushed the snow forward and a mounting pile moved toward Rob's house. Halfway down the driveway the huge snowdrift ground the truck to a halt, its wheels spinning on the slippery snow.

"There you go buddy, I did half, now you can do the rest," Moose gave a hearty laugh, backed on to the road, adjusted the blade, and with another long blast on the horn continued down the road, the plow pushing mounds of snow to the side.

What a jerk! Moose's idea of a joke usually had a mean twist to it. He remembered Moose bouncing a ball off the back of Rob's head at recess. Fortunately, in basketball, Moose reserved his worse meanness for the opposing team, a trait that resulted in more than his share of fouls, and occasionally ejection from the game. Amazing that a bully like Moose was the older brother of quiet, mild-mannered Skip Parker.

It was still cold, but the sun was shining, with only a light breeze off the bay. Rob wasn't lazy, but his attitude toward snow was that God put it there, and God could take it away. In the temperate climate and salt air of Cape Cod, snow usually didn't stay very long. Unfortunately, he didn't think he could wait out this immense dumping of the white stuff. He was going to have to dig out. He gave a sigh, and then went back to breakfast.

Two hours later, Chief Foster drove into the driveway and parked behind the dirty mound of snow. Rob was outside with a shovel, digging out the old DeSoto. He was stripped to a flannel shirt and sweating from the exertion, despite the temperature.

"Need to have a talk." Foster wasn't much for idle pleasantries.

Rob stuck the shovel into a snowbank, "Let's have some coffee. I need a good reason to let the sun do more of my work."

Foster nodded toward the driveway. "I see Moose was here."

Foster's bulk and Rob's height seemed to fill the tiny cabin. The wood stove had over-heated the room despite the cold, and he had taken advantage of the sunshine to open the windows and air it out. Rob put the coffee pot on the stove, "Reheated, OK? Made it fresh this morning, so shouldn't be too bad."

Foster just grunted in acknowledgement. "Rob, I need you to do something for me."

"Sure, Chief," replied Rob, and darned if he didn't feel like saying, *Howdy Partner.*

"Here's the deal. Somebody conked Proctor on the head hard enough to kill him. Doc says there wasn't any smoke in Proctor's lungs, so he was dead before the fire. It looks like the fire was started to cover up the murder. I've had the State Troopers here and by all rights it's really their case. They'll handle the investigation, the physical evidence and lab analysis. However, you, me and even the Troopers, know that nobody in Bound Brook will tell them anything useful. I can handle most cases, but I'm still an outsider here and this case is full of *old Bound Brook* feuds and bad blood. They're gonna stonewall me. No, you and Skip are the only ones that have a chance, and of the two, you've got the most experience."

About four years ago, Foster had married Miss Hilda Newcomb, who had been Rob's elementary teacher. He had retired from the Massachusetts State Police soon after the marriage, and almost immediately assumed the Chief's position in Bound Brook. Already in middle age, it was a first marriage for both, and a surprise to the town. The Newcomb family went back almost as far as the Proctors, but Foster was from off-Cape in Bridgewater, and four years in town bought you nothing.

Rob nodded slowly in agreement, "Yup, everybody in Bound Brook will have an opinion on Proctor. Most'll be glad he's dead, but none of them are gonna talk to any outsiders. I doubt they'll even talk to me."

"Right now you don't need to talk or ask questions, that will come later. I just want you to listen. Most folks in town are comfortable enough with you and Skip that they'll talk to each other when you're around. With me or outsiders, they'll clam up. So just listen and let me know what you hear."

"I can do that."

"Just to be upfront with you," continued the Chief, "I've got no money in the budget to pay either of you until summer."

"I'll keep my eyes and ears open," Rob agreed.

When Foster left, he went out and attacked the driveway with renewed purpose. The sun was helping, but he couldn't take the chance that the weather would turn Moose's snow wall into an iceberg. Four hours later the sun was getting low over the bay and his back and hands were screaming for a break. Rob had most of it shoveled. He'd finish it in the morning and hope the temperature didn't drop too much overnight.

A can of tomato soup and a grilled cheese sandwich served as his dinner. In a way he was glad for the shoveling. He'd needed the exercise, and the total exhaustion took the edge off his physical restlessness. He had spent his life playing sports, and his body craved the release that a workout gave him. This was the first winter that he hadn't played in the Men's Amateur Basketball League since he had returned to Bound Brook. His first few years back, he'd been in his twenties and still in great shape. His experience playing in college, and for his Navy basketball team, had given him an edge over the other men. At six-foot-three he could still jump, and for the first two years he had dominated, leading the Lower Cape Harbormen to two league championships, while being voted the league's MVP.

He had also become a marked man. It reminded him of what it must have been like to be a gunfighter in the old west. Every team had some young buck wanting to make a name against Rob Caldwell. Unfortunately, most of them had guts and grit, but lacked skill and savvy. They had compensated by grabbing, hacking and dirty play. One game against the Bourne Bridgemen, Rob had driven to the basket and made an improbable, off balance layup. On the way down, one of the Bourne scrubs had given him an extra push, and when he landed, he'd felt something in his knee give. The next day it had been the size of a balloon.

A trip to Doc Carter confirmed he had torn some cartilage and his season was ended. With a knee brace and a cautious attitude, Rob had returned to play the next season, but he no longer drove to the hoop with reckless abandon, and his jumping spring was gone. He had still been talented enough to be a good player, but it wasn't fun to watch lesser players drive past him and younger guys outleap him. Let's face it, he had a bum knee and was getting old at thirty. The game had lost its thrill. So this year he had hung up his sneakers, although he occasionally helped Coach Gilmore with the Bound Brook High School team.

Rob decided that in the morning he'd head over to Tyler Hill and have a talk with George "Coach" Gilmore, the teaching principal of The Bound Brook Consolidated School, grades one through twelve. In basketball-crazy Bound Brook, the coaching mattered as much as the teaching. It was school vacation week and Rob figured that Gilmore would be home.

Of course, the Coach's daughter, Rachel, might also be around. Rob sighed thinking about it, *if life had been different, he and*

Rachel would have been a couple. It had been hard when they had broken up after high school but was even harder these last four years. Now that he was back in Bound Brook, he saw her around town all the time. They never talked, just hello and a wave, both uncomfortable, both leaving so much unsaid. Was she the reason he'd returned home? If the war had taught him anything, it was that you couldn't get caught up in the past, you had to move on. But that didn't make it any easier.

The next morning, he found the temperature still cold, but the sun strong. He had started up the old '39 DeSoto Coupe the day before, not an easy task, but he'd learned a few tricks about old cars, back when he used to help out at the Flying A garage, and he was glad Hoopy had insisted he get a new battery before the winter. After Pearl Harbor there had been no new cars built by the auto makers. Everything had been converted to making tanks, trucks, Jeeps and other vehicles for the war effort. Only after the war were there any new cars. The result was most people in town owned cars and trucks from the thirties, since only a few could afford the new ones.

Neck Road was plowed, but still covered with a bumpy washboard of two inches of snow. The DeSoto spun, swerved and skidded until Rob got out to the newly completed state highway. The highway pavement was almost bare, and he suspected that the bigger plows of the state and county had done the job. Only a mile or so down the road, Rob pulled into The Flying A gas station run by his friend, Hoopy, and his brother Harold.

A teenager Rob knew from the basketball team came out to pump his gas. Corey Proctor, known as Junior, was the best player on the team. Rob noticed he was sporting a black eye.

"Wow, where'd you get the shiner?"

"Caught an elbow playin' some one-on-one."

"Just give me a buck's worth. Are Harold or Hoopy around?"

Junior shook his head, "Naw, they're out plowing, good chance to make a few bucks plowing out the old folks that can't shovel."

"Sorry about Cecil," said Rob, "what was he, your uncle?"

"Sort of great-uncle," said Junior, wiping the squeegee across the windshield. "I think he was my Dad's real uncle."

"So how is your family handling his death?"

"Well, you know, he was sort of a big deal, but he was older and you can't live forever."

"Did you know him very well?"

Junior paused and blushed. "Yeah, I did. He sorta took an interest in me a while ago. Wanted me to go to some fancy college. I think he wanted someone to take over after him. Guess he knew he was getting old."

"Doubt he expected to go this soon, or the way he did."

The teenager nodded, "Dad was pretty shook. Not sure how much he liked Uncle Cecil, but he was family, and way back I think they were closer."

Rob pulled out his wallet, while Junior continued. "By the way, some guy got gas about an hour ago and was asking about you."

"Really, who was he?"

"Never saw him before, not from around here. Real nice car… had a Rhode Island plate. Fancy dresser but talked rough. Kinda looked like a boxer, his nose and ears were all messed up."

"What did he want?"

"Just asked if you still lived around here. I told him you did, but I didn't like his looks, so tried to ignore him after that. He just paid and left."

"Thanks," said Rob, "let me know if he comes back. I went to college in Rhode Island, but that description doesn't ring any bells."

Junior finished pumping the gas, "Funny thing is I saw the same guy a few days ago talking to Harold. Harold said he was asking about my Uncle Cecil."

That caught Rob's attention, "When was that?"

"Must have been the end of last week, I know it was before the storm."

Rob paid the teen a dollar for the gas, pulled out onto the highway and immediately made the left turn toward Bound Brook Center. He thought about the mysterious Rhode Islander, but nobody came to mind. *That a stranger would ask about both Proctor and him was weird, but was it a coincidence?* With Proctor dead, he would have to follow up on all connections.

Past Bound Brook Creek, and the Olde Creek Inn, he had a choice: left on Lower Main Street, or straight up the hill on Upper Main Street to the town center. Deciding, he headed straight up the hill, past the Congregational and Methodist churches. Rob looked over at the building that had been the school before the new one had been built in 1936. Henry Newcomb had gutted it and turned it into a movie theater during the war. It was closed for the winter, and the talk was that he was going to close it permanently. With gas rationing ended, people could drive to the more modern theaters in the bigger towns of Orleans or Provincetown, and Henry couldn't keep up.

Rob drove slowly through the center. Some of the business owners were out shoveling the sidewalks. He waved to Agnes Perry, who owned the only year-round diner in town. The center had the Town Hall, A&P grocery store, pharmacy, news & tobacco store, liquor store, Agnes' Restaurant, Holcomb's Fish Market, the Post Office and several seasonal shops that opened for the summer tourist season. Not much, but the tourists found it quaint and picturesque.

The white marble obelisk of the Bound Brook War Memorial poked through the snow in front of the Town Hall. Last Veteran's Day the town had added a new plaque to the column, dedicated to Bound Brook's fallen military from World War II. There was Rob's cousin, Bogsy Tyler, who had died in France. Jeffrey Samuels, the younger brother of Rob's classmate Elaine, had joined the marines and died at Iwo Jima. Dick Towne, the only son of the Congregational minster, had died at Guadalcanal. Bobby Proctor, maybe four years younger than Rob, had joined the Navy and gone down with his ship in the Pacific. He had been Corey Proctor's oldest son, and Junior's brother. Hank Perry, Agnes and Joe's son, had been in the merchant marine, and his cargo ship had been sunk by a German U-boat in the early days of the war. Rob hoped the Korean Conflict wouldn't add any new names to the pillar. So far, Bound Brook had been lucky.

He turned the old coupe onto Holcomb Street and headed toward Bound Brook Harbor. The Town Pier came in view and Rob pulled into a small, plowed portion of the marina's parking lot. It had turned into a gorgeous morning, and the protected harbor of Bound Brook Bay glimmered like a sheet of glass, with barely a ripple stirring the surface. The Bay was one of the best natural harbors on Cape Cod. A half-dozen shellfish draggers were tied alongside the pier, and Rob noticed Tricky Tyler on the deck of the Mary Mae. Probably half the shell fishermen in Bound Brook were Tylers, while the other half were named Perry, Samuels, Costa, Joseph or some other name with Portuguese roots.

Driving along the beach, Rob slowed down by the recreation field. Bound Brook's crude baseball field was under a deep coating of snow. He'd played a lot of baseball there over the years, pick-up games, "flies and grounders," and a few high school contests. Bound Brook High always tried to field a team, but some years it was hard to come up with nine bodies. To make it worse, in the springtime, some of the boys helped out their fathers with shell fishing. Luckily for Rob, they had managed to scrape together a team for a couple of his high school years. Long, lanky and well over six feet, he had been an imposing figure on the pitcher's mound and could really fire a baseball, but it was a short season and the level of play pretty crude.

The road turned away from the harbor and, a quarter mile further, Rob took a right onto Tyler Hill Road. Way back in the old days some Tyler had owned the whole hill, with a large farm on the edge of the marsh. Now the farm was gone, and of the dozen homeowners, not one was a Tyler.

He pulled up to the Gilmore's house. A small figure was shoveling snow at the back of the drive, and there she was, Rachel Gilmore Curtis, wearing a light jacket and no hat, the sun highlighting her shoulder-length auburn hair. Rob felt a catch in his throat and gave a little wave. She looked up with a big smile, gestured toward the snow, and pointed for him to go to the house. The door opened before he could knock, and Margaret "Maggie" Gilmore, the coach's gregarious wife, grabbed him in a bear hug. "Rob, so good to see you, finally dug out?"

"Yeah, put it off as long as I could," he said with a smile. "You know how I feel about snow."

"If you're looking for George, you just missed him. Went to get the last four or five days of newspapers. You know how he has to get the Boston papers to check out the basketball box scores. Course, with the storm, don't know how many games were played, but he grew up in Medford and likes to keep up with the Boston news. They didn't get as much snow, nothing like what we got; we just got the power back. Knowing George, he'll be awhile. I'm sure there'll be someone or other he ends up chewing the fat with and catching up on all the gossip. Surprised you didn't pass him on the way in."

"I came in by the Bay. He probably went round the back way on Tyler Road," said Rob, referring to the back loop that connected to the center.

"Well, come in. Did ya see Rachel? Sure she'll be in soon, now that you're here."

"Actually, I'd like to talk with you and George," Rob blushed. "Not that I don't want to talk with Rachel."

"Sit down, I know you like coffee, but it's all gone. Oh, I hope George remembers to get some, but I can put water on for tea."

"Sure, tea will do just fine," smiled Rob as he sat down at the kitchen table.

"You know this is nice, reminds me of when you were in high school and spent a lot of time hanging out here. I've missed having you around, and I sure know George has. Having you help with the team this year has perked him up. You were the best player he ever had, and a pretty good kid too, if I do say so myself."

Rob flushed again. "Coach was the closest I ever had to a father. I mean, Ben is great, but he's like this terrific big brother. I don't know what I would have done without Coach. He taught me so much, not just sports and math."

"George loves teaching and kids, he always has a special few he takes under his wing. Not that he doesn't care for them all, but there are always some that can benefit the most from some guidance and support."

Rob just nodded as Maggie continued, "I know it's awkward, but both George and I would like to have you around more."

"Well, it's hard, you know?"

"Yes, I know, anyway, sorry to bring back old memories. Let's change the subject and talk about why you're back in this house after all these years." She gave him a knowing look, then reached over to add water to the tea kettle, "Terrible thing about Cecil Proctor, wasn't it?"

He paused, "It was. Aren't you related somehow?"

She lit the burner under the kettle, "Well, that's no secret, you ought to know that pretty much everybody in Bound Brook is related to everybody else. My father used to say that you couldn't throw a stone without hitting a relative, and sometimes that's just what you felt like doing. My father was a Snow, but he had Proctor connections way back, and my mother was from off Cape, Middleboro area. She had some distant Cape roots; I think a Newcomb or Harding connection."

"I know what you mean about throwing stones at relatives." Rob looked down at his hands on the tablecloth.

"Sorry, I didn't mean to bother you with cracks about family," She took a chair at the table and patted his hand. "So, are you here about Proctor?"

"Yes, it's about Proctor," Rob looked up at one of the few people in Bound Brook that he knew could keep a secret, "the word will get out in a while, but it looks like his death was no accident."

Maggie pulled back her hand and flinched. "Wow, you mean murder, in Bound Brook, I mean, I know lots of people resented, or even downright hated Cecil . . . but murder?"

"The post-mortem showed he died from a blow to the head, not the kind you get from falling down."

The door burst open, and a rosy-cheeked Rachel entered with a flourish. "I'm done shoveling, Dad can do the rest if he wants." She looked at the expressions of Maggie and Rob, "So, what did I miss?"

Before either could answer, the phone rang—two rings, the Gilmore's signal on the party line. Maggie got up and looked at Rob, who put his finger to his lips with a quiet shush sound. She nodded and went to answer the ringing in the dining room. "Hi Mabel," came her voice, "didn't even know we had the phone line back."

She peaked around the corner at Rob and rolled her eyes. Mabel Curtis was Maggie's best friend, the worst gossip in town, and she was also Rachel's mother-in-law.

Rachel sat down at the table, "OK, so much for *hello, how are you? where you been hiding yourself?* and other chit chat, tell me what's going on. I can tell something's up."

Rob lowered his voice and nodded his head toward the other room. "Proctor's death wasn't an accident. He got bashed on the head and the fire was started to cover it up. At least, that's what Chief Foster and the Medical Examiner are going to say."

Rachel reacted like her mother had. "Wow, hard to believe. You don't expect a murder in Bound Brook."

Rob looked at his high school girlfriend and knew he could trust her to keep the news quiet until the report came out. There were five, maybe six people he trusted to keep a secret, George, Maggie and Rachel, Hoopy, Ben Brown and maybe Phyllis. That reminded him of something a writer had said, maybe Mark Twain, or was it Ben

Franklin, something like, "Three people can keep a secret, if two of them are dead." He didn't need to keep it a secret long, he just didn't want the news to come from him.

Maggie now rejoined them at the table. "Mabel got a letter from Jimmy; she's going to bring it over in a little while."

Rachel looked at her mother. "I don't want to be here, if it's OK with you." Looking at Rob she added, "can we take a ride somewhere?"

A sad look came over Maggie. "Sure, I'll make some excuse."

Rob nodded to Rachel then looked at Maggie. "When I get back, I'd like to talk with you and George about Proctor. Funny, I lived here most of my life, but I never paid much attention to him. I'd like to get refreshed on how he got to be the way he was."

Chapter IV – Heartaches

They got in the old DeSoto. "Good thing the sun's shining today," joked Rob. "This old heap still doesn't have any heater." He felt awkward and avoided looking directly at Rachel. He knew the blue eyes, creamy complexion and gorgeous smile by heart. It was the first time they had been alone since the summer after graduation.

"Sorry, I just had to get out of there. I love Mabel, she's been Mom's best friend forever, and I'm married to her son, but I can't see her right now, especially not with a letter from Jimmy."

Rob just nodded and drove down Tyler Hill, took a right onto the back loop, and then a left out on Island Road past the Country Club. The roads were rough, but at least they had been plowed. Neither one spoke until he pulled into a parking lot overlooking a narrow body of water known as Bound Brook Gut.

"This may be the first time we ever parked here in the daylight," joked Rachel.

"Listen, you don't have to talk, I'll understand," Rob replied.

"No, I want to talk, god knows we've been avoiding each other for years. I can't keep going like this; I don't know about you, but I'm tired of pretending. I want to talk to you, but I need a minute. There's a dozen years of things I need to say."

The two stared out at the sight of Cape Cod Bay. In the distance you could make out the Provincetown Monument. Rob had seen a bit of the world, but he had to admit there wasn't a prettier sight.

They had been classmates since eighth grade when her father had become Principal of the new, state-of-the-art Bound Brook Consolidated School, built out on Pond Hill Road in '36. There were twenty kids in the combined seventh and eighth grade and Rachel made an instant impact on the class. All the boys had a crush on her and most of the girls were jealous. But Rachel was friendly, unpretentious, a tomboy, and without a mean bone in her body. She made friends with Cindy Silva and Mary Morris, the leaders of the girls, and soon she was accepted, even if she was from off-Cape and talked funny. Most every boy still had a crush, but Rachel settled in as friends with Jimmy Curtis, Hoopy Hooper and Rob Caldwell. They were all athletes; she was a tomboy and her Dad was the coach. It also helped that her father was a good teacher, terrific coach and generally nice guy.

Rachel was the best girl athlete, maybe even *the* best athlete, in school. Of course, that wasn't too hard, since Bound Brook never had good girls' teams. However, Rachel was in a class of her own. The few games they won were with Rachel carrying the team on her back, with very little help from her unskilled teammates.

The summer before eighth grade had also been the year that his mother died. She was out for a sail with an artist friend from Provincetown, when a squall, along with thunder, lightning and wind, rolled into Bound Brook Bay. It lasted less than thirty minutes, but it was enough. The Lighting class sailboat was found hours later off Curtis Island. The bodies of Roberta Caldwell and her friend had been discovered by some clam diggers two days later, not far from where Rob and Rachel now sat.

Rob was devastated and had floundered as the year started. He was lucky to have Jimmy and Hoopy, and the community seemed to rally around him. Ben and Phyllis took him in, and the rest of the Tyler clan looked out for him. When Moose Parker blindsided him on the field at recess, a half-dozen boys, Jimmy, Hoopy, and a bunch of Tylers stepped in front of Moose with their fists clenched. The message was clear, and Moose backed off.

Strange that the tragedy had been a driving force in his athletic achievement. Rob had always had athletic skill, speed and size, but he lacked aggressiveness. He had been double promoted in third grade because he was smart and tall for his age. This meant he was really a year younger than his classmates, even two years younger than some, though he towered over all of them. With his size and ability, it was impossible to avoid playing sports, and Rob was good, even though he played tentatively and with little passion.

With his mother's death, he got a chip on his shoulder. He'd always felt ashamed of being a "bastard," the word almost nobody said, but everyone knew. Sometimes Moose or Bunky Morris, the class bullies, used the word to taunt him, but mostly it was just there, in the air, always around, always a stain. It had made Rob quiet, shy and withdrawn. He'd avoided the spotlight and buried himself in books.

When his mother died he was angry, angry at the bullies, angry at being a bastard, angry at his estranged grandparents, angry at the town of Bound Brook, and angry at the world. One day, after the incident at recess, Moose Parker came up behind Rob in the lunch line.

"Listen String Bean, just you and me after school, without all your cousins around. Meet you at the sand pit."

Rob nodded. In the past he would've been terrified, now he just didn't care. He couldn't hide behind his friends and cousins, it was time he stood up for himself. There was something else: a strange feeling, he almost wanted a beating, some different kind of pain that would replace the empty feeling in his gut.

After school, a small crowd of kids sneaked through the woods to the sand pit. The word had gotten out, of course, as it always did. The sand pit was where scores were settled and everyone knew the rules: one on one, nobody jumps in. You had to be sneaky so the principal and teachers didn't find out. Well, maybe they knew, but mostly they never interfered.

A circle formed as Moose and Rob stepped out of the crowd. Moose had repeated first grade and so, even though they were classmates, he was at least two years older than Rob. His name fit him perfectly: a Bull Moose, short powerful legs, a thick torso, almost no neck, broad shoulders and powerful arms from lifting burlap bags of shellfish on his uncle's boat. Rob actually felt sorry for Moose. His father was a fisherman, but when he was on dry land, he was a mean drunk. Moose had looked out for his younger brother Skip and taken the brunt of the father's abuse. Maybe that was why Moose was such a bully himself.

Rob was a full head taller, and where Moose was built like an oak stump, Rob was more like a willow tree. All arms and legs, and lanky, but not skinny, he was agile, quick and surprisingly strong. He had never been in a fight at the sand pit. His only fights had been squabbles with Tyler cousins when tempers spontaneously exploded. He didn't even know how to start.

Moose had been here before. With a roar he charged at Rob. Head lowered, he barreled into him like a football tackler, shoulder into the gut, stubby legs pushing Rob off his feet, sending him crashing to the ground with all of Moose's weight landing on top. Rob was stunned.

Moose took advantage, flipped him on his stomach, administered a full-nelson headlock and threw his body over him. It was clear Moose had lots of experience, and his move rendered Rob completely helpless. The whole "fight" had lasted less than ten seconds.

Moose whispered in Rob's ear, "So *bastard*, want to cry? Miss your mommy? I'll let you go, just say 'uncle'."

Years of shame, fury at Moose for taunting him with his mother's name, and weeks of pent-up grief, rose to the surface. He felt a suppressed surge of power, like the rumble in a volcano before it exploded. Instinctively he pulled his legs up to his body, tucking his knees under him, and with a deafening roar, his arms and legs sprung upward. In a split second he was standing with a massive Moose attached to his back. Then he threw himself backward into a crashing heap on the ground.

A gush of air tore past his ear as all of Moose's breath burst from his lungs. Rob felt the headlock release, he spun over, grabbed

Moose's arm, stood up and twisted. Moose was helpless, gasping for breath and wincing in pain.

"Now, your turn, say 'uncle' or I'll twist your arm off!"

Moose looked at Rob with bulging eyes, still trying to catch his breath. Rob gave the arm another twist.

"OK man, you win, let him go," said Moose's friend, Bunky Morris. "He can't talk, so let him go."

The fight was a turning point. The word got around, and people looked at Rob differently, with pity replaced by respect. Now Rob began to pursue sports and physical activity with a passion. Coach Gilmore discovered he had a weapon. Still in eighth grade and not yet thirteen, Rob played basketball like a demon possessed.

The new coach, himself a former high school and college star, worked to refine the raw talent. Ben Brown replaced the sagging old hoop on Tricky Tyler's family garage, and Rob played pickup games or H-O-R-S-E, or just shot baskets until he collapsed from exhaustion. Coach Gilmore left the gym unlocked, and Rob arrived at school an hour or two early every day.

Rachel's voice now interrupted his thoughts, "Hey Rob, you still there?"

"Sorry, just thinking,"

"Yah, me too, but I need to talk, and it needs to be with you." She looked away.

"So, what's with you and Jimmy?"

"It's not good. I know the war changed all of you, but it changed him more than most. He saw brutal action: D-Day, Battle of the Bulge, bad stuff. The funny thing is he hated it, and he loved it. He misses the army, being part of a team, he calls it. I think his happiest days were playing sports with you and Hoopy. It was having friends who looked out for you, he said. The army made him part of a team again. The trouble is, lots of his team got killed. It was kind of weird—contradictory, you know? Maybe you can understand, being in the war yourself."

It made Rob think for a moment, before responding. "I sort of get it," he began, "but Jimmy saw a lot more action than I did. Hoopy was at Anzio, the Italian Campaign, and it was really bad. He never wants to talk about it. I saw a little action, but I started working as a shipping clerk, and then spent time on Shore Patrol, really a Navy cop. It was mostly away from the front lines, dealing with security, prisoners and things like that. Some of the sailors and G.I.s we dealt with weren't nice guys; they were almost as bad as the enemy."

"Well, the first couple of years we were married it was fun," she admitted, "even though Jimmy always thought he was second best," She looked at Rob and paused before continuing. "But it was good. We were still like the buddies from high school. My parents were ticked at me, dumping college and my dreams of being a teacher. I couldn't talk to them for weeks."

"We moved in with Mabel. She wasn't thrilled we had eloped, but she'd never expected Jimmy to do more than have a trade. Being a widow, I think she liked the company. It helped that she's known me for years. Made it awkward with my mom and her for a while, but gradually my parents accepted it. I mean, they always liked Jimmy, so it wasn't about him."

"Anyway, we played at being married, hung out with some of the other young couples and had a lot of fun. Not sure our parents approved, too much partying in Hyannis and Ptown, but we were just big kids. Of course, you were off at college, so that wasn't a distraction for either of us."

She stared out at the Bay. "After Pearl Harbor, Jimmy wanted to enlist right away. Our parents made him wait, but when the war got worse he signed up. I think he was already starting to feel a bit lost. Working at the Hooper's Flying A, fixing cars and pumping gas, wasn't very glamorous, and Jimmy always liked the attention he'd gotten from sports and being friends with the big star."

She look up at Rob, and he saw tears in her eyes. "He was so proud in his uniform! He wrote me all the time from boot camp. He was happy! He loved the regimentation, the schedules and the structure. He was part of a team again, just with drill sergeants instead of my Dad. He did so great that he qualified to become a paratrooper in the Airborne. I missed him, but his letters didn't sound like he missed me. Then he parachuted into the war on D-Day and I didn't hear much. When I finally got letters, he was different, still determined, but he had seen friends die, and somehow, I don't think he was ready for that. The army had been a game up till then. Sure, people died in wars, but not *his* friends."

Rob nodded, "War isn't like what we played as kids, it isn't pretend. When you get shot you don't get up when the game is over."

She continued, "When he came home, part of him was closed up. He was always fun, but not anymore. We drank and partied, but the liquor turned him mean. I'd never seen Jimmy mean, not to me, not to anybody. Pretty soon people started avoiding him, the parties went on, but without us. We just lived with Mabel, and never went out anymore, never left the house."

"You hadn't come back to Bound Brook yet, but Jimmy was still fixated on you and me. He blamed you for our relationship going bad, never himself. By the time you were back in town, we were just going through the motions of a marriage. He fixed cars, came home, had dinner, took a bottle and went to the basement to tinker and listen to the radio. I coached the girls' basketball team and worked the counter at the Pharmacy. We both had routines but having dinner with Mabel was about all we did together."

She paused and he took the chance to speak. "I tried to reconnect with Jimmy when I got home, but he either turned the other way like he didn't see me, or just grunted and walked away when I said hello. At first, I was mad. He'd been one of my two best friends since first grade, and now he wouldn't even talk to me."

"He felt guilty. He knew I'd married him on the rebound, and he couldn't face you."

"Pretty soon I just wrote him off. Plenty of other people in town were glad to see me: Hoopy, your Dad and Mother, Ben and Phyllis, even Moose in his own sick way. Mostly, I wished I could've talked to you with more than just *Hi* and *How Ya Doin'*."

"I know. Me too," she agreed. "But the way Jimmy was, I really couldn't do more than that; he was jealous enough already. When I tried to talk to him about it, he just got mad and clammed up even more. I started pushing it and we had arguments. A few got so bad that I left Mabel's and went to stay with my folks for a day or two—one time I even stayed a week. Jimmy never asked me to come back, it was always Mabel asking on his behalf. I swear I've stayed in the marriage more for her sake than for his."

Rob took a deep breath to hold his own emotions in check.

She looked him straight in the eyes before continuing. "Anyway, when Korea broke out, he couldn't wait to re-enlist. The army gave him back his Sergeant rank, sent him off to train the new kids, and then finally shipped him off to Korea. I moved back in with my parents, it was just too uncomfortable staying with Mabel. At first I got brief letters, but lately he just writes his mother and tells her to pass it on to me. Mabel brings the letters over so I can read them. It's killing her, because she knows we're so unhappy, and she feels guilty about the way he treats me.

"I've made such a mess of things. I never should have gotten so mad at you, you didn't even really do anything. It should have been you and me, Rob. It should have been us!" The tears flowed down her face and she leaned her head against his shoulder.

Rob put his arm around her and pressed his cheek against her hair. The sweet smell was so familiar. Rachel sobbed softly against his chest. So many nights they had parked in this same spot, talking about their dreams, and sharing kisses. The kids called it "watching the submarine races." They had been a couple, going steady and everyone had expected it to last. However, graduation had come and gone, and they were headed off to different colleges, although not that far apart. They had still expected to stay together, but then Elaine Samuels had gotten involved.

Elaine always had a crush on Rob, and flirted with him shamelessly. Petite, dark and voluptuous, she was eye-catching. By senior year she had a reputation. Boys bragged and winked about being with Elaine, who seemed to go with just about anybody, including some much older guys in town. Now that he was older, Rob could understand it better. Elaine's parents had both been drunks. Everybody in town knew but looked the other way. Elaine's life must have stunk, and who knew what she'd put up with. So maybe her fixation over Rob, the sports hero, wasn't such a surprise.

It had happened at the end of summer, a last celebration. Most of the senior class and a few others had a beach party out near Curtis Island. They'd built a bonfire of driftwood and joked about what they would do now that high school was over. A few were headed off to college or some other kind of school, and the rest had already started jobs in Bound Brook or the nearby towns, jobs that would likely last the rest of their lives.

Boys were working on the draggers or helping fathers with contracting, plumbing or other trades. Hoopy was joining his brother at the Flying A, Jimmy was headed to a trade school just off Cape, Moose was working on the town crew, and Bunky and Honk were fishing. Rachel was headed to Bridgewater State, and Cindy to hair dressing school, some of the other girls already worked the counters at the stores in town.

A sore throat and summer flu had kept Rachel at home. Rob hadn't planned on going at all, but Jimmy talked him into it. "The Last Hurrah" he called it, last chance for the team to be together. So Rob had gone, but planned to leave early. Moose, Bunky and Honk arrived with four cases of beer and some bottles of rye whisky. They were all under the legal age but getting liquor in Bound Brook was easy. Most everybody drank. You drank to survive the cold desolate winter, and you drank to party through the warm summer.

Rachel's absence, and the coming separation from his friends, made Rob sullen and sad. As an athlete, Rob had never touched liquor, but that night he quickly downed a few beers and took some pulls off the bottles of whiskey that were passed around. As the night wore on, couples slipped away from the fire and disappeared into the dunes. Most were steady couples, but a few were just couples for the night. Rob was pretty much out of it, and when he looked around everyone was gone . . . or almost everyone. He and Elaine were the only ones left.

He tried to get up and throw more wood on the fire, but he was tipsy and he just flopped back onto the sand. Elaine giggled. She stood, gave him her hand and tried to pull him up. Instead, she was pulled on top of him. The two laughed. Then she kissed him, and Rob kissed her back. The rest happened too fast. Elaine loosened her clothes and helped him with his. A voice in the back of his head told him to stop, but the temptation was too great. He and Rachel had never gone that far, and being a bastard himself, Rob had always had a fear. He never wanted to get a girl pregnant and stick some other kid with that label. This time those fears didn't stop him.

Drunk and spent, Rob rolled over and passed out. The next thing he remembered was waking up curled up on the sand with a partly naked Elaine cradled against his back. Several of the other kids had returned and more were drifting out of the dunes. He was groggy, but dimly aware of giggles, as the others took in the sight of them cuddled together.

Elaine got up, her shirt wide open, jeans unbuttoned and halfway down. She made a big production of pulling her pants up and buttoning her blouse. She leaned over and gave Rob a big kiss. "Thank you, sweetie! That was great!" Then she was gone and the party was over, in more ways than one.

Jimmy pulled him to his feet. "Come on Romeo, time to get you home. I'm driving."

Within twenty-four hours, the Bound Brook grapevine had the story all around town. Rob never knew who Rachel heard it from first, probably Cindy or Mary. There was no way to explain, it was a no-win situation. Rachel, still sick, refused to see him, and her parents kept him away.

Three days later he was off to college, at Brown University in Providence, Rhode Island. Rachel went off to Bridgewater State College and Jimmy to a trade school in neighboring Taunton. Two weeks later he heard that Rachel and Jimmy had eloped.

Rachel had stopped crying now. "Have you ever forgiven me for running off with Jimmy?"

"I guess I could ask if you've forgiven me? It was years ago, and I had behaved badly. Who knows what would've happened with us? We both were off to college, and not many high school romances last after that. I know Jimmy always loved you, and he was a good guy, so sure I was really hurt, but part of me felt I deserved it, and I thought you and Jimmy would be happy. I know he always loved you too."

"No, I'm the one that screwed up," she declared, "I know how Elaine felt about you, and the kids told me you were drunk, but I was angry. Instead of waiting to get over it, I just reacted. Maybe something in me was afraid to go off to school, I don't know. Mostly, I wanted to hurt you, and I did, but I also hurt Jimmy and myself. It was never fair to any of us."

"Rachel, one thing I learned in the war is to be glad to be alive. Life is too short for regrets. I've seen people who ruined their lives trying to undo what had already happened. I'm not saying it's easy, but you can't change things. We're thirty years old now, with lots of regrets. We can let them drag us down, or live our lives. . . . Look at me preaching! End of lecture, I'm sorry."

Rachel smiled at him, "No, you're right, nobody's perfect. I dragged you into this pity party, but now it's time to head home. I hope Mabel is gone by now."

"Rachel, you can talk to me anytime, I want you to know that."

"I know I can, always could, that's why I love you." She gave him a tender kiss on the cheek. "Now, please drive me home. I've been hiding long enough."

Chapter V – Proctor's Past

Rob and Rachel drove to the Gilmore house in silence. When they arrived, George's Chevy was the only car in the driveway.

"Mabel must be gone. I'm such a chicken, but it's a relief," said Rachel, slowly shaking her head, "Come in. Dad will be glad to see you."

"I hate to say it, but I need to talk to them about the Proctor murder. Your parents can give me a lot of background without the bias that most folks in town have."

After greetings, Rob and Coach Gilmore sat down at the kitchen table. "George remembered the coffee after all, so I'll make a fresh pot," said Maggie.

Rachel picked up an envelope from the counter, "I'm going to my room to read this."

Gilmore gave his daughter a sad smile and then looked at Rob. "Maggie filled me in on Proctor's murder. Still hard to believe someone in Bound Brook did it. Of course, we'll keep our mouths shut; if we can keep a secret from Mabel, with all her prying questions, I guess we can keep a secret from anybody. Maggie said you wanted some information about Proctor. How can we help?"

Before Rob could reply, the phone rang: ring-ring, pause, ring-ring. Maggie answered.

"Oh, hello, Bill. Yes, he's here. Just a minute. Sorry it took a while to answer; it's a party line, you know, had to wait to see if it was for us."

Maggie held her hand over the phone mouthpiece, "It's Chief Foster, he needs to talk to Rob. Rob, just remember it's a party line and Barbara down the street likes to listen in, so watch what you say. I tried to give the Chief a hint."

Maybe Rob should have wondered how Foster had known he was here, but this was Bound Brook, "Hi Chief, what do you need?"

"Barbara Spencer, if you are listening in on this line, get off now. This is official police business," said the authoritative voice of Foster. Rob heard a soft click.

Rob laughed, "Good job, Chief, I think we're free to talk."

"I'll make it brief: There was an attempted break-in last night at Doc Carter's office. Neighbor's dogs woke up Henry Newcomb, and his yelling must have scared them off. I think they might have been looking for the post-mortem report. Doc is releasing the results tomorrow. One positive thing is that Doc told the County DA, and the idea of someone tampering with official reports got the ball rolling. DA called me. He got some money from the Barnstable County DA's budget; said I can hire some help while the investigation is active. So, you available?"

"Of course! Joe Perry asked me to help with a foundation and some framing, but he's got to wait on the weather."

"Good, I know you were working on it anyway, but this way you're officially on duty. Meet me at the station tomorrow. Report will be out by then, and we can review the case. Oh, I got enough to bring Skip on too, but only part-time. See you at eleven."

Rob heard a loud click as Foster hung up, and suppressed an urge to salute the phone.

Maggie set the coffee out on the table and Rob thanked her. "The Chief just got some county funds to hire me for the investigation. You can help me with history and background. Tell me about Cecil Proctor. I don't know any specifics, just rumor and innuendo. How'd Proctor get to be so hated?"

George paused, and his voice took on his teacher tone, "As you know, the two biggest families in town are the Proctors, who founded Bound Brook, and the Tylers who settled here a little later. A lot of Proctors always considered themselves *above* the Tylers. The Tylers are individuals, they do their own thing, and go their own way. You know the Tylers make up many of the most solid citizens in town, but they also have most of the rascals and scoundrels."

Rob laughed. "Well, that's for sure. I wouldn't turn my back on a few of my Tyler cousins, and certainly wouldn't leave my wallet loose around them."

Gilmore continued, "The Proctors always seemed to have one patriarch, sort of a tradition of "Old Man Proctors" passed from generation to generation. It's kind of outdated now, but it mattered in the old days. Cecil Proctor was very rich, not that he showed it. Except for his Cadillac, he lived a frugal life. I think his money was a tool, not a goal. It'll be interesting to see where that money goes now that he's dead."

"You know," Maggie chimed in, "Cecil had a reputation of being mean, but most of what he did was pretty subtle. He didn't go around picking fights. In fact, he did a lot of favors for people, or least they seemed like favors at first. 'Course they didn't turn out to be favors, Proctor always got the better of those deals; the favors had strings attached."

"His father, Courtney," George continued, "started the family fortune. Way back before the turn of the century, Courtney Proctor bought the old wharf at the far end of the harbor, opposite end of where the town pier is now. Shipping, boat building and seafaring industries were slowing down. The town didn't need two wharfs, so he bought it for pennies on the dollar. Then he built a huge luxury hotel on the end of the wharf and named it The Bound Brook Inn. People in town thought he was nuts and called it "Proctor's Folly." Town folks figured nobody in their right mind would spend the fortune he was charging to come to an out-of-the-way, rundown fishing village."

"I remember it from when I was a kid," Rob commented.

"Well it was the golden age, with huge mansions in places like Newport, Rhode Island. The rich were so rich they didn't know what to do with all their money. I guess, looking back, you could say Courtney Proctor was a visionary." George paused, then continued.

"He billed it as a quiet, genteel getaway, more serene than Newport, and easier to get to than coastal Maine. Just take the train or sail right up to the wharf on the ferries, which Proctor finagled to make a stop before they landed in Provincetown. It did a good business and Bound Brook benefited. It created jobs and I guess it was the start of the tourist trade in town."

"So Proctor's father did some good for the town," remarked Rob.

Maggie laughed. "Proctors have usually done things that helped the town, but don't be fooled, it always helped them more, especially when Cecil took over. Not that you can blame someone for making a buck. Actually, the father, Courtney, cared about the town, and made lots of money, but people in town benefited too. Lots of folks got jobs and had business opportunities that hadn't existed before."

George continued, with a wink to Maggie for her input. "Well, Courtney died sometime in the twenties and Cecil took over. The Inn was very successful, but Cecil's best move was knowing when to dump it. In the Roaring Twenties it was jumping. It was Prohibition, but most folks ignored that, probably drank more than they had before, just because someone said they couldn't. Anyway, bootlegging was a big business on the Cape. Lots of folks with boats, and liquor was the cargo. Around 1927 Cecil shocked everyone in town. He sold the Inn. Not sure if he knew the Great Depression was coming, but his timing couldn't have been better."

"I barely remember," Rob noted. "I was real young. When I got older and my mother mentioned the sale, she always implied there was something bad about it, but she never got specific."

Maggie laughed again. "Well, that was probably because he sold out to gangsters!"

George chuckled as well. "Yup, mobsters wanted the Inn as a front, and to use the wharf to smuggle in booze. They paid big money for it. I'm sure it was a pittance compared to the illegal profits they were raking in."

Rob shook his head. "Wow, all that went right over my head when I was a little kid. So, Proctor got even richer from the sale?"

"Oh yes. I'm sure he was doing nicely before that, but the sale was big. Then the Depression hit hard! The rich people got hit as bad as the ordinary people, the stock market crashed, banks failed, people who'd been riding high, jumped out of buildings when they lost it all. The Inn turned into a seedy dive, no more high-flyers."

"Proctor was rich, didn't he lose out too?"

Maggie continued the story. "No just the opposite, Courtney had never trusted banks or stock markets, and Cecil continued on the same way. He believed in hard currency or precious valuables. When everybody else was broke, he had money. Kept it in a big old safe in his house."

"Cecil still had it," Rob interjected. "I remember from when we worked on his house a few years ago."

"Right," said George, "and he invested, but he invested in land, bought all the properties he could. People were hurting, and Cecil picked up property for peanuts. The sellers were desperate, and he was the only one who had cash."

"What about the Inn?" asked Rob. I remember it burned down in the early thirties."

"The rumor was it was arson, deliberately set by the mob," said Maggie.

"Probably was," George agreed. "The Inn wasn't doing any business, and the G-Men were shutting down bootleggers. At the same time, the rumor was the country was going to dump Prohibition to try to jump start the economy and give the government all the tax revenue they had been losing from liquor sales. Anyway, the result was, Cecil Proctor came out richer than ever, and owned half the land in Bound Brook and surrounding towns."

Rob slowly shook his head. "Wow, I knew he was a big deal, but I never knew the details."

"What he did with the land was interesting though," said George. "He used it to have power over people. He leased it out to them, and hardly ever sold any. That way he kept control. Lots of people in town didn't really own their property, Proctor was their landlord—still is, for a lot of folks. In other cases, they partly owned it, but Proctor held the mortgage. Some of his property abutted land that others wanted to turn to business use, but as an abutter, Cecil could raise a stink. Pretty much everyone in Bound Brook had to make him happy, or at least avoid making him mad; otherwise he'd find a way to get back at them."

"Yup, people have been kissing Proctor butt for years!"

"Maggie, watch the language!"

Rob laughed. "I've heard much worse. You know, I helped Ben install the plumbing in Proctor's house a few years ago. While we were working on it, there were lots of people coming and going. Proctor hardly left the house, but a bunch of people visited him every day, and I don't think they were social calls. I mean, now that I think about it, seemed like half the town: Proctors, Tylers, you name it, all kinds of people. I guess, like you said, they were coming to pay their rent or to kiss his butt, maybe to get his OK on some business deal. At the time it didn't sink in, now it makes sense."

Rob thought about the implications for a moment, then continued, "So Cecil's father died well before the Depression, right, and then he just continued on where the old man left off?"

"Pretty much," said Maggie. "Except I always thought Courtney was practical, all business, not really mean. But Cecil enjoyed the power. He liked to own people, that's the mean part of him you were talking about."

Rob paused to digest all the information, "What about more recently? Did you hear anything about anyone who was particularly mad at him, or had a bad deal?"

"No, not really." George seemed at bit uncomfortable. "I guess you might need to talk with Richard Caldwell. He and Cecil did a lot of real estate transactions together."

That caught Rob by surprise. Richard Caldwell was his estranged grandfather, the same man who had disowned his mother when she was unmarried and pregnant with him. Roberta Caldwell had refused to leave town, to have the baby in secret, or give it up for adoption. Instead, she had moved into the Tyler cottage by the Bay and then proudly, or stubbornly, had Rob, and had raised him in Bound Brook for the whole town to see. Hardly any words had ever passed between Rob and his "grandpa." Richard had treated Rob like he had treated Roberta, like he didn't exist.

"Well, that would sure be awkward." he commented.

"On the other hand," Maggie noted, "at least he'd have to talk to you, you know, in your . . . official capacity."

"Actually, he doesn't have to talk with anyone," George corrected her, "Might be better if Chief Foster talked to him anyway."

"I'll go over that with the Chief tomorrow," Rob said, but had one more question. "What would I be looking for if I do question *Mr. Caldwell?*"

"Well, your grandfather is, by far, the biggest Realtor in town, maybe even this part of the Cape. A lot of that is from doing business with both Proctors over the years. He's brokered most every deal they've ever done, going back to the Inn. You could say that the Proctors helped make him the rich man that he is today. He also helped them a lot. When your grandfather was Chairmen of the Selectman, he had a lot of influence, and combined with the power of Proctor, they could pretty much do anything they wanted. Of course, they had to agree, but since it meant money for both of them, they were usually on the same page."

"If Caldwell was Chairman of the Board, weren't some of those dealings a conflict of interest for him?"

George and Maggie looked at Rob with smiles. Finally Maggie spoke. "Rob, you grew up in Bound Brook, do you really need to ask that question?"

"Guess it sounded pretty naïve," laughed Rob.

"Well, Richard and Cecil did so many deals together, he might know if someone had a grudge," offered George.

Rachel now returned to the kitchen and joined them at the table. Rob noticed that her eyes were red.

"What did I miss?" she said, in a falsely cheery voice.

"Your Dad just gave me a lesson in Bound Brook history, with your Mom chiming in with the spicy comments."

George and Maggie laughed. "Well, I do teach math and science, but I love history. If I'd been a better reader in school, I would have figured that out earlier."

"Dad, you don't think all your Math students knew that. Every kid in school knew they could get you off Math and into some story about history."

"Getting you to talk about sports was even easier," Rob joined in.

Maggie laughed loudly and George blushed. "Guilty as charged, but you have to admit I did keep your interest enough that I could get the class back to exponents, eventually."

"Yes sir," said Rob, "You made Math a lot more interesting for a dumb hick from Bound Brook."

"Rob, you were never dumb—a hick maybe, but not dumb," joked George.

"Oh, another person I'm sure you'll talk with is the Reverend Duggan," added Maggie.

"Of course, but isn't he a little too obvious?" asked Rob with a grin. "I mean, who is going to be the biggest sinner in town now that Proctor's gone?"

George looked at Maggie. "I think what she means is something Mabel hinted at. The Reverend has been trying to acquire land to build his church, but guess who he had to deal with? Mabel commented that people had noticed that Duggan had been taking it easy on Proctor recently. Maybe he needed to mend some fences with the old sinner?"

"Well, that is interesting," Rob admitted.

"You have quite a mystery," Rachel concluded. "You ever dealt with something like this?"

"Not really. Oh, I handled plenty of murders, sad to say, but most of those were no mystery. Usually too much liquor involved, someone so drunk he thought his buddy was the enemy. We had a few unsolved crimes, but in the middle of the War, with so many deaths already, we didn't have a lot of time to search for the culprits.

"Well, I've had too much coffee already," he added, rising from the table. "I think it's time to hit the road. Hopefully, Moose and the crew did some more plowing."

"Heard down at the store that Moose was bragging that he'd *helped* plow you out, or should I say plowed you in," smiled George. "That move is one of his oldest tricks. Come back again, questions or not, you know the door is open."

"Let me see you out," said Rachel, as Maggie gave George a glance to indicate they should leave.

After her parents left, Rachel looked at Rob. "It felt good to talk. Dating aside, you've always been my best friend and I've missed you."

He looked at her reddened eyes, "Rachel, I don't want to get between you and Jimmy, but I agree, it felt good to talk with you too."

She gave him a peck on the cheek. Rob smiled back and went out the door to his coupe. Before he started the car, he took a deep breath. The emotions he had bottled since their breakup were threatening to spill out. He couldn't afford to let them out now, so, just as he had done when his mother died (and when Rachel and Jimmy eloped), he pushed them back down, into the place that stored the horrible sights from the war, that place for things he didn't want to feel.

Chapter VI - Meeting With The Chief

The next day Rob drove down Lower Main Street, past the footbridge that crossed over Bound Brook Creek, to the Public Safety Building. The Police Station was on the upper floor, over the double bay doors that housed the town's two fire trucks. He parked and looked at the familiar buildings on the street, the Masonic Hall, Auntie's Candle Shop and what had been Harvey's Hardware Store. Harvey's sign was gone now, replaced with a newer one; *Joseph's Hardware* had been in business since the war, and Frank Joseph and his family lived in the apartment over the store. Rob always got a kick that many Portuguese residents had last names that were also first names; Joseph, Samuels, Thomas and others. He had known and played against a Joey Joseph, a Sammy Samuels and a Tommy Thomas in his day. Joseph's Hardware had the closed sign in the window, and he hoped it was only due to the storm.

After climbing the stairs, Rob nodded to Diane Ellis, the dispatcher, and she waved him toward the Chief's small office, "Skip just got here."

Inside his office the Chief's large figure loomed over his desk. Skip Parker sat in one of the two chairs and Rob took the other.

"Good thing you don't have a bigger police force, or we wouldn't fit," joked Rob.

Foster just grunted, then began speaking. "OK, let me bring you up to date. First, Doc Carter, as the County Medical Examiner, released the official report this morning. It lists the cause as a fractured skull and rules the death as suspicious. What isn't in the report is that Doc thinks that Proctor may have died way before the fire started, maybe even before the storm. He sent the body on to the state medical lab to see if they agree, and if they can give us a better time of death. Also, we sent the fireplace poker and jerry jug to the state crime lab. Might be able to get some prints. It's a long shot, but worth a try."

"So, theoretically, anybody could've had access to kill him," said Rob.

Skip spoke up. "But from what witnesses said, it sounds like the fire started sometime in the middle to end of the storm, when the roads were really bad, maybe impassable, right?"

"Good point," said the Chief. "So it's possible that the two events, the murder and the fire, were separate, but likely related. We also can't assume that the same person, or people, did both."

"The murderer may have had clear roads, but the arsonist didn't," Rob noted. "So what about the attempted break in?"

"We found footprints in the snow. They tried to jimmy a window at the back of the office around 2 A.M. The temperature stayed cold, and the back area is shaded, so state troopers got a clear boot-print without any melting. It looks like your basic wading boot, probably owned by every man or woman in town. Best guess on the size is around a nine or ten, men's regular width. Shoes don't match exactly to height, but I'd estimate someone around five-nine to six-foot. Oh course, that assumes the boots fit properly; could have been someone shorter, wearing boots that were too big. The footprints ran down the hill to Whit's Lane, where they must have parked a vehicle, at a spot that has no houses and lots of trees.

"So as far as opportunity goes, most anyone could have killed him, but opportunity is far more limited on starting the fire. But what else the limited evidence seems to say is, the murder may not have been premeditated, or at least not well planned. We found Proctor's body in the middle of the living room, not far from the fireplace. The fireplace poker was fairly nearby, also on the floor. The head wound matches to that type of shaft, so it sure looks like we got the murder weapon."

"Ah, the murderer used a weapon that was at hand," Rob summed up. "Didn't bring a weapon, if they had they would've used it. So what are you thinking? An argument or crime of passion, something like that?"

"Could be," said the Chief, "which brings us to motive. Why kill him?"

"I think we have plenty of suspects," said Skip with a chuckle.

"Not really," continued Foster. "Sure, lots of people hated Proctor, but it has to be extreme and immediate for someone to kill. So maybe the person didn't go there intending to kill Proctor, but some motive pushed them to go to his house, perhaps have an argument, pick up a fireplace poker and hit him hard enough to crack his skull."

Rob completed the scenario. "Then the murderer leaves and later, maybe even a day or two later, that person, or someone else or the two together, go back to the house, probably on foot, and start the fire, hoping it will cover up the crime."

"But even that was rushed and not well planned," noted Skip. "They started the fire outside, used the jerry jug, and then threw it back in the shed where we could find it."

"Good point, Skip." Rob turned back to the Chief. "I've been told it would be a good idea to talk with Richard Caldwell. He and Cecil Proctor did lots of real estate deals together, and he might know if someone was angry or had a grudge to settle. I don't know if you want to talk to him or want me to."

Foster thought about it for a minute. "Well, I imagine it might be hard for you to talk with him. I gather you two never had much of a relationship. On the other hand, I always found that people talk more when they're thrown off balance. Talking to you might unsettle him. He's usually so composed and reserved, wouldn't be bad if you shook him up a bit. You want to give it a go? If he doesn't talk with you, I can always follow up."

Rob gave the Chief a hard look. "I have no desire to talk with him, but this is about a murder, and I'm a cop, so sure I can do it. I'll just keep it business. However, I want to poke around a bit first, see if I can find some specific things to ask him about, like you said, maybe get under his skin."

"Sounds good." the Chief looked at Skip. "Who do you want to talk with?"

"Well, it may sound nuts, but my brother, Moose, he's no genius, but he hears and sees lots of things. Driving around in the town truck, people tend to forget he's there, they do and say things in front of him they wouldn't in front of others. He gets around and talks to lots of people and doesn't exactly kill himself working on the town crew. I'll talk to him and the other guys, Bunky, Honk and the rest. Maybe Rob and I can split up the shopkeepers, fishermen and the others."

"Okay," said the Chief, "you and Rob figure it out. Rob will have to take more interviews; sorry I couldn't get enough money to put you both on full time. I'll talk with the relatives, certainly not every Proctor in town, that would take too long, but the ones who had the most contact with him."

"No problem," Skip explained. "My job delivering for Morris Fuel is flexible, but with a tough winter and this storm we're pretty busy. Probably don't have time to work on the murder full-time anyway."

"Chief, I was thinking," Rob interjected. "Proctor was a rich man. Do we have any idea who gets his money? That could be a motive, either someone who thought they got cut out of a Will, or who knew they'd get the money if Proctor just happened to die."

"I'm working on that, Rob," said Foster. "That's some of what I'll be asking the Proctors. Of course, we'll know more when we find out what's in the Will, but maybe we can learn something to get a jump on it."

"One other thing I was thinking," Rob added. "What if the fire wasn't to cover the murder, or maybe only partly? What if the fire was to destroy something Proctor had in the house? He probably had contracts, business agreements, and other things. Perhaps someone didn't want anyone to search the house and find something that would damage them?"

"We have to keep all options open," said Foster, then hardened his voice, all business. "Now, a few ground rules. Don't tell me, or each other, anything over the phone. Between party lines and operators, there are too many ears. Call me to set up a meeting when you have something, and we'll meet some place quiet. Like Rob said, this office is really small. Rob, your place is pretty deserted, not much bigger than this office, but it might work. Let's touch base every couple of days, even if there's nothing new. Any questions?"

Rob and Skip shook their heads and the Chief nodded. Rob felt like he and Skip should be told to "saddle up" and head out on the "posse" with Sheriff John Wayne.

"Oh, one more thing," said the Chief, "of course you know not to talk to the press, but this is a murder, and you may get contacted by some nosy reporter who wants to get an inside scoop by doing an "end run" around me. Those reporters can make "nothing" sound like news, so just tell them to talk to me, then clam up. We may get a break because the big story is the Coast Guard rescue off Chatham. Much better story than some old man's murder in little Bound Brook."

"There's one person I think we forgot," Rob broke in, "Reverend Duggan."

Skip laughed, "Don't think we forgot him, more like we were hoping someone else would do him. Since you brought him up, that means you will, right Rob?"

"Guess I walked right into that one."

Foster's grunt was the closest he came to a laugh. "If you'd talk to him that would be good, I'm afraid I might wring his scrawny neck. We already got one murder, don't need two."

"Skip, I do believe our Chief just made a joke," smiled Rob.

Foster actually cracked a little grin. "You two clowns get out of here; we've got work to do."

Rob and Skip went down the two-story stairway and stood beside the DeSoto. "So, you want to do the merchants in the center?" Rob offered. "I can do Flying A, the Harbor, South Bound Brook village and folks in the Tyler clan. I need to talk to Harold about a stranger who was asking about Proctor."

"OK," agreed Skip. "Think I'll start with lunch at Agnes' Restaurant. The regulars will be there and maybe I can overhear something, plus I get some lunch."

"I'm heading out to see Hoopy and Harold, then over to Ben and Phyllis. I want to get some more background before I take on the Reverend and . . . Mr. Caldwell. Maybe I can pick up something that will throw either or both of them off when I question them."

It was a short drive on Lower Main Street back to the highway to the Hooper brothers' station. Rob pulled into a space beside the garage, next to two cars that looked like they needed a lot more than engine work.

Harold waved from the office door, "I'm guessing you don't need gas, cause if you do, I'll need a longer hose."

"Where'd those cars come from?" asked Rob.

"The Snow kid was out joy riding with *our* boy, Corey Junior. Dumb kids got a kick out of sliding around the corners where the pavement was still snow covered. He took the corner of Whit's Lane too fast, and slid out onto Lower Main, just when Widow Sousa was coming along. They should rename it "Half-Whit's Lane" the way those kids drive too fast on it. Snow kid hurt his arm or shoulder, he'll be OK, but no basketball for him for a while. Junior's fine and the Widow got shook up, but, fortunately she drives real slow, even in good weather."

"What are their cars doing here? Didn't know you did body work."

Harold shrugged, "We don't, but Proctor's garage wasn't shoveled out yet, and it was already full before the storm. Still got a bunch of wrecks from winter fender-benders, and he needs to get the school buses out first. Howie Proctor asked if I could hold 'em for him 'til he juggled some cars around and made some space."

"Junior told me there was a stranger asking about Proctor last week," said Rob.

"Yup, Fancy dresser, but tough looking, asked me which way to Proctor's house. Didn't think much about it. Proctor always got off-Cape visitors. That was it, guy just paid and left."

Rob let that sink in, "Let me know if you see him again, and try to get a license plate number if you can without being too obvious."

"Will do, and if you're looking for Hoopy, he's under Milly's Ford," Harold jerked his thumb toward the closed garage bay door. "Do me a favor, don't slow him down. We're already backed up from the storm."

"So, what are you doing to help your busy baby brother?"

Harold laughed. "I'm covering the gas pumps. Don't you see all the cars?"

Rob went through the small office and took the side door into the garage. Boots stuck out from under a Ford sedan. "Hey Hoopy, your big brother says you've got to keep working while we talk. Says he's real busy pumping gas."

"He hasn't pumped gas in an hour. Oh well, we switch in a little while," came the voice from under the car. "Just got to tighten this exhaust pipe, then time for lunch. With the deep snow we'll be getting a lot of under-carriage and exhaust work."

"Guess somebody filled you in on Doc Carter's report?"

"Sure. Even under this car, I still get the news. Howie Proctor came by about the two cars out front. Don't know who told him, but word gets around fast. Bound Brook's never needed an official Town Crier."

"So you got any thoughts?"

"Bunch of people in town gonna be nervous with Proctor dead," came the muffled voice.

"Why's that?"

"Proctor had his finger in everything. We're probably one of the few businesses in town that didn't have him as a landlord or part-owner. It's gonna be pretty complicated sorting out his Will, if he had one. Unless he left it all to someone, which I doubt, it could be a mess. That'll make lots of folks jumpy. What if payments all come due?"

"Who was he close to? Anyone he might have left it to?"

"He wasn't close to anyone. Most of the Proctors turned their backs on him. A few years ago, he seemed to be grooming his nephew, Corey Proctor Sr., Junior's Dad. But then they had a falling out, must have been just after the war, cause I was back by then."

"What about?"

"Not sure, I think he wanted Corey Sr. to take over, someday become the next *Old Man Proctor,* but like everything with Cecil, I'm sure it came with strings attached. When Corey's oldest son died in the war it was pretty hard. I think he was a bit lost, maybe looking for something new. His wife, Delores, has never gotten over it, made her a nervous wreck. Now, Junior is her whole world. Anyway, he seems pretty content with his electrical business."

"Yah, it'll be interesting to see what happens when the will is filed," Rob agreed. "Oh, the Chief got some county money to hire Skip and me to help out during the investigation, but again you didn't hear from me, so act surprised when word gets out."

"OK, might take an hour or two," laughed Hoopy.

"Goes without saying, you'll let me know what you hear, right?"

"Of course. There we got it, last nut tightened. That should hold till Milly Harper scrapes it on some rut this summer," Hoopy slid out from under the car. "Want some lunch?" He wiped his greasy hands on his stained overalls.

Rob winced at the thought, "No thanks. No offense, but I'm heading over to see Phyllis. She always has something good, and a lot more sanitary."

Hoopy laughed. "See ya."

Rob headed back through the office and gave Harold a wave as he got in his car. Harold was pumping gas for Jason Flower's

"Honey" truck. Jason did concrete foundations, septic tanks and septic pumping. The "Honey" truck was a euphemism for the brown contents he pumped from the tanks. The truck displayed the colorful painting of a flower, with the slogan, "Flower Septic - Leaves You Smelling Like a Rose." Typical Bound Brook idea of humor.

Rob headed south on the highway toward the turnoff for Neck Road and Tyler's Tangle. Bound Brook was still covered in a blanket of snow, but the sunshine and salt air were having an effect, even though the temperature remained cold. Ben's truck wasn't in the driveway, probably a lot of burst pipes after the blizzard. Rob knocked and heard Phyllis telling him to come in.

"As usual you came just in time for lunch. I've got some beef stew left over."

"Beef stew made by the best cook in town, sounds just right on a cold day."

"You sure know how to butter up a girl," she laughed. "Before I forget, I got a call from Maggie Gilmore. She had a message from George; he asked if you could come to practice Monday and bring your sneakers. I guess he's down some players with the Snow kid injured. Probably needs you to scrimmage."

"Sure, I can use the exercise, been getting soft." Rob patted his stomach.

Ben Brown Jr. entered the kitchen. "Hey Rob, you going to scrimmage with us?"

Rob looked at the strapping figure of his eighteen-year-old cousin, "Benny, I will if you take it easy on me," he laughed.

"Oh, it's the other way around. It'll be good for the guys to see a real basketball player. Some of them think they're real cool, but they haven't got a clue."

"Well, practice is about you guys improving, not about me showing off."

"Speaking of practice, Coach Gilmore opened the gym to anyone who wants to shoot around. With the storm and vacation, we didn't get any practice this week, so I'm going with some of the guys to get a workout. Junior's picking me up, but I'll be home for dinner. Hey, Rob, you want to come?"

"Wish I could, but I got some work to do. I'll see you Monday."

Benny gave his mother a peck on the cheek and headed out the door.

"Wow, he's grown so much, he's a man now. I remember when I left for college, he was just what, six or so, just started elementary school."

"They grow up, just look at you! I remember a gawky, shy, bookworm teenager, and look at you now, Bound Brook's most eligible bachelor,"

Rob felt a blush. "Now who's buttering up whom?"

"Got a feeling this isn't just a lunch visit," she said as she stirred a big pot on the gas stove.

"Well, I am asking folks about Proctor, but I made it a point to make my stop here in time to get fed. Turned down an offer from Hoopy at the Flying A."

"A sandwich with Hoopy, or my beef stew. Boy what a compliment. How can I help?"

"You'll hear the news soon, Proctor was murdered, hit on the head, not an accident. I'm trying to figure who had a motive to kill him. We know the obvious suspects, and I've talked with several men, but I thought a woman who knows as much about this town as you do might have a different perspective."

"Can't say I'm shocked," she said, "Something seemed fishy about that fire from what Ben told me."

She put a steaming bowl and a chunk of bread in front of Rob, "A good idea to get a woman's viewpoint. There are things we don't share with the men, and there was talk about Proctor. Now, this is something that normally wouldn't be proper to discuss, but considering the circumstances, I guess I should tell you."

A soup spoon, butter dish and knife appeared on the table. "Proctor had a reputation among women in town. The word was, *stay away from him*."

Rob blew on a spoonful and savored his first taste, "You know I never knew anything about Proctor and women. Didn't even know if he was interested. Did he have any relationships with women in town?"

"As far as I know, not for many years. I heard that sometimes he had some women from out of town come stay with him. Heard they were women who did things like that, if you know what I mean. The way I heard it, way back when Proctor was young, he dated some girls from town, but the rumor was he liked to get physical with them, and I mean hurt them. Pretty soon the word got out, and no girls in town would date him. I guess he tried dating girls from other towns, but eventually nobody'd go out with him."

Rob was slurping down the stew, but this news made him choke. "Man, that's the first I ever heard about it. Unfortunately, I saw some of that in the Navy. We had guys who liked to beat up women, but mostly did it when they were drunk. Did the police know?"

"Only the women knew. It's not something you tell your men. Oh, I imagine a few fathers might have found out, but Proctor was not someone to cross, and they sure weren't going to the police about it. Even if they had, in those days, before Foster became Chief, the police were in Proctor's pocket. No, the women took care of it themselves, by spreading the word to stay away."

As good as the stew was, Rob had stopped eating. "So, any chance somebody decided to get even, an angry husband or father?"

"It could be, but I doubt it, I think Proctor turned his particular tastes to women who were used to that kind of treatment. He was rich enough to pay for what he wanted. However, you never know. I haven't heard anything, but in winter you don't get out to see as many people."

Rob finished his lunch in silence, while Phyllis chatted about the latest news: who had a baby, who was expecting, who had enlisted. There was a rumor that the Wellfleet Curtain Factory was finally going to close. That would put a number of Bound Brook folks out of work. Mabel Curtis probably had an edge in the gossip business, but not much got past Phyllis.

"That was a great lunch, as usual," said Rob. "What do you hear about the Reverend Duggan?"

"You mean other than he's a crazy fanatic?"

"Proctor liked to get dirt on people and use it as leverage. Anything he could've had on Duggan?"

"Well," She paused. "Duggan came to town from somewhere up north, Vermont or New Hampshire, maybe, so I don't know much about his background. The Methodists seemed to like him when he first got here, and other than his sermons he seemed to mind his own business. He visited the older parishioners and sick people and did the job a minister should do. There was some scandal in the forties, but it was hushed up and *even I* never heard the details. Seemed like it happened off-Cape, maybe even out of state. Somebody in the church knew something about it and next thing you know, Duggan was out of a job. There were people still loyal to him, and so he was able to hang around and eventually get his own church."

He thought about her comment. "You think Proctor knew about the cause of the scandal, and could have used it against Duggan in some way?"

She smirked, "Oh I think he had a hand in getting Duggan fired for sure."

"Just thinking that if Duggan went to see Proctor maybe they argued. Perhaps all those years of anger toward Duggan's insults got out of hand and they started fighting. Don't think a minister killing someone, even in self-defense, would be something a congregation would be too happy to hear.

"Word is that Duggan had gone easy on Proctor lately," he continued. "Also rumored that Duggan was having trouble buying land for the church and may have needed Proctor's help."

"Hmm," she frowned, "that could be something they had an argument about and perhaps it got out of hand."

"Well, I'll be talking to the Reverend soon, see what he has to say. You know where he's living these days?"

"Actually, not far from here. I heard he has a summer parishioner, a widow who lets him live in her house, sort of house-sitting for the off season. It's over on Bay View Point, name on the mailbox is Armstrong."

"That'd be a short walk through the woods to Proctor's house, from what I remember."

Phyllis raised her eyebrows. "Yes, it is, and the Reverend doesn't have a car that I know of. His *faithful* give him rides when he needs it, otherwise he walks everywhere. Says it's good for the body and the soul."

"You can use our phone and give him a call if you want, see if he's home."

Rob thought about that. "No, I'd rather surprise him. Of course, I'd rather not talk to him at all, if the truth be told."

"Amen," said Phyllis with a laugh.

Chapter VII – Repent Yee Sinners!

Before he surprised Duggan, Rob thought it might be good to talk with his own minister, the Reverend Lyman Towne. He had been the Congregational minister for as long as Rob could remember and was a respected fixture in town. He and his wife had been devastated by the death of their only child in the War, but carried on. Towne must have been well into his seventies and the word was that he was going to retire soon.

Rob parked at the Congregational Church and crossed the street to the parsonage. The diminutive Reverend Towne answered the door, "Why Rob, so good to see you. Haven't seen much of you lately."

Blushing, Rob replied, "I know, I'll try to do better. If you have a minute, I had a few questions."

"Sure, please come in."

Rob took a seat in the parlor that had been the meeting place of the Youth Fellowship when he was a teenager.

"So what can I answer for you?" asked the minister.

"Well, I wouldn't be asking, but this is official police business. I can't tell you the details and would appreciate it if you kept our conversation private. I wondered if you could give me your personal impression of Reverend Duggan?"

Reverend Towne frowned. "I'm not very comfortable talking about another clergy member, but if it's for police business I'll try to help."

"Well, I have to go talk with Duggan after we finish, and I hoped you could tell me more about what you thought of him when he was the Methodist minister, particularly his relationship with Cecil Proctor."

"Relationship with Proctor," Towne chuckled, "now that's funny. Proctor hated him. However, I honestly don't think that Duggan felt the same way. You know when Duggan was minister, the cooperation between our churches was strained. We had always worked well with the Methodists and the Catholics as well."

"What caused the problems?"

"Duggan is a difficult man," continued Towne. "He tends to believe that he is the only one who has all the answers on religion, and most other things as well. Everything has to be done his way. Proctor was just an easy target, in Duggan's mind it was nothing personal. Since I'm being candid, I always felt that he needed more humility, he has an awfully big ego for a man of God. I didn't appreciate that most of his targets seemed to attend *my* church. When I confronted him about that one time, *he told me to take better care of my flock.* Well, after that we had little or no contact, it was pretty mutual, and our Congregations rarely had joint activities. After a few years of being Duggan's whipping-boy, Proctor used his influence with the Methodist elders. I always suspected that he dug up dirt from Duggan's past as well. Proctor had the money and means to do some digging. That's about all I can tell you, except that since Duggan was replaced, the cooperation with the Methodists has been greatly improved. We do a number of joint activities. You should come to some of them."

Rob had to laugh. "OK, I get the hint, I'll try to be better."

"It would be nice to see you more often. I miss seeing so many of you after watching you all grow up over the years." The minister cleared his throat. "Helps me fill the void, you know what I mean?"

"I know," Rob paused. "Well, that's really about all I wanted to ask you, at least for now. I appreciate the background information." He walked to the door and shook the elderly minister's hand before heading back to his car, thinking about what he'd learned. So, not surprisingly, there was no love lost between Reverend Towne and Duggan. He wondered if Duggan knew that it was Proctor who had gotten him removed as the Methodist minister. If he didn't know for sure, he had to at least suspect it.

He drove down Neck Road to Proctor's Hollow Road, and turned off on Bay View. Driving the road was a roundabout route. It followed the shoreline and went around in a half circle. Taking the path through the woods, the one he'd used when he was a kid, made it a straight shot from Bay View over to Proctor's Point.

Almost at the end of Bay View, he saw a mailbox, with the name Armstrong, at the bottom of a long driveway that went up to the top of a bluff. The driveway was unplowed, so he parked on the side of the road and walked up the hill. The house was of modern design, and newly built: split level, with the first floor built into the side of the bluff, and the second story with more glass than walls.

When he got to the top of the driveway he understood why. Unlike most of the houses on Bay View that didn't even have a glimpse of water, the bluff had a spectacular vista of the Bay. Of course, with all that glass it must cost a fortune to heat in the winter. Rob suspected that the Widow Armstrong took care of the oil, so the Reverend didn't have to worry.

There was a walkway, shoveled just enough for one person to thread a way to the back entrance. Cape folks usually used the back door, the front was mostly for show. Rob took off his thick gloves and lifted the heavy brass knocker. No answer. He counted to ten and tried again, this time even harder.

A voice called out from somewhere deeper in the house. "Whoever it is, give me a minute!"

After several minutes the thin figure of Reverend Duggan opened the door. He was wrapped in an old bathrobe with at least a day's worth of stubble and unruly hair. Realizing his appearance, Duggan ran his hand over his head, patting loose hairs back into place.

"Mr. Caldwell, hello! I didn't expect any visitors, you have to forgive my appearance, started working on my sermon and lost track of time. Please come in."

"Reverend, call me Rob. There's a Mr. Caldwell in town, but he's not me."

"Ah yes, I get the reference," replied Duggan. "Come to the kitchen, I have tea and can make some coffee if you prefer. To what do I owe this visit?"

Rob entered the ground-floor foyer and followed Duggan up a flight of stairs that emerged into a large, open second floor. At the left far end was a kitchen area with gleaming modern appliances. Rob stood in the dining area. To his right was a large living room, modern furniture with bold print patterns providing the decor.

What was stunning was the openness and the view. Three of the walls were almost completely glass. The second floor hung off the back edge of the bluff, creating a feeling of being suspended in air. Directly ahead, and seemingly near enough to touch, was a panorama of Cape Cod Bay. Facing southwest, beyond the Bay, Rob could see the bending peninsula of Cape Cod, from Bound Brook, East Brook, all the way to Dennis and the Mid-Cape.

"Nice house, amazing view!"

Duggan seemed to blush. "Yes, I'm very fortunate. Mrs. Armstrong has let me stay here in return for taking care of things."

"I don't think I know her."

"Yes, she and her husband were newcomers. He was a heart specialist and medical school professor. They built this to be their retirement home and spent several years planning and working on it while they rented a summer house on the ocean side. Unfortunately, right after it was completed, and before they could move in, Dr. Armstrong had a massive heart attack and died."

"Rather sad, I would say."

"Yes, Mrs. Armstrong had a great deal of difficulty dealing with his death. It was hard enough to accept, but to be felled by the disease that was his specialty just didn't seem right to her. After years of working so hard, he was finally going to retire, relax and spend time with her. Instead, now she's really alone."

"So how'd you come to know her?"

"A parishioner friend of hers suggested that I might be able to provide some comfort. They'd never attended church regularly, but I think that was him more than her. After her loss, she needed to seek the Lord. I hope I've helped."

"And in return you have a beautiful home, and perhaps a generous donor?"

Duggan looked uncomfortable. "Oh, I don't consider it my home, but I am glad I can help by taking care of it for her. As for donations, that's up to the people who want to further the work of the Lord."

Rob noticed a pad of paper on the dining room table. "It must provide an inspiring view when you prepare your sermons?"

"Yes, a chance to reflect on the glories the Lord has created," said Duggan gazing at the Bay. "So, coffee or tea?"

"Thanks for the offer, but I'm fine. Actually, I'm here on official business regarding Cecil Proctor."

"Yes, a tragedy. As much as I preached against his attitude, I do hope his soul will find salvation. In fact, that's the topic of my sermon for next Sunday. It's never too late to seek the Lord."

Rob sensed the possibility of a long sermon, so he interrupted. "Yes, well you see there've been some developments in the case." He watched the Reverend closely for a reaction.

"Developments? What would those be? Anything that I should know before I finish my sermon?"

"Well, the official word just came out from the medical examiner. Proctor's death wasn't an accident, he died from a blow to the head."

Duggan's eyes opened wide. "My goodness, oh dear, that is shocking news. I didn't approve of the man, but none of God's children deserve to be killed. I've already prayed for his soul, but I must rethink my words for Sunday."

"Well Reverend, you see I'm here in an official capacity as a Bound Brook police officer, and I have to ask you some questions regarding your relationship with the deceased."

"What, you don't think. . . Surely you couldn't believe that I had anything to do with his death?"

"Reverend, your feelings toward Mr. Proctor were well known. I've heard he was making it difficult for you to buy land to build your church, and you certainly live close enough that you could have walked to his house, even in a snowstorm. So, it seems to me that you're a logical person to question regarding the murder."

The Reverend Duggan looked genuinely shaken. "I know I preached against Proctor's behavior, but it was never personal. I've known many sinners. I'm not without faults myself, but I don't wish them harm. On the contrary, I preach against their behavior as an example to others, but always with the hope that they'll see the error of their ways and welcome the Lord into their hearts. How can I hate them, if I want to save them?"

"Well, maybe we can start with you accounting for your whereabouts just before and during the storm. Did you see Cecil Proctor during that time? Is there anyone who can account for your whereabouts?"

Duggan shook his head. "During the storm I was here, like most people I was stuck inside. Nobody else was here, so I guess, no, I don't have anyone."

He suddenly gave a look of recognition, "Actually, yes, I did speak with him. The morning before the storm in fact. I walked over to his house."

"What did you talk about?"

"Like you said, building a church. There were two locations that would be perfect, both on land owned by Proctor over on the East Brook line. I was appealing for him to sell one of them to us, either one would be fine. He said he didn't want to sell, but that we might work out something like a long-term lease. I was afraid he might hold it against the church because of my sermons, but he didn't seem to have a grudge at all. In fact, just the opposite, he said he knew he was getting older and he wanted to make things right with his maker."

"Proctor talked to you about repenting?"

"Not exactly, but he seemed, I don't know, I guess nicer than I'd expected. He said he was worried about his legacy, or at least the Proctor legacy. He reminded me of others I've seen who are on the verge of making peace with the Lord and getting ready to repent. But, no he didn't repent, not then."

"Well I guess we'll never know now," commented Rob. "So how did you leave it with him?"

"He said he'd think about it. He told me to see your grandfather, I mean Mr. Caldwell. He said Caldwell was the realtor, and I should deal with him."

"Did you see anyone else there?"

"No, but maybe he was waiting for someone. His table was set for two people and he already had a full pot of coffee made, even though he hadn't known I was coming by."

"Did Proctor say anything to you that wasn't particularly *nice*?"

"I'm not sure what you mean."

"Well, according to you, the man you've been ranting against for years, who you screamed about as a sinner, who you said, *got what he deserved* at the fire scene . . . this same man and you, somehow had a calm, civil conversation about him helping you, to get property to build a church, so you could continue to preach about his sins. I'm sorry, Reverend, but that's kind of hard for me to believe."

Duggan blushed again. "I guess it would sound that way. First, I never should've behaved that way at the fire. I've been praying for the Lord's forgiveness, and it was uncharitable of me. Sometimes I get carried away, and the public sermons are dramatic—not that I don't believe in them, but to get attention I can be pretty extreme. I do honestly believe that the Lord has a plan, and having Proctor die in that fire was part of his plan. It was prophetic. I don't question God's intentions, but Proctor's death seemed no coincidence."

"Except the fire didn't kill Proctor, someone cracked his skull, and then someone set the blaze. The Lord didn't do that, a person or persons did it. It seems to me that Proctor burning in the *flames of hell* might serve your purposes perfectly. Prophesy fulfilled, church attendance rises, donations pour in, your church gets built, and all is right with the world, especially for Reverend Duggan."

Duggan's features hardened. "I'm trying not to get angry over your allegations. You are a policeman; it is part of your job ... You know, I always admired your mother. Like all of us she committed sin, but she faced her transgressions, I prayed for her soul and . . ."

"Reverend, please don't ever talk to me about my mother! I remember how you treated her *transgressions*." He had risen and his fists were clenched.

Duggan flinched. "Of course, I didn't mean any offense."

"Yes, you did. There's a part of you that's a righteous bully, using God to further your own goals. Until we find the killer you're on my list as a prime suspect. If you want to get off my list, I suggest you help us find who did it, *if* it isn't you. I wonder how being a murder suspect will help your donations?" He got up without another word. "I'll see myself out, *Reverend*."

Back at the bottom of the driveway, he reflected on his performance. Duggan wasn't the only one who could put on a show. The minister honestly did irritate him, but Rob had been looking for an opening to go on the attack. He wanted Duggan uncomfortable, and if he thought Rob was "out to get him" then that might work just fine.

Something about Duggan's story didn't ring true. Oh, most of it was probably accurate; the best lies have elements of truth. With Proctor dead, the Reverend's version of their conversation couldn't be checked. It was interesting that Duggan admitted to being at Proctor's house before the storm. However, it was also clever, there was a good chance someone else might have known, someone could have seen him, so better to admit it than to get caught in a lie. *And what about his claim that the table had been set for two, so did that mean Proctor was expecting someone? Was that the truth, or a smart way to open the possibility of another suspect?*

Duggan was leaving something out. At the very least he was putting his own spin on the conversation. Had the Reverend picked up the fireplace poker and clubbed Proctor, after the old man refused to sell him land? Had Proctor had some dirt on Duggan that he'd threatened to reveal? Maybe the minister had panicked, run back home, and later realized he needed to go back and destroy the evidence? It would be likely that neither event had been planned. The amateurish murder and arson would fit someone like Duggan.

Well, Rob couldn't rule him out, and right now he was about the best suspect he had. Motive, means, opportunity . . . they were all there. He wondered how the Chief and Skip Parker were doing.

Today was Friday, perhaps Sunday he'd go to church. Not to the Congregational Church where he'd been raised, but the Reverend Duggan's church at the Elk's Hall. Rob wasn't even sure what it was called. Might be a way to keep the pressure on the Reverend and could be interesting to see who his followers were. Could one of them have killed Proctor, perhaps thinking they were doing the Reverend a favor?

He drove the short distance to his cottage. He was glad to see that the bay breeze and sunshine had done some melting. He opened the unlocked door and threw his coat, hat and gloves over a kitchen chair. In the middle of the table was a note.

Knock, Knock, you weren't home. Chief says we should meet here on Monday morning, 9 a.m. You make the coffee and I'll bring some of Agnes's muffins. Skip

Well, if he was reporting his results Monday morning, he figured he better bite the bullet and talk with his so-called grandfather. Maybe he'd have something worth sharing at their meeting.

Chapter VIII – Family Reunion

Saturday morning saw further improvement in the weather and more melting in his driveway. Pancakes were on the menu with toast, butter and beach plum jelly. When he was little Rob had picked the berries, and his mother made the jelly. Now he relied on a cache of jars, tucked away for the winter, from Connie's Roadside Jams and Jellies out on the highway.

Over a mug of coffee and a full stomach, Rob reviewed his schedule. He was not looking forward to seeing his grandfather today. It was a part of his life that was an open wound. To have a relative, grandfather no less, who had been so cruel to his own daughter and shunned her offspring, it would seem bizarre if it wasn't true.

On Sunday he was curious to see Duggan in his home setting, and also to see if he knew any of his followers. He had the impression that Duggan had pulled in people from as far as Provincetown on the tip of the Cape, along with others from the elbow, around Orleans, Brewster, Chatham and Harwich. The Reverend's firebrand style was not common and, as far as Rob knew, it was the only church of its type on this end of the Cape.

Monday afternoon he was headed to basketball practice at Bound Brook High School. He wondered if there was any chance the teenagers of the town might have information. He doubted it. If his own youth was any indication, they were probably oblivious, but you never knew. Maybe with all his visits he could get something useful for the Monday meeting with the Chief.

Rob changed into his Bound Brook Police uniform, which fit a bit snug around the waist. He hadn't worn it since traffic duty last summer. He wanted to be completely official when he visited Caldwell.

He warmed up the old DeSoto and thought about seeing his grandfather. Before his mother had died, the only time he'd seen his grandparents was at the Congregational Church on Sundays. His mother and he had dressed in their best clothes and always arrived just before the service started. Ignoring the ushers, who tried to bring them closer to the front, Roberta Caldwell always took a pew near the back. With her head held high and chin thrust forward, she listened intently to Reverend Towne, and loudly sang the hymns with a lovely alto voice. As Rob had gotten older, he'd come to realize that the entire time his mother's eyes were aimed at the back of Richard Caldwell's head. Never once during the service had her father ever turned, but occasionally Rob caught furtive glances from his grandmother, Grace Tyler Caldwell.

Grace Caldwell was quiet and meek. There were a few occasions when Roberta and Rob had run into her in the grocery store. She seemed both eager and apprehensive. Her eyes had a pleading look, and although they had never spoken, there was a communication between mother and daughter that defied words. Sometimes, when Rob had been out playing with the Tyler cousins, he'd seen a parked car. A few times he caught a glimpse of a small figure in the back seat and sensed that he was being watched. One day he'd seen enough to recognize his grandmother, who'd quickly rolled up the window, and then the car had driven away.

Rob had asked his mother about what he had seen. Roberta had explained, the way she always did: When he had been born he hadn't had a father; his real father had gone away, and probably hadn't even known Rob existed. His grandfather had been very angry at his daughter for having a baby without a father, and they had a big argument. After the argument Richard Caldwell never spoke to either his daughter or his grandson.

"What about my grandmother?" Rob had asked. "Why doesn't she talk to us? Is she angry too?"

"No, she's not mad. Your grandmother is a good woman," Roberta had told him, "but it's hard for her. She always does what her husband tells her to do. Your grandmother Grace is just glad that we live in Bound Brook, and she can still see her daughter and grandson. Not all mothers are so lucky."

"Is that why she has someone drive her out here to watch me play?"

"Yes, I think so." Roberta had looked serious. "But this is important! Don't ever tell anyone that you see her watching you!"

"Why, Mama?"

"Because it would make your grandfather angry with her, and we don't want to get her in trouble with him. So promise?"

"I promise."

So the routine had continued, all through Rob's childhood. Encouraged by the preaching of Reverend Duggan, some people had snubbed his mother. But the Tyler clan had stuck by her. Roberta Caldwell had held her head high and refused to acknowledge the glances and snide comments those other people muttered under their breaths. In time, Rob had sensed a change, perhaps a grudging respect for her strength and determination. The comments had turned to tips of caps and greetings, until the day she died, still a young woman in her prime.

By now Rob had absentmindedly driven Neck Road to the Highway and was almost at his destination in North Bound Brook, at Hunter's Hill, his grandfather's house. In his thirty years, he had never been inside. When his mother had died there had been an outpouring from the Bound Brook community. The Congregational Church had held the funeral and the Tyler clan hosted a post-internment gathering, spread among several of the larger homes in "The Tangle." His mother had been buried among the many Tylers in the South Bound Brook Cemetery. Richard and Grace Caldwell had not attended.

After Roberta's death, Grace Caldwell had never left her house. Rob learned later that she'd almost never left her bedroom. She no longer attended church, although Richard continued faithfully. Rob had never again seen her at the store or spying on him and his friends. She had just disappeared. Then, exactly two years after Roberta's death, Grace Caldwell died. People had tried to keep the details from him, but he'd learned she had taken her own life with sleeping pills. Rob had been fifteen. He hadn't attended the service for the grandmother he'd never really known.

Rob turned off the highway at Hunter Hill Road. There was a dark car behind him, but too far back to recognize. He drove up the long, fully plowed driveway to Richard Caldwell's large, white, Victorian-style house. In high school there had been a big brush fire in the meadow on the edge of Hunter Hill. The volunteer fire department had rushed to the scene, and the older boys in the high school had been dismissed to help out.

It had been late fall during a dry spell, and high flames had leaped from the meadow and raced across the adjacent marsh. Fire trucks from surrounding towns had come to assist. It had taken hours to put it out, and at the end everyone was blackened with soot. Rob remembered looking at the figure of Richard Caldwell, on his third-story widow's walk, surveying the damage. Someone had hooked up a garden hose from the Caldwell house and they'd all taken turns washing off the grime. That was the closest Rob had been to the house, until today.

In contrast to many of the houses in Bound Brook, the Caldwell home was immaculately shoveled: driveway, walkways, roof, porches, all completely free of snow. Caldwell could afford to keep the house and grounds pristine. Walking up the extended walkway to the porch stairs, set on the top of a rise, Rob noticed the snow-covered expanse of what he remembered as a lush, green lawn. A large ornate front door with leaded, stained-glass panes marked the entrance. He pushed the doorbell and heard the sound of chimes resonating inside.

After a short wait, the door opened to reveal the striking presence of Richard Caldwell. His grandfather was tall like Rob, and at around seventy years old still carried himself with a ramrod posture. Even on a Saturday morning, he was clean shaven, groomed and wearing slacks and a cashmere sweater. Rob had never noticed it before, but the posture, facial features and thrust-out jaw reminded him of someone: his mother.

Caldwell's perfectly composed demeanor crumbled slightly as he realized who his visitor was. Looking genuinely perplexed and disturbed, he took a step back, and regarded the uniformed figure of his grandson. Rob said nothing, just stood in the door waiting. Finally, Caldwell seemed to gather himself, and the composed look returned.

"Yes, officer, what can I do for you?"

"We are investigating the death of Cecil Proctor, and given that you were involved in many of his business and real estate dealings, I need to ask you some questions. May I come in?"

"Of course." Caldwell seemed bothered by his presence and the reason for it. "I doubt I can tell you anything."

"You may have heard that his death was no accident," Rob began, staring intently at his grandfather. "Perhaps you can shed some light on someone who might have had a conflict or disagreement with Mr. Proctor."

Still standing in the doorway, he asked, "So, may I come inside?"

"Yes, yes, do come in."

He led Rob through a large entry foyer and into a small parlor with heavy brocade curtains and oriental carpet. Caldwell gestured him to an upholstered settee, while he took a seat in an antique rocker. Rob looked at the opulent furnishings, acutely aware at how little of the house he was actually viewing.

"Very nice house," he said, with a slight twinge of irony. If his grandfather wanted to continue the thirty-year charade that was fine by him.

"Thank you," said Caldwell brusquely. "So, how can I help the Bound Brook Police Department, and why isn't Chief Foster here?"

OK, that was designed to put Rob in his place, "We're dividing up the people in town, and the Chief thought it might be a good idea if I spoke with you instead of him. He thought that given our *connection. . .*" Rob paused to let the words sink in, and Caldwell actually winced. "I mean, the fact that we are both Bound Brook natives, it might be easier for us to communicate, you know, given our shared *heritage*."

Caldwell smiled. Maybe he was enjoying this game. "I see. Well, ask your questions, I have a lot planned for today."

Rob took out a small notebook. He didn't need it, but he might as well play this game to its fullest. "You were the broker for most of Proctor's real estate dealings, correct? Can you think of anyone recently who had a grudge, or felt they got a raw deal?"

Caldwell chuckled. "You're probably aware that the town is full of people who had a grudge against Cecil. Most thought they had a bad deal, but at the end of the day, the reality was it was the best deal, sometimes the only deal they were going to get. Cecil was tough, but he was willing to do deals that banks and others wouldn't even consider. Of course, he could always repossess the property if need be. Mind you, even when he was the only one willing to make the deal, that didn't make people happy."

"As his business partner, didn't any of those bad feelings spill over onto you?"

Caldwell cleared his throat. "Ahem, well, I was merely the real estate broker who facilitated the transactions. I wasn't the owner or the seller."

"Were you aware of Reverend Duggan trying to purchase some land owned by Mr. Proctor?"

"I heard about it, but not directly."

"So Mr. Proctor never talked to you about selling or leasing land for Duggan to build a church?"

Caldwell thought for a moment. "Not that I remember."

"And Reverend Duggan never spoke with you about acquiring land for the church?"

"Well, several months ago the Reverend inquired at my office about any land that might be available. He asked me to be on the lookout for some appropriate locations."

"So, did you tell him about land that Proctor owned over near East Brook?"

"I may have, I don't remember."

"But you didn't mention that to Mr. Proctor?"

"I already told you I didn't." The smile had gone now.

"Were there other dealings that you and Proctor shared where you were partners, rather than you just being the broker?"

Perturbed, Caldwell leaned forward. "Are you implying something?"

"Not at all, just trying to get a handle on Proctor's business affairs, and who better to talk with than you?"

Caldwell seemed to weigh his answer. "Yes, Cecil and I were occasionally partners. We owned a few properties together. Mind you, compared to all the property that he owned, it was a small fraction."

"I believe you also did business with Cecil's father. I heard he didn't believe in banks, and kept his money in a large safe in his house. Did Cecil feel that same way?"

Caldwell smiled, actually more of a smirk. "Well at first Cecil kept everything in the safe just like his father, but that changed after the Depression. Cecil was pretty cautious, but banks are insured these days. We learned something from the bank failures of the Depression. Cecil used the Bound Brook Bank, and I believe he had a few "blue chip" stocks and government bonds. He didn't take risks, he liked *sure things*, but most of his fortune was invested in property."

"Do you know all the properties that he owned?"

"Well, I brokered most of them, but I don't have a list, if that's what you mean. I suppose his lawyer, I think it's Attorney Winters in Provincetown, will have that information. I imagine I'll hear from him, given that we owned a few properties together."

"When you bought property together, did you use another broker, other than yourself?"

Caldwell didn't answer.

"Like I said, did Proctor always use you as his broker, or did he use other realtors sometimes?"

Now Caldwell looked angry. "Look, young man, I don't think I need to answer all these questions. That's my private business and has nothing to do with any murder."

"Okay," Rob conceded, "but speaking of the murder, can you tell me the last time you spoke with Proctor?

Caldwell didn't answer.

"Oh, and would you please account for your whereabouts during the blizzard and for the two days before?"

"That's it!" Caldwell rose abruptly from the rocker. "I don't need to answer impertinent questions from a snippy, young . . ."

"Grandson?"

"Get out!"

"Of course, I'm leaving. Why shouldn't you shut me out of your house and life? You have for thirty years, so why change now? You can shut out your grandson, but you'll still have to answer for your business dealings with Proctor to the Police. For your behavior toward your daughter and wife, you'll have to answer to a higher power."

Caldwell clenched his fists and looked poised to strike. "How dare you?"

"You want to hit me? Is that what you did to your wife to keep her in line? Is that how you threatened your daughter because she defied you? What would happen if you tried to hit someone who'd stand up to you?"

"This is not the end, I'll be speaking with Chief Foster about your unprofessional behavior. You won't have your job long."

"Probably just long enough to find Cecil Proctor's murderer. You better hope you're not involved, because I have extra motivation, you despicable bully. I don't know how you can live with yourself in this big, empty mausoleum. Who do you have to boss around?"

Caldwell's face was beet red and he looked ready to explode.

"I can find my own my out. Oh, and thank you for the tour of your lovely home." Rob strode out the door, leaving it open behind him. As he walked down the stairs he heard the door slam, but not before he heard Caldwell exclaim, "By God, you're just like your mother!"

****

The black sedan was parked a hundred yards away. The driver had pulled into a short loop off the main road left over from the old twisting highway. He came out on the edge of route 6, and stayed back enough to be hidden by scrub pine trees. The car was invisible through the trees, but the driver had a clear view when Rob's car pulled out rapidly and turned back south toward Bound Brook center. The driver waited until the car was almost out of sight, then eased out and accelerated. In this *Podunk* town, in the middle of winter, it was almost too easy to trail a car. Most of the time the highway was deserted, and there were so few cars around that the driver could stop tailing the DeSoto, and just drive around until he spotted the distinctive old car again.

The driver saw Rob take the turn for Bound Brook Center. He tapped the brakes and slowed to a crawl, then pulled the powerful sedan to the side of the road. He'd give the old coupe a huge lead and then slowly cruise through the town. If the driver spotted the car he would stake it out; if not, it was easy enough for him to find the car later. After five minutes he pulled out and drove cautiously, glancing into driveways along the road for Rob's car. In the town center, the driver checked the parked cars and then pulled into the parking lot beside the Town Hall. There it was!

The auto crept past the DeSoto, through the lot, and found a parking spot on the street where the driver could see any car that left. He waited patiently, but the only traffic was a young girl who walked up the street from the opposite direction and entered the pharmacy. About ten minutes later, Rob exited, and held the door open for a young woman in a plaid mackinaw. The driver watched the two cross the street to the car. Rob glanced around and looked directly at the black car, then started walking in his direction. The driver started the engine and pulled out quickly before Rob could get to him.

He didn't need to follow him, he'd done his homework. He knew who the girl was and where she lived. His work was done for the moment, but he'd be back.

Chapter IX – Rachel

After he left his grandfather's, Rob took a minute to gather himself before he started the car. He had planned for two possibilities. The first, and unlikely one, was that Caldwell would be more than superficially cooperative, that he would volunteer information that would be helpful. Instead, he had been the second possibility: pompous, arrogant and acting like he was above the investigation. When Caldwell had taken the uncooperative route, Rob had deliberately provoked him. He knew he had nothing to lose, and maybe it'd be easier when Chief Foster followed up. Just like with Reverend Duggan, Rob wanted possible suspects to be nervous. As he thought about the conversation, *he realized Caldwell had stopped answering when he'd asked him specific questions about deals with Proctor and when he had last seen him alive.*

As for Caldwell's threats, Rob was unconcerned. Honestly, if he got fired it wasn't a big deal. It wasn't like he was making it a career. However, he expected Chief Foster would resist the pressure. Foster already had a state pension, and Rob knew he had taken the position on the condition that the Selectmen promised to leave him alone and let him do the job his own way. After years of political Chiefs who did favors, the Selectmen were under scrutiny and needed a professional.

What he hadn't expected, but should have, was the real anger that came pouring out of him by the presence of the man who had done so much wrong to his own family. Rob knew he had been denying his feelings of hostility toward Caldwell. However, once the emotion came pouring out, it was hard to bottle it up again.

Rob drove to Bound Brook center without any conscious plan. Parking by the Town Hall, he found himself entering the pharmacy, and then realized who he was looking for. There she was, working behind the counter of the soda fountain, her back turned and her hair pulled back in a ponytail. He took a stool next to two young boys and remembered the times his mother had treated him to a root-beer float, or for special occasions, a hot fudge sundae. Rachel turned around with a sundae in each hand, and placed them in front of the youngsters. The boys pushed their quarters toward her, but Rob pushed them back. "My treat, boys! Mrs. Curtis, would you please make one of those for me too?"

She gave him her radiant smile, "Whatever you want, sailor," and gave him a wink.

He laughed. A hot fudge sundae and Rachel's smile were just the medicine he needed.

"I'm sorry, Mrs. Curtis, but you seem to have confused my attire. This is the uniform worn by Bound Brook's finest!"

One of the boys looked at Rob with awe. "Yes, Mrs. Curtis, he's a policeman."

"Thank you, Johnny, now I see, I was confusing him with one of those sailors my mother always warned me about."

"Thank you for the treat, sir," said the second boy, while the first just continued to stare.

"Mrs. Curtis, I wondered when you get off work, and whether you needed a ride home?"

"Well, actually, after I finish taking care of you and these two gentlemen, I should be finished. Mary will be here in about fifteen minutes. Given that you're a policeman, and not a sailor, I guess it'd be safe to accept a ride."

He put a dollar on the counter while she started making his sundae. The two boys seemed to inhale their treats and finished before Rob got his. With a quick round of thanks, they were out the door.

"Wow, now we still got our quarters, we can get some comics at the News Store," said one of the boys.

Rachel put the sundae in front of him. "My, my, a policeman, *and* a big tipper! Good thing I gave you an extra cherry on top!" She started cleaning the ice cream scoops and the boys' empty cups and spoons, "You sure made those two happy. I told my father I'd call him if I needed a ride."

The jingle of the little bell over the front door drew their attention as a high school girl bustled in. "Hi, Rachel, hope I'm not late. Oh, hello Officer Caldwell, don't see you in uniform very often."

"Not late at all, Mary, you're actually early," Rachel gave her a smirk and a wink. "Don't you love a man in uniform?"

Mary Joseph got the hint. "Yes, Officer Caldwell looks very handsome. No wonder all the girls have a crush on him." Noticing Rob's discomfort, she warmed to the game. "Good thing I'm going steady with Junior, or I'd be batting my eyelashes like crazy."

"OK, you two, I might have to arrest both of you for dangerous flirting, very serious crime you know."

Mary giggled.

"Mr. Williams," Rachel called over to the man behind the pharmacist counter, "Mary's here, so I'm going to head along," "Officer Caldwell has offered to provide me a police escort."

Bob Williams looked up from filling a prescription and gave Rob a wave.

"Probably stop by a little later, Mr. Williams," said Rob. "Like to talk to you about recent events."

"You know where to find me," replied Williams.

Rachel came out from the back room wearing a heavy, red plaid mackinaw, her hair tucked into a blue stocking cap with a white pom-pom on top, "I'm ready."

"Look at that hat. Bound Brook High School colors, you look like you still go there."

"Why, thank you, I guess. Either that means I haven't aged, or else I'm still immature."

Rob laughed. "A little of both, I'd guess."

These few moments of silly banter with Rachel reminded him of what he had missed all these years. It felt good to joke and flirt, instead of just awkward hellos and side-long glances.

The two went out the door and crossed Upper Main to the Town Hall parking lot. "That should be all over town in about two minutes," laughed Rachel. "Between Mr. Williams and Mary, the town and high school will be buzzing."

"You're right. Sorry if it causes problems for you."

"No, I didn't mean it that way at all. I'm sick of trying to please people. The truth is they're happier when they've got something to talk about. Besides, I'm the one started the joking, not you. If they want to talk, let 'em."

"So, is something going on since I saw you last?"

She looked at him as she got into the car. "Drive by the harbor, would you?"

He nodded, but something caught his eye. A shiny black car that didn't look like it belonged in Bound Brook in February was parked along Main Street.

"Stay here," he said. He closed his door and started walking toward what looked like a new Chrysler. The vehicle's engine started as he approached. Before he could get close, the car had pulled out of the space and accelerated down the street, leaving Rob looking on in frustration.

"What was that all about?" asked Rachel when he got back in the car.

"That car has been all around town and involved in some suspicious activity."

"Suspicious?" asked Rachel. "Meaning something about Proctor?"

"Could be, I don't know. But what were you saying before I interrupted you?"

"Well, talking to you got me thinking. I've been stuck in a rut for years, trying to be a good wife to a man who doesn't want to be a good husband. Trying to be a good daughter to the school principal, and not cause him any embarrassment. Something you said sunk in.

I've been trying to make up for all my regrets, but it's time to move on."

"Rachel, I don't want to cause problems between you and Jimmy, or with your parents."

"You aren't! I'm thirty-one years old and I should start acting like a grownup—you know, living my own life? Time to stop being the principal's daughter and going through the motions of a marriage. In Jimmy's last letter he said if he survives this war, he's going to try to stay in the army. I guess that tells you a lot about what's important to him, and where I stand."

"Maybe he wants you to stay with him, you know, go to whatever base where he gets stationed?"

"I don't think so. That wasn't the message that I got!"

Rob just listened as they drove slowly past the marina and along the beach.

"This isn't about you, and it's not about the two of us; that ship sailed years ago. This is about me getting on with my life. Twelve years ago, I was headed off to college to become a teacher. Then I chickened out, used getting mad at you as an excuse, and then played at marriage. I've decided that when Jimmy makes it back, and I pray to God he does, I'm getting a divorce. Honestly, I think he'll be relieved. Meanwhile, I'm going to go back to school in the fall, not teaching, but something related to business. At least if some college will take me."

"Of course, they will, you were the smartest in our class, well, actually maybe second smartest after Joanne,"

"You mean third, after Joanne and you in a class of twelve. What an accomplishment," she replied with a smile.

"Well Joanne was brilliant, in a class of her own, that's why she went to Columbia. Probably a toss-up between the two of us for second," he laughed.

"Rob, I want you to understand something, I want to be friends with you again, and right now I don't want more than that. Don't get me wrong, I still got the hots for you," she laughed, "but whatever happens with us, I need to put my life first."

By now they were pulling into the Gilmore driveway. He stopped the car, but left the engine running. "Rachel, whatever you want is fine by me."

"Still bottling things up, I see. I tell you what, let's go on a friend date. The movie *Greatest Show on Earth* is playing in Orleans. Want to take me?"

"OK . . . You sure?"

"Never been so sure, pick me up around 6:00. I know mom will have enough for dinner. Movie starts at 7:30, won't take long to get there, and you can have a little visit with my folks. One condition, though, no talk about Proctor or murder. Is it a deal?"

"Dinner, a movie, and the best company in town. How can a guy say no?"

"See you tonight!"

He watched her go in the door, and she turned and gave a little wave. He wasn't sure how to take all this, but Rachel was right, he still kept things bottled up, and he thought he better keep it that way. Rachel was trying to find herself, after years of treading water. If he let his real feelings out, he wasn't sure how either of them could handle it. With a deep sigh, he backed down the driveway.

Rob spent the next two hours visiting some of the businesses in town. Even though he expected Skip had already talked to Mr. Williams at the pharmacy, he stopped in and chatted with the genial, pipe-smoking pharmacist. They talked about things in general, and it didn't seem like Williams had anything useful, at least not yet. Next he stopped at the Flying A, and got some gas for the trip to Orleans that night. He bantered with the Hooper brothers, but again, nothing new. He headed to the South Bound Brook General Store, got a cup of coffee, *on the house* because he was in uniform, asked a few questions and listened to the chatter.

Mostly folks seemed to be digesting the information about Proctor's murder. Lots of vague comments: "Terrible wasn't it? What's the world coming to? Sure, he was an SOB, but who would murder him?" Some sick humor too— "What if every SOB in town got murdered? Probably be nobody left."— that one from Harold Hooper. Nothing useful, but Rob wanted to keep the pot stirred.

His last stop was at Ben and Phyllis's house before he headed home. It being a Saturday, Ben's truck was in the yard. Some Tyler cousins had shoveled the driveway at Tricky's house, and six boys were shooting baskets, despite the cold. Rob saw Benny and his brothers, 13-year-old Jack, and 10-year-old Tim. They were playing 3 on 3 with some Tyler cousins. One thing great about growing up around the "Tangle" was he'd always had lots of playmates.

Rob let himself into the house and called out, "Anybody home?"

"Back here," came the voice of Ben.

Rob went the through the kitchen and small dining area to the living room at the back of the one-story, three-bedroom house.

"Well, look at you in your spiffy uniform. I suspect you've been out shaking the bushes."

"Yup, you it hit on the head. Talking to people, seeing what turns up. Biggest thing is I spoke with Richard Caldwell."

That got Ben's attention. "Oh, I wish I could've been a fly on that wall. How'd it go?"

"I bet you could guess," chuckled Rob.

"Let me see, hmmm, very stuck-up, never let his guard down, treated you like dirt, or at least just a town flunky, and you got little or nothing out of him. How did I do?"

"Pretty close, but he did let his guard down, after I poked the hornet's nest a few times."

"Oh, now I really wish I'd been there. You got under his skin?"

"After he told me some pretty basic stuff, things got a little heated, ended with a shouting match, and me storming out of the house. However, he was the one who slammed the door, not me. Of course, before he slammed it, he paid me a high compliment, said I was *just like my mother*."

"Man, oh man, you really got to him! Not sure I've ever seen Caldwell lose his cool. Was that your intention, or just a pleasant result?"

"Mostly intended, but a mix of business and personal. The man really is despicable. I'm ashamed to be related to him. Imagine if he'd raised me? Don't even want to think about that! Overall, things turned out for the best for me. But I'll never forgive him for my mother and grandmother. Someday he'll answer for it, but it won't be to me."

Ben nodded. "Well, if you're wondering about Proctor, I haven't heard anything that would help. People seem to be having a hard time getting their heads around the fact that we have a killer in town."

"Oh, one thing you can tell Phyllis. Rachel Curtis and I are going to the movies tonight. I'm willing to bet she'll hear about it, so she can hear it from me first. People can put any twist on it they want, but it's two old friends doing something fun together. We're both sick of avoiding each other, time to get on with our lives."

"OK, sounds good to me. I'll let Phyllis know, she loves it when some old biddy tries to surprise her with gossip and she's already a step ahead. Likes to rub it in, you know, probably say something like, *You've just heard that? That's old news, I've known that for days!*" Ben imitated his wife's tone like a professional mimic.

"Yes," Rob laughed, "I can hear her now!"

Ben gave him a serious look. "So that's all it is, two old friends going to a movie? You sure that's all you want it to be?"

"Let's not got down that path, OK? Right now, that's all it is, and all it's going to be. She's married to my best friend, you know."

"You mean *former* best friend, who stole your girl, and treated both of you like dirt ever since, hides his sorrows in a bottle, and runs off to war to avoid his real troubles. You think people don't see past his patriotic front? You mean that best friend? Sure, I get it! Listen, you deserve happiness, and I'll punch anybody in the nose who stands in your way!"

Rob felt a lump in his throat. "Thanks, I know you'll always look out for me." Then he pulled himself together. "Lay off the punching in nose part, OK? I don't want to have to lock you up for assault."

"You got it, buddy, you do what you want to do, don't worry about this dinky town. There's so much dirt going on behind the scenes it ain't funny! You know the old saying, *People who live in glass houses . . .?*"

"Well, I hope you don't have a glass house, 'cause I need to use your shower."

Ben smiled. "You know, I *am* a plumber. Maybe you'd like some indoor plumbing in that cottage?"

"Then I'd have to think of a new excuse to visit."

Chapter X – Another Saturday Night

Back at the cottage, all showered and shaved, Rob put on his nicest slacks, shirt and sweater. He was looking forward to both the date, as well as the dinner with George and Maggie. When his mother had died, Phyllis and Ben had taken him in, but it was the Gilmores who had mentored him. George had been his principal, coach and teacher, while Maggie had been a mother figure. George had guided him, taught him the intricacies of basketball and convinced him to go to college. Maggie had been nurturing, but also practical and down-to-earth. She was always candid and blunt, and never afraid to burst your bubble when she thought George, Rob or anyone else were a little "full of themselves." Rob had missed them almost as much as he'd missed Rachel.

George had been instrumental in getting Rob his scholarship to Brown University. When Rob had arrived in Providence, Rhode Island he'd been a fish out of water, an orphan from a backwater fishing village with no money and no pedigree. He had suddenly been thrust into a world of boarding-school graduates and old family connections. Within two days he'd been ready to pack up and head home. Fortunately, the freshman basketball coach had looked him up, and invited him to the gym to shoot baskets and meet some of his fellow recruits. It had been a turning point as he found that he liked most of the guys he met.

When he had heard the news about Rachel and Jimmy eloping, he'd done what he always did, pouring his energy into his classes and mostly into basketball. Even in pick-up games and shoot arounds he'd played with an angry edge. His level of play had even caught the attention of the varsity coach.

Sports has a way of leveling the field. You can't fake it, you can't buy it, and you can't use your connections on the court. You can either play, or you can't. And Rob could play. The freshman team was separate from the varsity, and was a small, cohesive group. They stuck up for each other and hung out together.

The freshman basketball season was exciting for a boy who'd never left Cape Cod. They played games all around New England and the Northeast. The level of competition was far beyond anything he'd ever experienced. At first Rob had been a bit overwhelmed, but once the games started, he felt at home. He moved from the first sub off the bench to a starter at forward. At six-foot-three, he was versatile. He mostly played forward, but he could also spell the starting center and, a good dribbler and passer, could even fill in as a tall guard. Passing, ball handling, and most of all defense, were his main talents, and he owed that to Coach Gilmore. The Brown coach had discovered he could also shoot, and by the end of the season he was the team's leading scorer.

Rob now pulled into the Gilmore driveway exactly at six and Rachel opened the door before he had a chance to knock.

"Punctual as usual," she said.

"Been looking forward to it all day. I mean, it's been a long time since I've been treated to your mother's cooking," he smirked with a wink.

"Wow, you really know how to flatter a girl."

Maggie gave him a hug, "With me, flattery will get you anywhere. Unfortunately, *somebody* didn't give me any advanced notice, so I had to make do. I hope you like *le boeuf,* ground to perfection, combined with special herbs, hand-shaped with *pome de terre puree, petits pois,* all served *au jus.*"

Rob smiled. "Yes, meatloaf, mashed potatoes, peas and gravy will be great."

"Glad to see you remember your Latin," said George as he entered the kitchen.

"It's French, you ninny," laughed Maggie. "Good thing you're good at math and science."

"French, Latin, whatever, they all sound Greek to me," said George, puffing on his pipe. "Let's take a seat in the living room while Maggie performs her French cuisine miracle with hamburger."

He settled into his stuffed chair while Rob and Rachel sat on the couch. "Rob, you know with circumstances being what they are, I never really got a chance to hear about your Navy experience. Rachel told me you promised not to talk about Proctor, so can you fill us in on how you ended up in the Shore Patrol?"

Rob cleared his throat. "Well, I'll try to keep it short. When Pearl Harbor happened, I'd just finished the first semester of my sophomore year. I wanted to enlist right away, but the basketball season had just started, and I felt I had a commitment to the varsity coach. He already had lost a couple of experienced players. As soon as the second semester ended, I enlisted in the Navy. After basic training I got posted to Newport, Rhode Island Naval Base. It turned out the Executive Officer of base operations was a big basketball fan. He'd gone to Brown games all the time and had seen me play. He got me stationed at Newport and assigned me to shuffling papers, but my main job was to play for the Naval Station's basketball team."

"Did they really do stuff like that?" asked Rachel.

"Sure they did," George affirmed. "Honey, lots of major league baseball players played for the military teams and did recruitment publicity, especially early in the war."

"Honestly, I was a little irritated at first," Rob admitted. "You know, join the Navy to do my bit for the war effort, and I'm typing, shuffling papers and playing basketball. Of course, once I got to Newport, I realized it takes a huge support system to purchase materials, track supplies, and all the other stuff that it takes to run a Navy. The ships don't get out to sea all by themselves, and somebody has to do it. On top of that, Newport was expanding fast, and it was really challenging. There wasn't any time to do things gradually. The war wasn't going our way at first, and we needed to get ships and men to sea as fast as possible. After a while I found it pretty interesting and challenging. People know about sailors and ships, but they don't realize that the Navy is a complicated business."

George puffed on his pipe. "So how was the basketball? Was it a competitive level?"

"The most competitive, I ever played! All the guys were college starters, many of them stars, and some had played pro or semi-pro. To be honest, I was mostly outclassed. Stuck around because I was versatile. A little like in college, I could go in and give a forward or guard a breather. In college I even subbed for the center sometimes, but in the Navy, the centers were older, taller and stronger than a 20-year-old kid. What the Navy coach liked about me most was, I would go in and play tough defense. By the way, I owe that to you, Coach. Most of the other players didn't like to work that hard on the defensive side."

"So how'd you end up in the Shore Patrol?" Rachel asked.

"Most guys do Shore Patrol as a rotating duty, not a regular posting. I drew my turn doing a Shore Patrol shift and the Master Chief took a shine to me. Meanwhile, the Executive Officer, the same XO who liked me, got shipped out, and the basketball coach got a fresh bunch of new players who shipped in. So I was somewhat expendable. The Master Chief got me assigned to long-term Shore Patrol duty. Every big base needs some guys to do it full time and supervise the part-timers."

"What did the Master Chief like about you? That you were an athlete?" asked Rachel.

"Well it helped that I'm tall, but no, I tried to calm things down instead of stirring them up. Some Shore Patrol guys liked it because they get a baton, and they got to bust heads. Gave them an excuse to act tough and throw their weight around. I tried talking first, next I used my height and leverage to subdue sailors and lastly, I pulled out the baton. Even then I tried to use it more as a threat. I'm really not crazy about clubbing people. Besides most of the time they were falling down drunk, it didn't take much to get them under control.

"After D-Day they shipped me to France and put me back working on shipping, cargoes and transports. Then the Master Chief from Newport showed up and got me regular shifts on Shore Patrol. The Shore Patrol provided security and kept order in the ports. That was about the closest I got to the fighting until the last couple of months of the war."

"Dinner is served," called Maggie from the kitchen.

Rob felt a comfortable, nostalgic feeling, sitting at the kitchen table as he had so often during high school. "I told you about my Navy experience, now your turn, Coach. How've your teams been since I was away?"

"Rob, your team was our last really good one. We won the Cape Small School title and lost a close one to Barnstable for the Cape Cod Championship. You, Hoopy, Jimmy, Jerry Tyler, Moose and Johnny Sousa, best team I ever had."

"Closest knit team I ever played on," Rob said.

"Now we're always competitive with the other schools our size, but it's tough against the big towns. This team is the best I've had in several years. Ptown is loaded and they are killing almost everybody, and Wellfleet and Sandwich are struggling. There's a close battle for second with us, Orleans, Chatham and Harwich. I've got a couple of good underclassmen, but don't see much after that. Maybe I'll get lucky and have some tall kid move into town. You've seen the team, what do you think?"

"Junior Proctor is your best player, and my cousin Benny is solid. Bobby's your tallest kid and a pretty good center, but you got a problem now that he's hurt. Of the juniors, Johnny Webster is a steady guard and Tony Oliver, at the other forward, he has some promise. That freshman, Vinnie Costa, has a lot of potential, nice soft touch and very coachable, but he gets pushed around by the older, bigger guys. When he fills out, he'll be a top player. The rest of the team are nice kids and try hard, but not real ball players."

George smiled, "Good breakdown. Monday, we have to start adjusting to the loss of Snowy . . . dumb kid. Vinnie moves into the starting lineup, and if you get to practice early, I can fill you in on the other adjustments. Just hope nobody else gets hurt, and we don't get into foul trouble, cause you're right, not much talent on the bench."

"Whatever I can do to help," replied Rob.

The rest of the dinner they chatted about Bound Brook gossip, repeatedly praised Maggie's cooking, and talked about the movie they were going to see. Rob was enjoying the company, and engrossed in the conversation, when Rachel kicked him under the table and gave him a look. "Rob, we've got to go or we'll be late. I hate to miss the beginning of a movie."

"Bundle up. Remember the DeSoto's got no heater."

Rachel grabbed her heavy coat, blue and white stocking cap, and some warm-looking mittens, "Mom and Dad, don't wait up for us, OK? We're grownups now!"

Maggie and George both laughed. "Have fun, you two," said Maggie.

The ride to Orleans went quickly. The roads were clear and there were almost no cars on a freezing night in late February. Rachel seemed lost in thought and Rob was quiet most of the ride. It wasn't an awkward silence though; in fact, to Rob it felt very comfortable. They pulled into Orleans Center and parked in a half-empty parking lot a few minutes before seven-thirty.

"Should be in time to see the previews," said Rachel. "Sometimes I think there're my favorite part of the show."

Rob bought two tickets, two cokes and a big bag of popcorn. Out of the corner of his eye he saw a Bound Brook couple, who whispered to each other after seeing Rob and Rachel together. Oh well, might as well get it over with. Rob nodded and they gave a wave.

They settled into seats, closer to the back in the less-than-half-full theatre, just as the lights dimmed and the preview of coming attractions started. *Singing in The Rain* burst onto the screen in living color, and Gene Kelly, Donald O'Connor and Debbie Reynolds sang and danced through snippets of several cute numbers.

The screen switched to John Wayne, slugging it out in the mud with Victor McLaughlin, in *The Quiet Man*. For a quiet man, Wayne seemed to spend most of his time in fistfights and arguing with Maureen O'Hara. Rob was distracted by Wayne's resemblance to Chief Foster, and not very impressed with the narrator's description of an American boxer in Ireland trying to win the heart of the lovely Irish colleen.

The screen went to Black and White. It was *High Noon*, and Gary Cooper was in the middle of a western street with a gun belt and a tin star. Then Grace Kelly was pleading with him not to go out there, and the narrator talked about nobody standing with the Sheriff against the outlaw gang. Then the lights went from dim to black, and the soundtrack trumpeted the start of the main attraction, *The Greatest Show on Earth*.

For the next two hours, manager Charlton Heston tried to keep the struggling circus from bankruptcy, while competing for the love of his aerialist girlfriend, Betty Hutton, with her rival trapeze artist, Cornell Wilde. Jimmy Stewart, always in clown makeup, was a man with a secret, and a sleazy con man, named Harry, got revenge against the circus by causing a train wreck.

The love triangle, or maybe quadrangle, made Rob uncomfortable. Heston and Wilde vied for the love of Betty Hutton, while Dorothy Lamour tried to lure Heston away after being dumped by Wilde. Maybe it hit a little too close to home, but at least Rachel seemed to be enjoying it.

The credits rolled, the lights came on, and the cokes and popcorn were long gone. Rob realized Rachel was now snuggled against his arm with her head on his shoulder. During the movie it had felt so natural, but now in the light, it felt wrong. Rob eased himself up out of the seat and stretched, before the Bound Brook couple turned and headed toward the exit.

"Don't worry about it," said Rachel. "Everybody'll know anyway."

Braced against the cold, they made their way to the car. "So what now, I just realized that it's almost ten on a Saturday night in February, and nothing is open except a few dives. Not sure I want to go to some noisy bar."

"I want to go to your place," said Rachel. "After twelve years of avoiding each other, we have a lot to catch up."

A quick ride on an empty highway and they were turning down Neck Road. For people who had a lot of catching up to do, they didn't say a word. In the cottage, Rob got a lantern lit, put some newspaper and kindling in the wood stove, started a fire and added some logs. "Once the fire gets going," he assured her, "this place is so small, it'll warm right up."

He looked at his tiny home: a round kitchen table with four wooden chairs in the kitchen/dining area, an antique rocker, an upholstered couch against the outer wall of the living area, and a day bed that doubled as a sofa, against the facing wall.

Rachel sat on the couch, still wearing her coat, hat and mittens. Rob sat facing her on the day bed.

"So, I gather you finished college after the war?" she asked.

"Right. I went back to Brown and finished up."

"You came back to Bound Brook in '48 right? Did it take you that long to finish college after the war?"

Rob blushed. "No, with summers and extra courses, I finished in a year and a half. The fact is, I didn't start right after the war. When I was in France, I met some people, and got offered a job. I had to go back to the states to get officially mustered out, but then I went back. Stayed there a year, and things didn't work out that great, so I came back and went to Brown."

Rachel gave him a deep look. "I have a feeling a lot just got skipped over, but if you're uncomfortable it's alright."

"I never could hide anything from you," he laughed. "Yeah, I've skipped a lot. It's a very long story, and I'm not going to tell it all, but it involved a girl. After D-Day we made another landing on the southern coast of France called *Operation Dragoon,* we needed the big ports there to supply our troops. In September of '44, I was sent to Marseille, France's largest port.

"One night on shore patrol we found some drunken sailors harassing a French girl. We broke it up; it was something that happened all the time, nothing special, sad to say. But this *was* special, turned out that the girl was the daughter of an important shipping tycoon. The girl remembered me, probably because of my height, and a few days later, I got an invitation to their home. Her father was very rich, and to cut to the chase, Marie and I developed a relationship."

He paused and cleared his throat. "After the war ended, I got contacted by her father and offered a job in Marseille working for him. I knew about supplies and the nuts and bolts of shipping from my days in Newport and Marseille, and also about security from the Shore Patrol. Marseille can be a dangerous place. Anyway, he wanted me in the business, and I spoke enough French to get by. The pay was extremely generous, and of course, there was also Marie.

"So I went back to France, and spent about a year, but it all ended pretty badly. Turns out Marie's father was a gangster and a collaborator. He was running a black market, and wanted my inside knowledge and Navy connections. I should have known no legitimate businessman could've survived the war and come out of it with his villa intact and richer than ever. I was twenty-three, naïve, easily flattered . . . and I thought I was in love.

"There was a really bad scene when it ended. Next thing I knew, I woke up on a ship, with a black eye, aching all over, my passport stamped, a ticket to New York City, a hundred bucks in my pocket, and a note that said; *Don't come back, don't ever try to see her!"*

"I'm sorry," said Rachel. "I had no idea all that happened to you. Here I am feeling sorry for myself, stuck in little Bound Brook, and you've been through so much. It sounds like a movie plot. Does anyone else know all that happened?"

"Not really, Ben knows a little. Ben and Hoopy are the two guys I tell stuff, but Hoopy and I have a deal: we don't talk about the war."

She got up now, took off her hat, coat and mittens, "I said we have a lot to catch up on, but I didn't necessarily mean just talking." She crossed the room and sat down next to him. Rob reached his arm around her and pulled her close. She nestled her cheek against his chest and wrapped him in a hug. Rob put his hand under her chin and raised her face. He kissed her lips lightly, then harder.

She looked into his eyes. "I want you to make love to me."

He started to say something, but she put her finger to his lips. "Sssh, don't talk, just listen. I don't want this to be the start of something, I have baggage to sort out, and I'm not jumping into another relationship until all that gets settled. I just want this one night."

She pulled her sweater over her head, took Rob's face in her hands and gave him a deep kiss.

"Rachel, are you sure?"

She smiled at him, "I'm positive! It should've happened years ago. Now blow out the lantern, put another log on the fire and get back here!"

He did as he was told. "Rachel, I didn't expect this, and it's been awhile, I don't have any, you know, protection."

She laughed and held up a small, foil package, "You mean this? You do know I work in a pharmacy."

They kissed again, slowly unbuttoning each other's clothes, her body glowing in the light from the fire. "Show me something you learned in France, sailor," she whispered.

Tenderly they caressed and held each other. Rob went slowly, wanting the moment to last forever. Then passion took over, and they rocked in each other's arms, a dozen years of yearning unleashed.

****

Rob woke with Rachel cuddled in his arms. The fire had burned low, but the cottage was still warm. She stirred in her sleep, and he eased himself off the bed. Naked, he tossed two logs into the woodstove, and wrapped himself in the old quilt on the rocker. Last night didn't seem real. Now, he felt embarrassed and ashamed.

"Hey sailor, where're you going? You want to come back to bed?"

He smiled at the beautiful face he'd loved since eighth grade. She peeked out from under the covers, her hair all the redder in the glow of the fire. He wasn't sure how to feel. Could he afford to get his hopes up? Was what they had done right? He felt a catch in his throat and paused before he answered.

"I'd like nothing better, but I'm afraid if I do ... I'll never want to leave. That was amazing, but I think I better get you home. We've scandalized enough people tonight."

"You are way too logical, but OK, I probably better get home. You're right though, it was amazing!"

Rob grabbed his clothes and took them into the frigid little bedroom. He dressed and waited a little longer before going back. Rachel was dressed and putting on her coat. "The clock says one, so I guess technically, I spent the night."

"We'll get you home long before *dawn breaks, o'er yonder mudflats.*"

"You're so poetic," she laughed.

They went out into the frigid night and snuggled close in the cold car as Rob drove the three miles to her house on Tyler Hill.

"Don't pull into the driveway, just stop at the end. My father will be out cold, but my mother will be half-awake. Probably not fooling anyone, but I'll try to sneak in quietly. I know I'm a grownup, but some habits die hard." She gave him a big smile and a kiss on the cheek.

"Rachel, I don't know what to say . . ."

"Don't say anything. I meant what I said in the cottage, we are friends again. I don't know if what happened last night is going to happen again. I have lots of stuff to sort out. It was wonderful, but right now, I'm glad I have my *friend* back. I just know that this is the happiest I've felt in years."

She hopped out of the car and with her light, athletic stride jogged down the driveway, slowly opened the house door and slipped inside. The door closed slowly, and the outside light went out.

Rob sat in the car with the engine running. He was still stunned, like he hadn't woken yet from a dream. The whole evening was more than he could sort out right, now. Tonight, his long-suppressed emotions had awoken, but he had to take Rachel at her word. Tonight was special, but he still had to keep his feelings under control, for her sake.

He turned the car around and drove home. In a few hours he'd be headed to church, how was that for irony? He hadn't been to church since the war. Now, of all days, he was going to hear *hell, fire and brimstone* and be called upon to repent. Would he come forward and confess his adulterous deed? No, that wasn't going to happen. He reminded himself he was going to church for only one reason; to see if he could catch a killer!

Chapter XI – Sunday Service

Rob tossed and turned until the sun came through the kitchen window and light filled the cottage. Even then he resisted waking up, pulled the pillow over his head, and tried to go back to sleep.

****

In his dreams, he was back in Marseille, and an unseen figure was chasing him down a street. Rob was in uniform, and as he ran, he kept stopping to break up fights between drunken sailors. Then he resumed his flight from his pursuer, but all the time he kept hearing a woman's voice calling him to hurry. The woman was beyond his reach; as he got closer, she drifted further away. Then his pursuer would get closer, and another fight would start, and he'd break it up. All the time the woman's voice called his name. He struggled to recognize the voice, at times, it sounded like Rachel calling "Rob"; at times it had a French accent and called him Robere, but whenever he tried to answer, no sound came out. Then he was making love to a beautiful woman. Instead of being aroused, he felt confused and threatened. The woman now faded away, and unseen hands yanked him from the bed. Then the pursuer got closer, a shadowy figure that spoke French and growled, "Never see her again."

****

He jerked awake! The woodstove had burned down, but despite the chill, Rob was sweating. The clock on the table said nine. He reminded himself he was headed to church at ten and better get moving. He relit the fire, started a pot for coffee, and found some bacon and eggs left in the ice box. Normally he'd wear his only suit jacket with a white shirt and tie, but he didn't want to blend into the congregation, he wanted to stand out, so he was going in his Bound

Brook uniform. He wasn't worried about being late; in fact that was his plan, a late arrival so that everyone would see him.

After breakfast, Rob drove leisurely down the Highway, heading south toward the hall that Duggan rented for his services. It was a little after ten when he pulled into the parking lot that held a dozen or so cars. At the front steps he heard the hymn, *The Old Rugged Cross*. He knew they'd all be standing, so he waited. He wanted everyone seated when he entered.

The singing stopped, and he heard Duggan's preacher voice: "So we pray for the soul of our earthly brother Cecil Proctor. Like all of us on this earth, he was a man with flaws and faults, he was a sinner, but we all have sinned. We pray that he has found redemption, and in the words of the scripture, *he will dwell in the house of the Lord forever,* amen!"

"Amen," repeated the congregation, as Rob stepped through the door. The small gathering barely filled a quarter of the space. Duggan stood on a riser behind a podium in the far-left corner. Folding chairs were set up diagonally, facing the makeshift pulpit with a center aisle down the middle. The set up allowed light to come in from two sides and made the gathering more compact and intimate.

"We have some announcements," said Duggan.

Rob walked down the left side of the seats, and found an empty chair halfway down, as twenty-five sets of eyes followed his tall frame.

Duggan looked up from his notes, and his brow furrowed. He took a moment to digest what he saw. "Why, Officer Caldwell, what a pleasant surprise. You're welcome here. We usually introduce newcomers, so if I may, please welcome Robert Caldwell to our service today. He's a Bound Brook native, who fought in the War against the evil Hitler. He has returned to our beautiful area to pursue the truth, and find the killer of our brother, Cecil Proctor. Please welcome him!"

The small congregation gave Rob a round of applause as they regarded him with curiosity. With all eyes turned his in direction, he was able to scan the gathering. As he suspected, he didn't recognize many of the faces. The majority were older couples or individuals, and there seemed to be two families with younger children. Of the faces he did recognize, none were very familiar, with one exception. Moose Parker stared at him with wide eyes.

He kept eye contact until Moose looked away. His presence clearly had surprised Moose; he could see it in his first glance. But there was something else after the surprise passed. Moose's expression hardened, and turned to a stern, almost defiant, gaze. He wasn't sure if Moose's presence or expression meant anything, but it was interesting.

Rob tried to make himself comfortable in the metal folding chair. He remembered daydreaming and dozing off in the large pews of the Congregational Church. He smiled to himself, at least Duggan had solved the problem of keeping his congregation's attention. If anyone dozed off, they'd end up on the floor.

He turned his attention back to Duggan's words. The preacher finished announcements; he thanked some members for helping with church activities, asked them to pray for two members who were ill, one of them in the hospital, and to send their prayers to the large number of congregation members who were unable to travel to the service, due to the weather, or who had gone to warmer climates for the winter. The last announcement seemed aimed at Rob, judging by Duggan's glance in his direction. The Reverend wanted to make it clear he had a larger following than what was here today.

Duggan now cleared his throat, looked out at the gathering and waited until all eyes were fixed on the podium before continuing. "Evil takes many forms, and those that battle evil are often cursed for their efforts. The Devil is sneaky and duplicitous, he uses seemingly innocent individuals to do his bidding. We have a situation in our glorious country that brings great spiritual danger to all of us. While our brave boys are in a distant land, fighting against the heathen Asian communists, we have a great danger here at home.

"Fortunately, we have a prophet, a man who has alerted us to the dangers of godless communism, not just within our country, but within our government, and even within our armed forces. Make no mistake, communism is the Devil's work, and Senator Joseph McCarthy is a messenger sent by our Lord to warn us of the danger.

"However, it is hard to be a prophet. Look what happened to our Lord and Savior, Jesus Christ, so while the godly Senator McCarthy leads the good fight against the evil of communism, there are those who attack the messenger. Is Senator McCarthy a perfect man? No, no man is perfect. Senator McCarthy is a Catholic, not a Protestant or of our denomination. But the Senator is leading a Christian cause, and we must follow.

"There is no easy way to defeat the devil! Evil must be exterminated, stamped out and driven from our god-fearing landscape. I say *praise Senator McCarthy;* we need more fearless men like him. The Senator is a common man, like you and me. He doesn't have an *Ivy League education*, like the communist sympathizers in our own State Department, but he knows the Devil's work when he sees it."

Duggan had Rob's full attention now. People said Duggan always needed a target, someone or something to personify evil. For years, Cecil Proctor had filled that role, but now he was dead, his sinning days done. The Reverend had a new cause, a new hero, and a new evil. Joseph McCarthy had risen from obscurity to political power when he'd claimed he had a list of Communists within the government and the army. Our former World War II ally, Russia, was now the second strongest power in the world, and our avowed enemy. Russia's dictator, Joseph Stalin, now occupied and controlled all of Eastern Europe and half of Germany. China was led by the communist dictator Mao Tse Tung, and now Korea threatened to fall to Communism.

Rob had no doubt that Communism was a great danger, and a clear enemy of the United States of America, but he had an inherent distrust of politicians. Many Americans had that same feeling, and it seemed to Rob that McCarthy was playing on that fear and distrust. However, he kept reminding himself that the Senator was a politician also, and there was something about that man that seemed sneaky. Meanwhile, the worst thing that could happen to an American citizen was to be accused of being a *commie, pinko,* or *commie sympathizer.* Once you were accused, it seemed to be a stain that wouldn't wash away. Now Duggan was jumping on that bandwagon.

While Rob was thinking, Duggan was bringing his sermon to a close, "So my fellow Christians, we have seen the pattern. When a prophet stands up against the misguided *powers that be* that infest our government, those officials try to tear him down with false accusations. When a *true Christian* fights against evil, there are over educated intellectuals, *communist sympathizers,* all too eager to cast aspersions on his character and intentions. We as *true Christians* must defend those prophets, we must defend Senator McCarthy in his holy crusade, and we must defend any other god-fearing man against unfounded charges, so that God's work can continue in his fight against the demon Devil! Now let us pray."

Had Rob interpreted this right? Was Duggan doing more than defending McCarthy? Was he setting himself up against future allegations*? Was Rob the Ivy League government official who was being used by the Devil to attack Duggan with charges of murder?* It seemed that Duggan was preparing his defense, not with a lawyer, but with the court of public opinion.

"Hear our prayer, oh Lord, defend and protect those who proclaim thy holy name and smite those who would hound and harass thy servants who do thy work . . ."

A loud voice interrupted, "What about charlatan ministers, who bilk old widows out of their life savings? Are they doing the Lord's work?"

Rob looked at a man about his age with reddish hair, standing in the back of the hall. The man's face was flushed, and his cheeks puffed with anger. "You've bedazzled and brain-washed my grief-stricken mother into giving you a house, an income, and a huge endowment to build a new church for this mindless unwashed pack of hicks. You say the Devil is tricky and uses people as his instruments. I say that sounds a lot like you."

Moose Parker moved quickly. He grabbed the man in a bear hug, lifted him off the ground and carried him toward the door. All the time, the red-faced man jabbed his fist in the air and kept shouting. "You're a fake, an opportunist and a thief. My lawyers will be serving you with papers next week. Don't get too comfortable in that house, and don't go signing papers on any land deals. Your gravy train is coming to an end. . ." His last words faded as Moose carried him out of the building.

"My fellow Christians, did I not tell you? Here in our own midst are the agents of the Devil, come here to defame and confuse. Now is the time to pull together and be steadfast . . ."

Duggan's voice faded as Rob darted out the door. In the parking lot Moose dropped the man on the pavement and stood over him with a raised fist. "If I ever see you near the Reverend again, you'll be sorry! How dare you talk like that to a holy man? He's twice the man you are . . ."

"Moose, back off! I'll handle this."

Moose looked at Rob in confusion and then glanced at his uniform. He backed away from the man. "Remember what I said!"

"Enough, Moose, not another word. Don't get yourself in any deeper. Go back inside now. Go take care of the Reverend."

The last words seemed to register with Moose. "Right, the Reverend needs me."

As Moose left, Rob turned to the man who had risen to his feet, "Are you alright? I assume you're Mr. Armstrong?"

"Yes I'm fine. I'm sorry, and, I'm not sorry—know what I mean? Are you one of that fake's followers?"

Rob shook his head and smiled. "No, not at all. Short story, I'm here on duty, following up on a murder investigation. Just doing my job."

"Well, good thing you were here. I should've expected that a man like that would be protected by thugs. I should press charges against that oaf."

"Sir, you have the right to do what you please, but it sounds like you have a bigger issue than Moose throwing you out of church."

Armstrong smiled. "Yes, you're right. I see by your name tag it's Officer Caldwell. My name is Bruce Armstrong. You know, I'm a devout Presbyterian, but guys like him give all religion a bad name."

They shook hands. "Mr. Armstrong, the service is ending, and I'd rather not have another scene. Can we meet somewhere to talk? I'd like to hear what you have to say about your mother and Duggan. I'm trying to get all the information about him that I can. There's a diner in Orleans, The Fair Wind, right in the center. Could we meet there after I wrap up here?"

"Sure, I know the place," replied Armstrong. "I'll meet you there." He got into a new burgundy Buick Special and pulled out of the parking lot. Rob turned as the gathering started to leave the service. Suspicious eyes glanced his way, and he had a feeling his initial warm welcome had worn away.

After almost all the cars were gone, there was still no sign of Duggan or Moose. Rob walked to the door and quietly entered. The small, frail figure of Duggan was talking to a contrite looking Moose. Rob hadn't heard Moose called by his given name since teachers called the roll back in high school.

"Arnold, I know you meant well, but I can take care of non-believers like Armstrong and Caldwell. If you keep your faith in the Lord, and listen to me, everything will be fine."

Moose's head was lowered in shame. "I'm sorry, Reverend, you know I love the Lord and you. I'd never let anyone hurt you. It's just, you know, what he said, it just got me mad."

Duggan turned to the doorway, suddenly aware of Rob's presence. "Officer Caldwell, thank you for coming to our service. It seems your presence was fortuitous, and thank you for helping with that poor deluded man. And my sermon, I hope the message was clear and enlightening?"

"Oh, I think I heard the message loud and clear. I gather that Mr. Armstrong has heard a different message, I think it's along the lines of *beware of false prophets.*"

Duggan gave him an even stare. "Well, his mother has seen the light and heard the call, and she is a grown woman and can make her own decisions."

"That's between you and the Armstrongs. I need to have a talk with Moose. I don't think Armstrong is going to press charges, but if he wanted to, he has grounds. Moose, can we talk outside?"

"Sure, Rob." Moose glanced at Duggan before following him out the door.

In the parking lot, Rob glared at his old teammate. "Look Moose, you can't physically grab someone and threaten them. That's assault and battery. I'm going to talk to Armstrong. I don't think he's going to press charges, but if he does, I'll remind him that he could be charged with disturbing a public gathering. He was pretty out of control in there himself."

"Sure Rob. Anything you can do to help, I'll be mighty grateful."

Rob patted Moose on his bulky shoulder. "That was quite a move you pulled. Where did you learn that Bear Hug Carry? I've seen bouncers do it to drunks but didn't know you knew how."

Moose laughed. "Well, actually I learned it from a bouncer. I work some weekend nights at a club in Ptown. The other bouncer showed me how to get down low, wrap your arms around some drunk, carry him to the door and drop him in the parking lot. First time I ever had to use it in a church."

Rob cracked up. "Moose, you're always full of surprises. Tell me, how did you become one of Reverend Duggan's flock?"

"Well, it was in Ptown, actually, I was getting something to eat, before working at the bar, and sat down beside him at the counter. He started talking to me about how we're all sinners, but it's OK, you know, if you find the Lord and repent, he will forgive you. I never met anyone who made me feel so good—no, I think *hopeful* is the word. I don't have much of a life, you know, working on the town crew, hanging out. It was the first time I felt a connection to someone, and that maybe God had a purpose for me."

He turned and looked him directly in the eyes. "Rob, I hope you're not gonna make trouble for him. You aren't, are you?"

"Moose, you know me. I don't make trouble, but I don't shy away if somebody does something wrong. If the Reverend hasn't done anything wrong, he'll have no trouble from me."

Moose brightened. "OK, Rob, glad to hear it. You need to talk to me anymore?"

"Yes, I do. I know Skip must've talked to you, but we're all trying to get to the bottom of the Proctor murder, so can you tell me if you talked to Proctor before the fire?"

Moose blushed. "I didn't tell Skip, but yes, I went to his house just as the storm started. Look, I didn't touch him, as God is my witness!"

"Why'd you go see him?"

"I had talked to the Reverend. I knew he was going to ask Proctor about getting land for the church, and the Reverend told me it didn't go so great. I've known Proctor my whole life, I thought maybe I could convince him that it'd be a good thing. You know, he'd be helping a lot of people."

He gave Rob a pleading look. "I swear I didn't threaten him. That's probably hard for you to believe, knowing me like you do, but since I met the Reverend, and found the Lord, I'm different. That was part of what I told him, you know, I was trying to tell him the good the Reverend does, how he changed me for the better."

"So what did he say?"

"He listened. I'll give him that. But then he said he was a businessman. He didn't see where business and religion were a good mix. He promised he'd think about it but didn't think it was a wise investment."

"Did you go into the kitchen? Did you see a table setting for two people?"

"No, we never got out of the first-floor hallway. Wasn't much of a conversation, didn't take too long."

"Did you see anybody else?"

"No, mostly I talked, and he listened. Must have been less than five minutes. When I left, I could tell a big one was coming, you know you could see it in the clouds and feel it in the wind. Figured I better get the truck ready, make sure the plow was attached, you know? Oh, there was one thing. When I was going to Proctor's I passed a fancy black car on the road. Looked out of place on the road in the middle of February. Might see a car like that in the summer, but not this time of year."

"So, that was on your way to Proctor's. Did it look like the car was leaving his house?"

Moose scrunched his brow. "I wasn't near his house yet, so I couldn't tell where it was going or where it had been."

Rob paused. "That's it for now Moose. If there's any problem, tell Skip or me, don't take matters into your own hands. I'll be honest with you, I don't like Duggan, but I promise if he hasn't done anything illegal, he'll have no trouble with me."

Moose nodded. "Thanks Rob, I'll tell the Reverend."

Rob left the makeshift church and headed to Orleans, trying not to think about the previous night. Instead, he thought about Duggan and Moose. He sure hadn't seen that one coming!

At the diner, he spotted Armstrong in a corner booth reading a menu. "Thanks for meeting me." He slid into the booth across from the man.

"I guess the thanks are mine," Armstrong grinned. "You were right, I got a little out of control back there. I just slipped in the back near the end of the service. I wanted to see for myself what he was like. I didn't plan on interrupting. You know, I somehow hoped that maybe if I saw and heard the man myself, I could see what she saw in him; maybe he was some backwoods Billy Graham or Bishop Sheen. Maybe he was truly a good man. But it took about two minutes: he looks and sounds like a carnival barker. What a phony! And what was all that defense of that numbskull, Joe McCarthy. That man is a menace! I've got to admit he's got everyone scared, though."

"Don't underestimate Duggan. I don't like the man a bit, but he's smart and shrewd. He's got a knack for survival. The way he operates is that he always has a *boogie man,* some actual personification of the Devil. For years it was the guy that just got murdered, name of Proctor, but now he seems to have found the perfect evil, Communism. Who can argue with that? If you do, he just labels you a *pinko,* and then you're stuck. Of course, part of his message, was a warning to me. I'm an Ivy League graduate with a government job, and he would love to label me a *commie,* if I try to stick him with a crime."

"You mentioned a murder. Do you think this Duggan is involved? Is my mother mixed up with a murderer?"

"Right now we're just touching all the bases. Duggan and Proctor had some issues, but nothing that shows he murdered the man."

"What about that thug, Moose? He sure sticks up for Duggan. Could he have done it, you know, get rid of Duggan's enemy? You said Duggan made Proctor sound like the Devil, right?"

"I've known Moose all my life. He's not too bright, and he's a bully, but one thing I know about him is that he's a terrible liar, at least if you ask him the right question. I could always see right through him. No, I doubt Moose did it."

The waitress came. Rob didn't need any menu: stack of pancakes with maple syrup, hash browns, English muffin and coffee. He'd eat breakfast three meals a day if he had the chance.

He asked Armstrong about his mother. The man told the sad story of the lonely wife of an over-worked, dedicated doctor. She'd kept busy with social clubs, bridge and charities, but always waiting for the day when he retired, and they'd finally have time together. They'd discovered Bound Brook a few years ago and fallen in love with the picturesque town. He'd never seen his mother happier than when they'd bought the land on the bluff and started planning the house.

When his father had died, she'd fallen apart. He really worried about her physical and mental health. Some Cape acquaintance had mentioned Duggan's church, and his mother had gone. She'd been ripe for his slick message. Somehow, he'd known she was well-off, talked to her about plans for a new church, mentioned a stained glass window and plaque dedicated to Dr. Armstrong, and all the good he could bring to the poor people of the Cape. She was hooked!

"You know, it's not the money, both my brother and I do fine. If she gave all the money to the Red Cross or Home for Little Wanderers, I could live with that, you know, as her choice, but money for this sneak? I won't stand by and let it happen! Originally, I was going to go to Duggan's church service last weekend, but the storm cancelled those plans."

The two men finished eating and the conversation wound down. Rob walked out with Armstrong and watched the man drive away. He had a feeling that Armstrong was a strong match for the Reverend. He sure hoped so, he'd love to see the man put in his place. Meanwhile, unless it had something to do with the murder, he had plenty to keep himself busy.

****

A set of eyes peered through the brush and studied the cottage. A faint wisp of smoke rose from the chimney, but otherwise everything was silent and still. The DeSoto was gone and the house seemed empty. He took another look before leaving the shelter of the woods and creeping through the snow to the back of the cottage. He tried to stay on the small path, but once behind the house all the snow was still fresh. Quietly, the watcher moved to the south side window and took a peek. Assured there was no movement, he moved toward the front door, removed something from a coat pocket, opened the latch, and stayed less than a minute before emerging, tracing his steps back into the brush and disappearing into the woods.

****

Driving back to his house, Rob went over the events of the last twenty-four hours: His dinner with the Gilmores, his date with Rachel, their night together. He wanted to think about her, but he forced himself to review the morning's events: Duggan jumping on Senator McCarthy's bandwagon, his veiled threats to Rob, Armstrong's accusations and Moose's reaction. Moose's total dedication to the devious minister was the most disturbing. God knows, Moose was a total pain, but Rob hoped he wasn't getting himself involved in trouble.

Then there was Moose remembering a shiny black car on the road to Proctor's house. Couldn't be two cars like that in Bound Brook this time of year. Something else dawned on him. The Reverend had said that his conversation was cordial, and Proctor hadn't ruled out selling him the land. However, Moose had said that Duggan had told him the meeting didn't go well, so Moose went to see Proctor to try to talk him into selling. *Significant difference in their stories? Rob wasn't sure.*

He pulled into his driveway, parked and went inside. He hung up his coat and noticed a paper on the table. Another message from Skip? Maybe the meeting got changed? He picked up the white-lined page and saw large, crude, block lettering written in black crayon.

IT WAS AN ACCIDENT
LEAVE IT ALONE
NOBODY WILL MISS HIM

Rob ran out of the cottage and looked around in the snow for footprints. Maybe the writer had just left. He saw prints in the snow that circled around the house. The footprints turned and faced the window, as if the writer had peeked inside before entering. He followed the trail into the woods; in the snow the tracks were clear and easy to follow. The trail connected to the common path all the kids used to travel between Tyler's Tangle and Proctor's Hollow. It was impossible to stay with the trail. It could have headed toward Tyler's or Proctor's; there were too many prints and the snow was packed down.

He retraced his steps and looked at the clearest print he could find. It looked fresh. He stepped down hard with his own boot, and compared them side-by-side. At six-three, Rob had big feet, usually a size thirteen, often a problem when he tried to buy shoes. Comparing the prints, the writer's foot seemed two or three sizes smaller, Rob guessed around a ten. The tread looked familiar, the bottom of a common rubber boot. They were around the same size and pattern as the prints outside Doc Carter's.

Back at the cottage, Rob thought about the note. Because he had gone to lunch with Armstrong, he couldn't rule anyone out. Duggan, Moose or anybody could have taken the back path to the house, made sure he wasn't home and left the note. The paper had been ripped from a spiral notebook. It looked like the paper Rob had used in high school and college. Did that mean anything? Probably not, likely the most common paper around. The block lettering and crayon would disguise any handwriting. He was careful handling it. He didn't know if they could get fingerprints, but he'd turn it over to Foster in the morning. He thought about the black car: coincidence, something connected to the murder, or just his imagination? No, he didn't see any clues here, but it did tell him something. *Someone was getting nervous about his questions.*

Chapter XII – Comparing Notes

Monday morning at nine, two cars pulled into Rob's driveway. Chief Foster and Skip got out of Bound Brook's only police cruiser, and a State Police vehicle parked behind them. A trooper got out and grabbed his hat. Rob stepped outside to greet them.

"Rob, Trooper Don Stewart. Already filled him in on who you are." Foster made the introductions in his usual terse manner.

"Well, I got the coffee made, and good thing I happen to have four kitchen chairs. Don't get much company out here." Rob pulled down some mugs from the cabinet.

"And I've got Agnes' muffins," said Skip, producing a large bakery box. "Got an assorted baker's dozen. I've got an appetite and judging by the size of the three of you, I bet you can pack away at least three apiece."

Trooper Stewart took off his hat and ran his hand over his close-cropped blond hair. He looked to be about Rob's age, maybe a little older, over six foot and in good shape. "Chief Foster told me what you two have been doing, and I appreciate it. As you know, homicides fall under the State Police, but I'm glad to get all the help I can get. Not all my colleagues feel that way, but I come from the Upper Cape, grew up in Falmouth, and I know how people are around here.

"The blizzard really put everything behind schedule. The lab will run tests on the poker and the Jerry Jug, but I'm not too hopeful. Even if we get some prints, I doubt many Bound Brook folks are in our records. However, prints might help prove the case, if we can make an arrest."

"Now I remember you," said Rob. "Played for Lawrence High in Falmouth, couple years ahead of me. Pretty good player."

"Thanks," blushed Stewart, "I was OK—not in your league, but decent. I remember trying to guard you, wasn't easy."

"Alright, introductions complete," interrupted Foster, "Skip, can you fill us in?"

Skip Parker pulled out a small notebook and proceeded to go through the list of people he had talked to within the last few days. Most of them were merchants in Bound Brook Center and whatever customers happened to be there at the time. He had also talked with his brother, Moose, the rest of the highway crew and people who worked in the Town Hall and Post Office. Most were shocked at the murder, most didn't like Proctor, most said they had no idea who hated him enough to kill him, and nothing had leaped out of any of the conversations.

"I asked people if anybody was mad at him over any business dealings," he added, "and I got the names of a couple of people. He held their mortgages and had foreclosed on them. But it was ancient history, all several years ago. They weren't really locals, and both parties have moved away. I'll give Trooper Stewart the names, maybe he can check them out.

"I got more gossip and dirt than any of us really want to know," he concluded. "Right now, none of it seems to fit, but maybe when the Chief and Rob fill us in, something might click."

"I'll go next," said Foster. "I talked with a whole bunch of Proctor kin: Howie Proctor at the garage/body shop, and the guys that work for him, Kenny and Chandler. Howie said he never could stand Cecil and tried to avoid him. He said he was embarrassed to be related, and thought Cecil gave all the Proctors a bad name. Kenny and Chandler couldn't add anything, but pretty much agreed.

"He did tell me I should talk to Corey Proctor, Sr." Foster looked at Trooper Stewart. "He's a local electrician and the victim's nephew. Evidently, there was a time when the old man tried to take Corey under his wing. So I went to see him."

"Corey said Cecil had tried to interest him in the business. Corey had lost his oldest son in the war and it had hit the family hard. He said Cecil had always been kind to him when he was a kid, so he was open to the idea. Cecil showed him some of his properties and explained how he operated. Corey said the more he learned, the less he liked it. He also said he saw Cecil in a different light, saw what a mean SOB he was, not the kind uncle he'd thought he was. Anyway, they had a falling out. Corey got out of the business and Cecil didn't take kindly to it."

"He told me, after he did Proctor's electrical work, they hadn't spoken in years, until about six months ago. Seems that Corey's son, Junior, told him Proctor had been talking to him when he was getting gas at the Flying A. Well, Junior said at first, he'd been flattered; you know, an important, rich man showing an interest in him. Started talking to Junior about college and said that he could help out. Dropped some hints that he was looking for a younger Proctor to take over the business someday."

"Junior finally told his Dad about it, and Corey admits he hit the roof. He didn't want Cecil to get his claws into Junior—those were his words, get his claws into him! So he'd gone to the house and had a big argument with Proctor. Told him that Junior was off-limits. Corey admitted he was really ticked-off, but that was months ago, and says he hadn't talked with him since."

"I talked to Junior. The kid was nervous talking to a cop but told me pretty much the same thing. I asked him if he had any more contact with Proctor. He said after his father told the old man to back off, Proctor still tried to talk to him when he got gas, but Junior ignored him, or got Harold or Hoopy to fill his tank instead. He said after a while Proctor had given up."

Rob spoke up now. "Not to interrupt, but Junior told me pretty much the same thing when I was getting gas."

The Chief nodded and continued, "I checked with the bank and town officials, to see if there were any pending legal or financial issues, but nothing that seemed pertinent to the murder, at least nothing obvious. Talked to a bunch of other Proctors and town folk, but nothing, at least for now. Got a feeling something might click if we keep following up."

He looked at Rob. "Been saving you for last. You had a couple of interesting people to talk with, and I'd be lying if I didn't admit that I've been anxious to hear how your talks with Duggan and Caldwell went."

Rob looked at the others. "Well, first I've got something to show you." He carefully opened a manila file folder to reveal the crayon note. "Got back yesterday and found this on my kitchen table. Tried not to handle it much, once I realized what it was. Maybe your lab can get some prints off of it, Trooper."

The other three stared at the crayon note with wide eyes, before Stewart used the end of his spoon to tuck the paper back into the folder. "I'll take it."

Rob told them about following the footprints, how they had disappeared and what they looked like. "Checked them this morning, they're still there if you want to compare them."

"I'll look before we leave, but prints in snow don't tell us much, especially such a common tread and size," said Stewart.

"Now I *really* want to hear what you discovered," said Foster. "You're making somebody nervous!"

Rob went over his visits, mentioning getting background from the Gilmores and Phyllis Brown, his visits to Hoopy and Harold, the brief talk with Junior, the Pharmacist and folks in South Bound Brook General Store, as well as the comments about the suspicious black car.

"I surprised the Reverend Duggan with a visit at the fancy, new house he's living in, courtesy of a rich congregation member. Let me fill you in on that." He gave them the details. "The next day I went to his church, and I'll tell you more in a minute on that, but first let me tell you about my conversation with the *other* Mr. Caldwell. Trooper, just so you know, he's my grandfather, but before Saturday, he and I have never had a conversation in my entire life. It's a long story, but you can imagine he was surprised to see me."

He gave them a summary of his conversation, and Caldwell's defensiveness, and included the abrupt departure. "Chief, I provoked him on purpose, must admit I got some satisfaction out of it, but I was hoping it might help you when you follow up. Of course, I expect you'll get an earful about me, if you haven't already. He threatened to get me fired."

Foster actually chuckled. "Wow, now I can't wait to talk with him. Don't worry about the job, not that you probably even want it, I'll handle him. After all, this is a murder investigation, not some parking ticket."

Next Rob gave them a detailed description of his visit to church, Moose's attendance, the appearance of Bruce Armstrong, and the interesting topic of the sermon. "Also it seems Duggan gave me a different impression of how his conversation went with Proctor. Told me it was cordial, and Proctor wasn't closed to the idea, but Moose got a different version."

"So, Duggan's jumped on the McCarthy bandwagon," Foster sighed. "Just what I need, bunch of citizens labeling each other commie/pinkos. The man is a piece of work."

"Can't believe Moose is one of his followers," said Skip. "He never said a word to me. You know, I should have noticed though. He's been acting different lately, now that I think of it. Course, I never directly asked him about it, if I had he would have given himself away. Terrible liar - always has been. Guess I didn't ask the right questions."

"There's another angle I'm checking out," added the State Trooper. "Rob mentioned that Proctor had a business connection to gangsters when he sold the old Bound Brook Inn. It seems that Cecil still had occasional dealings with the Providence crime family. His connection with women of "ill repute" might have been another connection; they control most of that type of activity. I'm not saying he was part of the mob, but it's enough of a connection for me to explore. Wouldn't be the first-time gangsters did away with somebody who got in their way or crossed them on a business deal. In fact, arson would be right up their alley. Maybe they sent someone to threaten him and it got out of hand. I also know that I'll have to check out this black car. If it turns out this does involve the mob, I want the three of you to back off and let us at the State Police handle it. Those gangsters are more than you want to deal with."

The three Bound Brook men looked at each other with concern, then Foster broke the silence. "Well, that would put a whole different spin on it. Guess we'll leave that for you to sort out."

Trooper Stewart nodded, then continued, "Leaving out a possible Providence gangster connection for now, who do we have for suspects, and what do we have for motive and opportunity?"

The Chief cleared his throat. "Well, Reverend Duggan might have done it, with the motive being an argument over buying land for the church. He doesn't have a solid alibi for the murder; Moose says he saw Proctor after Duggan had left, but Duggan could have gone back again. He also could easily walk back to light the fire, even in the blizzard, and he could've left Rob's warning note. He doesn't have a car, so maybe he didn't try to break into Doc's office."

The Chief looked at Skip. "Then there's Moose; hate to say it Skip, and honestly, I doubt he did it. However, he may have been the last person to see Proctor alive. Sounds like he'd do anything to defend the preacher. He drives the town plow and might be the only person in town who could have driven to Proctor's in a storm. He could have left Rob's note, and could have been the one trying to break into Doc's. Like I said I doubt it, but we can't rule him out."

Skip gave a little smirk. "Well, I can practically guarantee he didn't write Rob's note. I can tell, 'cause everything's spelled correctly. Don't think he could spell *accident* if his life depended on it."

The other three burst out laughing. "Good point, Skip," said Rob, "When we had spelling bees in school, Moose was always the last one picked. I think he can spell his name, but not much more."

"What about Armstrong? Any chance he tried to stop Proctor from selling to Duggan?" asked the Trooper.

Rob shook his head. "Doubt it. Duggan and Moose both said that Proctor didn't say he'd sell. Armstrong lives in Wellesley, and that would've have been a tough drive in a blizzard."

"Now, if Duggan turns up dead," Stewart chuckled, "we might want to check on Armstrong first."

"What about Corey Proctor?" Skip asked.

"I don't see a current motive," the Chief replied.

"So, of the known suspects, Duggan looks the most likely," said Stewart. "But we also have the unknown. Rob mentioned some nasty history Proctor had with women. Maybe it connects to that? Sounds like we still don't know all his business dealings either. We need to be careful not to zero in on someone like Duggan so much that we close out other possibilities."

"There's Caldwell, but I don't see him as a murder suspect yet," the Chief added. "However, he might know something he's not telling us. The two of them were tangled up in so many deals, he might be protecting his interests. Anyway, I'll be following up with him."

He gave Rob a serious look. "Rob, you seem to have stirred the hornet's nest, and I need you to do a couple of things. First, get a lock on that door! Second, you are out here with no phone, I can't reach you, and more importantly, you can't reach us. I want you to stop at the station whenever you're near the center. The dispatcher will radio me and keep me updated, and I can pass along any messages to you. I need you to do that at least once a day, more frequently if you can. Skip, at least you have a phone, but will you check in regularly also? Just remember, no details over the phone."

His voice took an ominous tone now. "Let's not forgot that we've got a murderer out there. They already killed once, so they've got nothing to lose." He let that sink in. "Let's meet every morning same time, same place, until further notice. Skip, I got the muffins tomorrow. Stewart, feel free to join us whenever you can, but meanwhile I'll keep you posted either way.

"Today I'm following up with Caldwell. Skip and Rob, drop in places around town, start conversations, just see what you hear. People have a way of remembering things after they think about it for a while. One more thing, and this is important, nobody else, except us and the murderer, knows about Rob's warning note. Let's keep it that way, not a word to anyone, got it? Might come in handy down the road."

Rob noticed the empty muffin box, good appetites. He shook Don Stewart's hand. "Good to meet you, still shoot any hoops?"

Stewart laughed. "I wish I could, but this job makes it hard. Show me those footprints, just for the record."

The four men circled the cottage, looking at the tracks, "You're right, they look like the ones at Doc's, but that doesn't prove anything," said Foster.

With that, Skip, Foster, and Stewart went on their way. Back inside, Rob realized that it was almost noon already. The muffins were good, but he figured he'd better get some lunch before he went to basketball practice at the school. Probably need all the energy he could get to keep up with those teenage boys.

Chapter XIII – Hardware & Basketball

After a quick lunch of a cheese sandwich and milk, Rob packed his knapsack with his sneakers, shorts, tee-shirt, socks, jock, towel and knee support. He had some errands to do before heading to practice. He parked in the little lot next to the Public Safety Building, across the street from Joseph's Hardware, which now had an *OPEN* sign in the window. A small bell over the door signaled his arrival.

Frank Joseph emerged from the backroom. "Hey, Rob, what can I get for you?"

"I need to get some kind of lock for my front door."

"How quick do you need it installed?"

"Today would be good."

"What do you have now?"

"Just a basic latch, no doorknob or anything."

"How fancy or pricey you want to go?"

"Basic and cheap!"

Frank thought about that for a moment. "Well, quickest thing is to get a sliding bolt for the inside. If you want to lock it when you leave, I would say a hasp and padlock for the outside. Both you can put on yourself with a drill and screwdriver. You want a real locking doorknob, it will take longer to install yourself, or you might get somebody to put it in for you. Need to drill out the right size hole, but the locking doorknobs really aren't that expensive."

Rob considered his options. "Give me the works. I'll put the bolt, hasp and lock on myself, and when my cousin Ben has time, he has the tools for the real knob."

"You got it." Frank knelt down under the counter and rummaged around.

"Glad to see you're open. Saw a closed sign the other day, was that because of the storm?"

"Partly," came Frank's voice from under the counter, "it's sort of a long story, not sure it matters now that Proctor is dead."

"Skip Parker was talking to merchants in town about Proctor's murder, didn't he talk with you?" asked Rob.

"No, I was out of town for several days."

Rob's interest perked up, "So what was going on with you and Proctor?"

Frank emerged from his search with a heavy inside door bolt, "Proctor holds the mortgage on this place, and a part ownership in the business. Never totally understood the legal side of it, but when I wanted to buy it a couple years ago, the banks turned me down. Proctor made me an offer, the only option I had."

"What happens now that he's dead?"

"Well, just before he died, Proctor told me he was calling the loan due and exercising his ownership share. He told me I had to close down, and he was going to sell the place."

"Wow! What was he going to do?"

Frank came from behind the counter and headed down one of the aisles, "The word will get out now, although I guess the deal is dead with Proctor gone. Barnstable County Lumber Company wants to open a branch here in Bound Brook. Proctor was going to sell them this lot and the two beside it, Snow family next door and the Jenkins couple two doors down. Both of them rent from Proctor. Also included the rooming house across the street. The BCL was going to put in a hardware store and lumber yard, like the two they've got in Bourne and Barnstable. Even if I didn't have to sell, they'd put me out of business anyway, no room for two hardware stores in Bound Brook."

"So, what happens now?"

"Well, I called Attorney Winters in Ptown, just this morning. He says everything stays the way it is for now. Proctor's estate has to go through a bunch of legal stuff, and nothing is likely to happen until all that's settled. I was out of town before the storm, went up to see my brothers in Wareham and got stuck up there until after the blizzard.

They run a fish market, and I've got a standing offer of a job if I ever need it."

"You must be relieved."

"I'd just broken the news to my wife and daughter. They were pretty upset, especially Mary. She's a junior and had her heart set on graduating from Bound Brook High like her older sister. Now I guess we can stay here after all."

"So what about the Lumber Company?"

Frank pulled out a hasp and lock combination. "Here you go, now we'll just get you a locking doorknob you can put on later. Well, I guess the BCL has to wait or find a different location. All the properties could be tied up until everything is settled. Attorney Winters said it could take a year, maybe more, if there are claims against the estate. If BCL finds another location in Bound Brook or nearby, of course, they might put me out of business anyway, but for now I can keep going."

"Did anybody else know about this?" Rob was sensing something he might be able to use.

"Well, besides Attorney Winters, there's Mr. Caldwell, he's the Realtor, plus my wife and kids and anybody they told. I said to keep it a secret, but you know kids. Anyway, we don't have to worry about it, at least for now."

"Did the Jenkins and Snow families know?"

"Not from me or my wife, but Mary's friends with Bobby Snow, and she might have told him or else somebody else could have. As renters, they had to put up with the chance that Procter might move them out anyway."

He grabbed a box and headed for the counter. "OK, here we go, these should take care of it. You got the tools you need?"

"Sure, I've got a screwdriver set and a hand-drill and bits, think that will do it?"

"It should, except for the doorknob, but you said Ben has the tools for that, right?"

Rob paid for the locks, said goodbye to Frank Joseph, and left the store. Since the Police Station was across the street, he figured he'd better check in. Going up the stairs he noticed the Chief's Chevy Special Cruiser parked behind the building.

Diane gave him a nod and jerked her thumb toward the office door.

"Hey Chief," he said, "I know we just talked, but there's something you should know. You haven't talked to Caldwell yet, have you?"

"I just got off the phone with him, heading to his office in a few minutes. By the way, he gave me an earful about what a pushy, rude, blankety-blank, you are. I told him it sounded like good police work to me. Why, what's up?"

Rob filled in Foster on his conversation with Frank Joseph. "The point is that Frank says Caldwell knew about it, but he never mentioned it to me."

"Good timing, I'll definitely ask old Caldwell about that! He probably has some slick answer, but I'll see how he handles it."

"I'm heading to the school, helping George with basketball practice. I'll keep my eyes and ears open. Doubt the kids know anything, but you never can tell. See you at my place tomorrow at nine." He gave Diane a nod on his way out.

He had some time to kill, so he decided to check his mail at the Post Office. Bound Brook didn't have mail delivery; you had to pick it up at one of the two Post Offices. His cottage was halfway between the locations, but he used the main branch in the center of town. Some people rented a P.O. Box, everyone else picked it up, *general delivery,* at the counter. Rob got very little mail, so he didn't check there often. Skip had already talked to the postmaster and clerk, but Rob hadn't been there since way before the storm, and who knew what he might learn?

He parked in the Town Hall parking lot and walked across the street to the little Post Office building. Suzanne Taylor finished waiting on a customer and gave him a smile.

"Hello stranger, wondered if you were ever going to come get your mail. I got two letters for you. One's been here awhile, and the other just came in Friday. Let me get 'em." She ducked out of view, but kept talking, "Funny thing about the first one, just addressed to you at *Bound Brook, Cape Cod, USA*. Surprised it even got here, looks like it got shuffled around. It was originally postmarked three weeks ago, somewhere in New York State."

She returned to the counter with the letters. "Another funny thing, there was a guy here last week, Thursday or Friday, asking for directions to your place. Told him postal regulations don't allow me to give out that information. Were you expecting anyone?"

"No, what'd he look like?"

"Big guy, fortyish, well dressed, dark, slicked hair, maybe Italian or Mediterranean, I'd guess. His clothes didn't match his looks or speech, real rugged looking, cauliflower ears and broken nose. Friend of yours?"

Rob shook his head. "Don't think so."

"Just thought I'd let you know. I'm not allowed to tell him, but lots of other folks might give him directions."

He thanked Suzanne and took his letters back to the car. One was hand printed, no return address, but Rob recognized the writing. Inside was one page and a short note written in French. He translated as he read.

Dearest Robert,
I have left France and am in the USA. My father will not be happy and will try to find me. I cannot tell you why or any details. I cannot live under his roof anymore. I do not know if you still want to see me, or if this letter will find you. If you are still in Bound Brook I will find you and we will see. I still love you.

Marie

It had been, what, seven years? And now a letter from Marie, in the United States and looking for him. He glanced at the other letter, in an expensive envelope, with his address typed, and an embossed return address from *LaVache LTD, Marseille, France.*

This letter was typed in English.

Mr. Robert Caldwell,
This letter is to inform you that my daughter, Marie, has left France and is believed to be in the United States of America. It is possible she may try to contact you. If she does, I expect to be informed immediately, and for you to make every effort to return her to her home. You will be provided with contact information in person in the near future. Do not ignore these instructions! To do so would not be in the best interests of either you or Marie.
Emile LaVache, Chairman
LaVache, LTD

Letters from a bittersweet past. One a lost love and the other her ruthless father, not a man to treat lightly. Two weeks ago, he had been practically a hermit, living in his little cottage, working odd jobs, and reading books. Now he was investigating a murder, involved with his high school sweetheart who was married to his best friend, awaiting the possible arrival of his French girlfriend and threatened by her powerful and dangerous father. So much for living a quiet life on Cape Cod.

He thought about the mystery man. Now it made sense; was this the individual who would contact him "in the near future," but, in fact, was already in Bound Brook? But why was this person interested in both Proctor and him?

There was nothing he could do about Marie. He had no contact address for her, and he was confident he would hear from the man with the broken nose very soon. Nothing to do except wait and see.

He tucked the letters into the glove box and headed back on Main Street to Pond Hill Road and the Bound Brook Consolidated School. He parked on the traffic circle and walked to the gym. There was an elementary gym class just finishing up, taught by the district Physical Education teacher, who Rob didn't know. When he'd been a kid they didn't have P.E. class, just recess. He went down the back stairs to the cramped boy's locker room and changed.

When he got back upstairs, the class was gone and the gym was empty. He pulled out a bag of basketballs from the equipment closet and started shooting foul shots while he waited for Coach Gilmore. The letters were still on his mind, but the familiar feel of the basketball brought some comfort.

"Still got your touch, I see," came the voice of Gilmore as he walked through the swinging doors, "I've got a trig class of juniors and seniors, started them on their homework and Miss Richards is watching them so I can meet with you."

Rob snapped a two-hand bounce pass to Gilmore as he crossed half-court. George, still in his white shirt and tie, scooped up the pass, took two dribbles and stopped outside the foul circle arc. He pulled the ball to his chest and put up a two-hand set shot. The ball traveled to the backboard, hit the spot just below the red square and ricocheted into the basket.

"Looks like someone else still has his touch," laughed Rob.

"Back when I played, my coach would have benched me if I ever tried a shot from that far outside. Only took a shot like that if time was running out."

Rob retrieved the ball. "So you want to bring me up to speed before practice?"

"Sure do. With Snowy hurt, we don't have a real center, so we're going to improvise. Your cousin Benny will play center on defense, and Tony Oliver is the center when we have the ball. Ben is under six foot and will give up inches, but he's rugged and knows how to use his body and plays tough defense. He'll make their center work hard. Oliver is taller, but skinny, and he's got a nice shot, particularly that hook shot of his is hard to block. With Vinnie Costa in the starting line-up we really have three natural guards. So, we've got to pass the ball around fast, keep it moving, run some outside weaves and take advantage of our speed."

"What about on defense? Zone, man to man or a mix?" asked Rob.

"Mostly man to man. With our height disadvantage, we have to pressure them, and try to use our quickness to disrupt and make them uncomfortable."

"What do you need me to do?"

"Two things: first, help me demonstrate the outside weave—we've run it, and they know it, but with three quick guys, I want to move it faster—you know, pick up the pace? Second thing is, help Benny and Oliver with playing center. We'll alternate between a high and low post and a double-low one, try to incorporate it into the weave by setting screens."

Rob nodded his understanding. The strategy made sense for a short, quick team.

"One other thing," George added. "Junior is our best player, but he also tries to do too much—you know, takes it on himself, instead of working with the team. I'm worried that with Snowy hurt, he'll feel he has to take on even more. He's not really selfish, just overestimates his ability, and he's got a short fuse. After his brother died in the war, his parents really spoiled him. He was always the baby of the family, of course; must have been nine years younger than his brother. Anyway, I think he tries to be perfect, maybe to please his parents, or make up for his brother."

Rob nodded. He'd noticed the same thing when he watched the home games. "Who're we playing?"

"Orleans tomorrow afternoon at their place, and Sandwich on Friday night at home. Sandwich is a make-up game from a snowstorm earlier in the season. Wellfleet and Sandwich are at the bottom of the small-school league right now, and Provincetown is totally dominating everyone. It's a close race for second place with Orleans, Harwich, Chatham and us all fighting it out. Next two games decide the season. Two wins and we could slip into the playoffs."

As they talked the bell rang and school ended. Rob heard the familiar bustle of students in the hallway as they got ready to board the two school buses, walk home, or, in the case of a few older kids, drive their own cars. Of course, about half of the high school boys were on the team.

The guys filtered into the gym and headed for the locker room, with lots of goofing around, bantering, and friendly teasing. Rob was reminded of his own days playing for Bound Brook High. The last player in was Bobby Snow, his arm in a sling. He dropped down on a sideline seat with a glum expression.

George headed over to his injured player. "Snowy, I know how disappointing it is to get hurt, but I've got a job for you. Benny is playing center on defense and Ollie on offense. I need you to watch their moves. Give them some pointers and mostly encourage them. It's going to be an adjustment for them. Can you do that for me?"

"Sure, Coach," said Bobby, brightening a little.

Leave it to Gilmore to encourage an injured player and make sure he stayed involved. It was one of the many qualities that Rob admired about the man. He hoped he had picked up a few of Gilmore's traits.

He went back to shooting foul shots until the team started to come upstairs from changing. Then he switched to shagging rebounds for the kids, so they could warm up and practice their shots. Like he'd said to Benny, this was their practice not his.

Rob noticed that Gilmore had pulled Junior off to the side and was calmly talking to him while the teenager nodded. "Orleans is going to key on you, you can't try to do too much. Sometimes you've got to be a decoy, so they think you'll shoot, but you've got to pass it off to the other guys if you get double teamed."

The coach finished his pep talk. Junior joined his teammates and Rob grabbed a rebound and flipped the ball to Junior, who put up a nice, smooth shot.

"Tweet," came the shrill sound of Coach Gilmore's whistle. "OK guys, circle up over here."

The boys each grabbed a basketball and gathered around the coach. They all knew not to interrupt him by bouncing a ball. That indiscretion was good for five laps around the gym.

"Listen guys, you all know Rob Caldwell. Rob's going to help us out again today. It's not going to be easy making up for Snowy, but we're going to make some changes, and Snowy is going to help me coach instead of playing."

Gilmore went through an explanation of the changes to the team, who listened intently. Then they broke up into their regular warm-up drills, starting with a layup line. Finally, they went to their positions on offense and practiced the outside weave.

"OK guys, that's it, but you need to pick up the pace, move the ball faster, move your feet, be quick. You want to leave your man in the dust. We need Orleans to be so confused they don't know who they're covering. That's it, that's the idea."

Next, they moved to a controlled scrimmage. Rob played center for the second team against the starters. It was fun being guarded by Benny when Rob's team got the ball. Benny played him tough, used his body to move Rob out of position, and really cracked him up with his incessant line of chatter. Even Coach Gilmore had a hard time keeping a straight face.

"Gee, it's such an honor to be guarding the great Rob Caldwell. Too bad you got so old. I remember watching you play when I was just a baby. What was it like playing in the real old days? Tell me if you need me to slow down, OK? Don't want you having a heart attack."

Whenever Rob got the ball in the post he made a pass back out to the open man. The goal was to keep the ball moving and make the first team hustle on defense. When he was on defense, Rob guarded Tony Oliver. He gave the kid a challenge but held back just enough so he didn't ruin his confidence.

As Rob ran down the court on offense, he passed Gilmore who gave him a wink. "Give your cousin a lesson."

Rob knew what that meant. He flashed to the top of the foul line in a high post, with Benny clinging to him like glue. The ball came to him up high. He grabbed it, faked left, faked right, spun back to his left, pivoted around Ben, took two quick dribbles, stretched his tall frame high in the air, and laid the ball off the backboard and into the basket. Several players broke into applause.

"OK, I let you have that one," laughed Benny. "Didn't want you getting discouraged."

Gilmore laughed as hard as anyone. "That was a reminder, Ben, at least one of us old timers has still got something left in him."

The rest of practice went well, and Benny ceased his chatter. The team grasped the changes and practiced with intensity. Vinnie Costa seemed to be fitting in nicely, and Junior was meshing with the team, not trying to do too much. It was getting close to the end, and the girls' team started to drift in for their practice. Rob recognized a few of the girls, including Mary Joseph, and tried not to get too distracted when Rachel appeared.

The first team was on offense, running the weave, when Junior passed the ball to Johnny Webster, who passed to Vinnie, who put up a little set shot from outside that circled the rim and spun out. Junior grabbed the rebound and fired the ball at Vinnie's head. "You're supposed to keep the ball moving, freshman, not take a long shot!"

Junior charged at the freshman player, but Benny grabbed him in a bear hug, and held on tight. "Cool it, Junior," he barked.

Coach Gilmore blew his whistle. "OK, practice over, I should've wrapped it up already. Everybody hit the showers, except Junior and Vinnie. I need to talk to you guys!"

Ben let go of Junior and headed to the locker room. George walked over to the two remaining players. "Junior, that was unacceptable. You were right, but that's no way to handle it. He's your teammate and still learning, teach him, don't attack him."

Junior's face was still flushed with anger and he screamed, "I can't take this right now Coach. I just can't." With that outburst he ran out of the gym, through the outside double doors and into the cold, still dressed in his practice shorts and tee-shirt.

"Junior, come back," yelled Mary Joseph. Then she turned to Gilmore. "I'll go talk to him. He hasn't been himself lately." And she too went out the double doors.

George gave Rob a look. "He's a good kid, but that temper of his, it just breaks loose sometimes. About now he'll be feeling embarrassed and too ashamed to come back in. I'll get an apology call from him tonight, but I'll have to do some sort of discipline. Great timing with the game tomorrow."

"Rob, do me a favor," he continued. "Go ask Johnny Webster if he can grab Junior's clothes, car keys and stuff and bring them out to him. I'm sure he'll find him freezing to death in his car, with Mary trying to calm him down."

Rob went to the locker room and conveyed Gilmore's request to Johnny. Most of the guys were still getting dressed. Benny gave Rob a glance. "Junior just loses it sometimes, thinks he's better than he is. I don't know what gets into him."

Rob took a quick shower and changed into his street clothes, then headed up to the gym where the girls were starting to shoot around. Rachel had a whistle around her neck and was talking to her Dad. Rob couldn't help being distracted by her trim, athletic figure.

Trying not to stare, he turned to Bobby Snow, who was waiting for the last guys to finish changing.

"Hey, Snowy, can I ask you a question?"

"Sure, Rob."

"Your family lives next to Joseph Hardware, right?"

"We do."

"Did you hear anything about your family maybe having to move?"

Snow looked uncomfortable. "I heard it from Mary, she said Old Man Proctor might kick us out and sell the house. I didn't want to believe it, but when I asked my mother, she said it was true. Guess it doesn't matter now that he's dead."

"Who else knew?"

"You mean of the kids? Well, Mary told me, because it was our house, and of course she told Junior. I don't know who else knew, with the blizzard and losing the power and telephone for days, I don't think the word got around too much."

Rob thanked Snowy and took a seat on the sideline. He watched Rachel run her team through their drills. Mary Joseph came back in the gym and joined the team. Rachel was doing the best she could, encouraging and demonstrating, but it seemed to Rob that she didn't have many skilled players. The exception was Mary, who was quick and had a nice shot from her forward position.

George came over and sat down. "Rachel's done a great job coaching but continuing in the tradition of Bound Brook girls' teams, she doesn't have much to work with. The girls in town have always had more enthusiasm for being on the cheerleading squad than on the basketball team."

Rob nodded and Gilmore continued. "I think I'm going to have Junior sit out the beginning of the game. Just hope we don't get behind too much before he goes in. The team bus leaves for Orleans at 2:30, girls' game at 3:30, boys' around five. You know the routine; if you're coming, you want to join me on the bench?"

"I'll drive up, try to make it in time for your game, maybe catch some of the girls' game. You mind if I don't join you on the bench though? I think I need to be free to move around."

George nodded in agreement. "The Proctor murder?"

"You never know what I might pick up from conversations." Rob got up to leave. "See you tomorrow." He gave Rachel a wave and headed to his car.

Chapter XIV – Sorting Things Out

It was getting dark as Rob left school. The boys were all gone, and only a few cars remained. He stopped to look at the school building where he'd spent his high school years. The fading light, the coating of snow and the stillness of the winter air, all created a picture that stirred memories. The Bound Brook Consolidated School had been his haven, an oasis of stability in a tumultuous life.

The building fit the Cape environment; a weather-beaten shingle exterior, and an entrance of solid, square, white columns, it was simple, yet dignified. It was a split level, taking advantage of the back slope of the hill. The entrance was on the main floor, and the basement level faced the back, looking out at the playground with swings, seesaws and a small paved basketball court. Rob remembered elementary grades at the old school near the town center. The whole school had gone to recess at the same time. He had particularly loved the swings: swinging as high as he could go, the feeling of flying as the chains lost their tightness, and then snapped back. He remembered jumping off the swing, the tingle of the fear he felt, the exhilaration of flying through the air, and the sense of achievement landing in the soft sand. It was a rite of passage, and he had repeated the leap again and again, each time swinging and jumping higher and higher.

Looking at the building brought him comfort, but he realized it wasn't the building that was his haven, it was the community of stern, but caring teachers, and the constancy of the same group of children who had progressed with him year after year. Even the jerks, the bullies like Moose and Bunky, were part of the familiarity. Their stupid tricks, like luring a younger child onto the seesaw, then suddenly jumping off when the youngster's end was at the top, and laughing at the little one's jarring landing—even those were part of a rhythm, a routine that had given Rob a sense of belonging.

He got in his car and made the short drive to the Hooper brothers' gas station. He didn't need gas, but he did need to talk. He parked next to the building and noticed that the damaged cars were gone. Howie Proctor must have towed them over to his body shop. They were replaced by another car, a shiny, new Cadillac that looked like Old Man Proctor's. He found Hoopy sitting in the small office.

"Hey Hoop, just came back from practice. Is that Proctor's Caddy?"

"Yup, they needed it away from the fire scene so they could clean up the mess. I told them we could store it here. Hey, you seen Junior?"

"Sure, he was at practice, but had a bit of an incident right at the end. Lost his cool and took it out on the Costa kid. Took off in a huff."

"Well, he's late," said Hoopy, "supposed to spell me, so I can get some supper."

"Don't know what to tell you."

"Well, my wife will be miffed; doesn't like the dinner getting cold or dried out from reheating. Can't say I enjoy it much either."

Hoopy was a relative newlywed, married about two years now, to a young woman named Susan Coogan, from Brewster. As it turned out Rob and Hoopy had played basketball against her older brother, Jim Coogan. Like lots of folks on the Cape, they were distant cousins, a Doane or Nickerson connection. Hoopy had met her at a relative's wedding in Harwich and been smitten. It was a short courtship, and Rob had been the best man. Susan was pretty, smart and pleasant. Rob was pleased for his friend; she was just what Hoopy needed.

A car pulled off the highway, its beams lighting the office, and parked in the space next to Rob's coupe. Junior Proctor jumped out and walked briskly to the office door. "Geez, Hoopy, sorry I'm late, got hung up at practice," said Junior.

"So, I heard," said Hoopy, looking at Rob.

Junior now noticed Rob for the first time, and just blushed and lowered his head.

"OK, you're here now, but don't let it happen again. I'll be back at seven. Everyone who had repairs picked up their cars already, so just handle the pumps. You should be able to get some homework done, not very busy."

"Let me walk you to your car," said Rob.

"Just don't hold me up," said Hoopy, heading out the door. "Susan's going to be mad enough already."

The men got in the 1950 Packard, and Hoopy started the car.

"I won't keep you long, but a few questions. Junior really lost his cool at practice, and for no obvious reason. You ever see him act like that?"

"He's a good kid and usually reliable. Not the most sociable, a bit moody, but does a good job. Family went through a lot, losing his brother in the war. I know he has a temper, but I've never seen it. I think going steady with Mary Joseph has been good for him. Nice girl, cheerful and smart, kind of perks him up in more ways than one, if you know what I mean." Hoopy winked with the last words.

"You ever hear anything about Frank Joseph closing the hardware store?"

"Junior came in one day in a bad mood, said Mary might have to move. Not sure why, he didn't elaborate, and I didn't ask. Young love, you know, has its ups and downs."

"When was that?"

"Must have been just before the storm. Speaking of young love, what's up with you and Rachel? Think you've got the whole town buzzing."

Rob shook his head. "Nothing really, just two old friends finally reconnecting. We've been avoiding each other for years, decided it was time to stop tippy-toeing around."

Hoopy gave him a long look. "Really? Listen, if it matters, everyone I heard it from thinks it's great. Oh, I'm sure some of the old, self-righteous biddies in town will be wagging their tongues, but, you know, most people genuinely like Rachel, and they feel sorry for her. Jimmy's been my friend forever, and he worked at the station, but, honestly, people are pretty sick of him, and you can include me in the group. So, whatever happens with you and Rachel, I say, good for you!"

Rob nodded. "Thanks buddy." He got out of the car, "Now you get going. If Susan's ticked, blame it on me. Tell her you were part of an official police investigation and couldn't get away."

Hoopy laughed. "If she knows it's you, that won't work. No, I think Junior's my best excuse, I'll leave out mentioning you. It'll only get me in deeper."

Rob watched his friend pull away and went back in the little office. Junior had a fat textbook open, and was staring blankly at the page, doing his best to ignore him.

"So, you ready for the Orleans game tomorrow?"

"Sure," grunted Junior, his eyes still on the page.

Rob's voice got serious, "Did you call Coach Gilmore?"

Junior looked up sheepishly, "Yeah, how'd you know? Oh, I guess Coach knows me pretty well. I was really stupid! Poor Vinnie, never should've done that to him."

"So what did Coach say?"

"I'm not starting, sitting out the beginning of the game. Said he'd put me in at one of the first time-outs. I deserve it. Feel bad though, letting down the team."

"Junior, did you hear something from Mary Joseph that her dad might close the hardware store?"

Junior looked surprised. "Yeah, Mary told me they might have to move."

"Did she tell you why?"

He looked uncomfortable. "Kind-a, she said that Old Man Proctor might sell the place. Guess he was a part owner. She was pretty upset, but I guess it wasn't definite."

"Who else knew, did you tell anyone?"

"Well, Bobby Snow knew, Mary told him, don't know who else did. The only ones I told were my parents. And oh, I guess I told Hoopy when he asked why I was in such a bad mood."

"What did your folks say?"

"My Dad was pretty ticked! He said something about the SOB always messing with people's lives."

"You're pretty serious about Mary, I guess."

The teenager brightened. "Sure, Mary's great. I mean she's a junior and still got a year of school, but I was thinking that I might apprentice with my father, you know, get my electrician license and stick around Bound Brook."

"I guess she'll be staying now that Proctor's dead."

"Guess so. I got a history test tomorrow. Better read this chapter or Mr. Keane will flunk me, and I won't be graduating." He put his head down and started reading. Rob gathered that their conversation was over.

"Good luck with the test. Mr. Keane's not such a hard grader, but you've got to at least read it. I'll see you at the game."

He went out and got in the car. Typical Bound Brook, everything that happened was connected somehow. That was life in a small town, he guessed. As he drove, he pondered which culinary masterpiece he would make for dinner. Whatever it was, it would come out of a can!

He lit the lantern and got the woodstove going, and he kept his coat on until the cottage warmed up. Next, he found a screwdriver and hand-drill, grabbed the bag of hardware and took out the sliding bolt for the inside of the door. By the time he finished, the cottage was warm. Dinner was not completely out of a can, Rob fried three eggs, heated a can of beans and buttered two slices of bread. After all, he hadn't had a real breakfast yet today!

He was finishing his meal when a car pulled into the driveway. He went to the door and saw the Gilmore Chevy. Rachel hopped out and Rob held the cottage door open.

She took off her coat and hung it on the hook. "I need to talk to you."

Rob nodded, "Sure."

"When I got home, there was a letter to me from Jimmy. To get to the point, Jimmy says that he wants us to get a divorce."

He was stunned. "Wow, where'd that come from?"

She pulled out a kitchen chair and sat at the table. "It was a long apology letter, really, I think it started with his mother. He said Mabel wrote him a letter a couple of months ago. She really blasted him, told him she was sick of him feeling sorry for himself, and what it was doing to me. Guess she told him I was wasting my life waiting for him, and unless he straightened himself out, he wasn't worth my time.

"He said he knows how mean he's been to me and everybody. He said he hates himself when he's around Bound Brook. Guilt and shame make him drink too much and act the way he does. In his words, in the Army nobody knows or cares that he stole his best friend's girl. He said that's one reason he feels better in the service. Jimmy said he wants to try to make a career in the army but isn't sure they'll need him when the war ends. Either way, he said he probably won't come back to town."

Rob sat and looked at her before speaking "I don't know what to say."

She reached out her hand and put it over his. "You know, I'd decided to get a divorce anyway, but I didn't want to do it when Jimmy was still fighting. I didn't want to write the classic *Dear John Letter*. I don't think that's fair to someone whose life is in danger."

"So, what now, where do you go from here?"

"Well, I'm not sure about the divorce legal stuff. First off, I told my parents, and Jimmy said he was writing to Mabel. I guess I'll talk with a lawyer and go from there. You know, as bad as he feels, I feel just as bad. If I'd never run off with him to get even with you, none of this would've happened."

"It happened, too late now. It sounds like Jimmy is getting things straightened out. I think that's a good thing for him. I still want the best for him, and this might be a start."

"Rob, you're so damned fair! Most guys would be so mad at him and me for what we did, but you're almost too kind for your own good."

"Well why wouldn't I care about two of my best friends?"

Rachel got up and went over to his chair, leaned over and gave him a deep kiss, then pulled away. "Whoa, I better stop right there! You know I love you, always have and always will, but I need to figure some things out. Right now, I'd like nothing better than for you to take me over to the bed and make love to me."

Rob gave her a deep look. "Sounds pretty good to me."

"Hold on, lover boy. I've made one decision. I'm not going to jump into another commitment. I want you to stay in my life, if we can work that out, but like I said before, I've had my life on hold for twelve years, and it's time for me to find myself, before I give my life to anyone else, even you. Do you understand that, does it make sense?"

"Completely."

"Good, that's great. I better go now, before I get tempted again." She grinned, then grabbed her coat, opened the door and blew him a kiss, "See you at the game tomorrow."

He had stored his love for Rachel away in that safe place. He'd locked it up and hidden the key. Oh, there'd been girls he dated in college. He was a basketball player, tall and good looking and girls were interested. Some had dropped him quickly when they found out he was a poor kid from a backwater town. Others had seemed to find it exciting, dating a boy who didn't fit the prep school model of so many of the Brown guys. He'd never gotten the sense that any of them were interested in bringing him home to meet mother and father.

That was OK with him. He hadn't been ready for anything serious, and he'd known he couldn't take the pain of making a commitment and getting hurt. Besides, how could he love someone else, when he still loved Rachel?

Marie had been different. Maybe because he was in a foreign country. Maybe because all around him were people who faced death in the war. Whatever it was, when he met her, he didn't think about Bound Brook or Rachel. Then there was Marie's father, Emil LaVache; cultured, powerful and controlling, he had swooped in on Rob, welcomed his relationship with Marie, and talked him into joining his shipping business after the war. It was like the father and daughter had taken over two different aspects of his life and, at that point, Rob had been glad to surrender control.

When the war had ended, he had found himself returned to the States, mustered out of the Navy, and then back in Marseille. He had a job with an exorbitant salary. He'd known that Marie was crazy about him and been dazzled by her and his new lifestyle. Her father had shown him around the business, rotating him through the different operations, treating him like a partner and a son.

Monsieur LaVache was a dominant personality and Rob had found himself swept along. LaVache peppered him with questions about the Navy and port procedures. Eventually, he had become involved in things that made him uncomfortable. He tried to press the older man for answers, but the shipping tycoon had brushed them aside. Finally, the reality had dawned on him. LaVache was involved in the black-market trade and had been pumping Rob for information to help with his smuggling operations. When he confronted LaVache, it had all come crashing down. Rob had never known what hit him!

Then, back in the United States, all he had wanted was to get on with his old life. Fortunately, he had saved a year's worth of his huge salary and was well set financially. The G.I. Bill passed in '44 covered most of his college costs. The result was that Rob had his college degree, with no debt and more than enough money left to support his modest lifestyle.

Since returning to Bound Brook, he had worked odd jobs. He'd helped Ben with his plumbing business when he needed an extra hand, had done some labor for Joe Perry when he needed a strong back, and occasionally filled in as a substitute teacher at Bound Brook. In the summer he'd worked traffic duty and tended bar on weekends at Art's Bar & Grill on the harbor. He made enough money to get by, and never needed to dip into his large savings account. Meanwhile he had played basketball in the Cape League and kept himself in reasonable shape until the knee injury.

And there had been other girls, but like in college, he dated casually: summer girls, college waitresses and barmaids, never letting anything get serious. In the last two years there hadn't been anyone. He was getting too old for the college girls—not that they weren't interested, but it didn't feel right to him. He had to admit, part of it was that Rachel was still around.

So he'd settled into a dull, but stable routine. He didn't think about the future, didn't think he was underachieving by not using his degree. He went through life one day at a time, immersed in the ordinary business of Bound Brook, Cape Cod. It hadn't been exciting, but it was comforting. Now that routine was in tatters. He was investigating a murder, reunited with the love of his life, and threatened by his past in France. Would Rachel be available? What would he do if Marie showed up? The possibilities left him confused and overwhelmed.

He looked at the pine bookshelf in the corner for a distraction. Should he take another crack at Melville? He'd read the first half of Moby Dick five times before finally finishing; it usually succeeded in putting him to sleep. In contrast, he'd read Tolstoy's epic *War and Peace* twice. Victor Hugo's *Les Miserables* wasn't a good idea right now. He'd just finished rereading *The Tell Tale Heart* for at least the sixth time. Now, if Proctor's murderer would confess like the one in Poe's story, it would make things a lot easier. Ah ha! Arthur Conan Doyle, *The Complete Works of Sherlock Holmes*, seemed perfect.

Maybe Sherlock could give him a clue about Proctor and take his mind off other topics.

Chapter XV – New Directions

Rob tossed and turned most of the night. He dreamed the same dream: the man chasing him, the sailors fighting, the woman's voice calling him, it was all there. But this time, somehow, Old Man Proctor was there too. He kept smirking and laughing at Rob's ineptitude, taunting that his Ivy League education didn't help him much there.

Then Proctor disappeared, replaced by Duggan, ranting at him to repent for his sins. Moose and the congregation chanted, "Repent! Repent!" But then Duggan was gone and in his place was LaVache. The Frenchman laughed hysterically at Rob's discomfort while a broken-nosed man smirked in the background. Then all three figures, Proctor, Duggan, LaVache, stood on the altar laughing, while Moose shook his head and wagged his finger at him. All the voices spoke in unison, "and you think you're so smart!"

Then the dream changed. Hoopy and Susan were smiling happily, along with Ben and Phyllis, and even Junior and Mary, with all three couples telling him to join them, as the woman's voice still kept calling his name. . . .

****

He woke early to a dreary, foggy dawn. He'd always been a morning person, which hadn't fit great with summer bartending, but this morning he was groggy and cranky. He put the coffee on and thought about Rachel's news. Part of him wanted to jump in his car, drive to the Gilmores', yank her out of bed and take her away, somewhere, anywhere. All these years it had hurt, but he could manage it, because he knew she was unavailable. Now suddenly she was available, but not ready to make a new commitment. Logically, he understood what she was saying, but that didn't mean he had to like it. Even worse, he wasn't sure he could keep his true feelings under control, now that the door had opened a crack.

After his morning ritual with the woodstove and coffee pot, Rob took the hasp and padlock out of the bag. He grabbed the screwdriver and drill, stepped out the door, and started installing his outside security system. While he worked, the dizzying events of the past week rattled around his brain.

By the time he finished the sun was burning away the fog, and it felt like the temperature would melt more of the snow. He took out the padlock, read the directions, set the combination, and dropped it into his pocket. That should keep out intruders and letter writers.

Back in the kitchen, sipping his coffee, he wallowed in his mood, enjoying a moment of self-pity. The sound of a car, crunching on the oyster-shell driveway, snapped him back to reality. He opened the door and saw the tall, erect frame of State Trooper Don Stewart.

"Hi Rob. Sorry, I'm a little early. Made good time on Route 6, and figured I'd come straight here."

"Trooper Stewart, come on in. I got coffee, but we'll have to wait for the muffins."

"Please, call me Don."

The two men agreed to hold off any discussion of the Proctor case until Skip Parker and Chief Foster joined them, so they could all share at the same time. Instead, they talked about high school basketball, players they knew and had played against. When they had finished comparing who they knew in common, Rob asked Stewart how he had become a State Trooper.

"Well, when I got out of high school, I went to Bridgewater State for a while, but college wasn't really for me, and I only lasted a semester. Came back to Falmouth and worked odd jobs. Like you, I got appointed as a part-time special cop. Then came Pearl Harbor, and like most of us I was in the war, served in the Army Air Corps as a gunner on bombers. Somehow, I survived, not sure how, we lost so many planes. Anyway, when I got out, the State Police just seemed natural, it's a lot like the military, and I already had a little experience with the Falmouth P.D.

"I started out in western Massachusetts in the Berkshires," he continued. "I got lucky when a spot opened up on the Cape. Actually, I got the opening when Bill Foster retired and took the Bound Brook Chief job; everyone in the Cape Office moved up a notch, and I came in as the new low man on the totem pole. Gave me a chance to work in my home territory, although that has its plusses and minuses."

"So, did you know Foster when he was a Trooper?"

Stewart smiled. "Only by reputation. *Bull* Foster they called him, and he was a bit of a legend. It wasn't just because of his size that he got the nickname. He was also a bull when it came to working a case, determined and dogged. He pushed his way through red tape and BS until he solved the case. Sometimes that ticked off some higher-ups. Bill doesn't play politics, probably why he took an earlier retirement, he had some people just waiting to pull the plug on his career. I'd say Bound Brook was lucky to get him.

"In fact, because this case is a murder, I should be having a senior Sergeant or officer working on the case with me, but we're bit shorthanded, and when the Lieutenant heard that Foster was the Chief here, he said it would be fine for now. Some of the department command may not like him, but they all respect him."

They heard the sound of another car pulling into the driveway and waited for Skip and the Chief to enter the little cottage. Skip came in carrying two bakery boxes. The Chief paused in the doorway to inspect the door's new locks.

Skip put the boxes on the table. "I guess the Chief left here hungry yesterday, I only got us a baker's dozen, but the Chief's a big spender. He got us a dozen and a half."

"More like a big appetite," grunted Foster, "any complaints?"

Rob and Don both laughed. "Napoleon said, *an army travels on its stomach*. I guess we can apply that to a police force too," Stewart quipped.

Foster jerked his thumb toward the driveway. "I got the cruiser window open, and the radio volume on high, so can we keep the door open a crack? Diane gave me an earful yesterday; said she couldn't reach me if there'd been a call."

"Was there a call you missed?" asked Stewart.

"No, but that doesn't count with Diane. She did a radio check, and got no answer, so now she's got me on *probation*."

"Hell hath no fury . . ." quoted Skip.

Rob poured the coffee and the four men pulled up chairs and dug into the muffins. "So I'll go first" said Foster. "Thanks to something Rob found out from Frank Joseph, I got more information out of Mr. Caldwell. It seems that Proctor was working on a big deal involving the Barnstable Country Lumber Company. They're looking for a Lower Cape location, and Caldwell said he expects a huge building boom of summer houses, now the state highway is finished. Anyway, Proctor was offering them a large tract of land on Lower Main Street. It would have taken Joseph's Hardware, two houses that Proctor rents out to the Snows and Jenkins, and also the rooming house Proctor owns across the street. The plan was to put in a large hardware and plumbing store with a big lumber yard. Caldwell claims it would've been a huge boost to Bound Brook's economy."

"I had to push him hard to get details. When I asked him if he was involved, he was hesitant, but then admitted that Proctor had left him out of it. I gather that was pretty unusual. When I asked him the last time he saw Proctor, he said he couldn't remember, but when I asked if he had talked to Proctor about why he left him out, he got really uncomfortable."

The Chief leaned in a little more. "Here's where it gets interesting. After a long pause, he admitted that he had called Proctor, and said he needed to talk to him. He had set up a time to go over the next afternoon. The next day the storm had started, but Caldwell drove over. He says he knocked several times and yelled for Proctor, but nobody answered. Swears up and down that he never went in and didn't see Proctor at all. I asked if he saw Proctor's car, and he said he did. When I asked why he thought Proctor didn't answer the door he got even more hesitant. Finally, he said he thought Proctor had figured out that Caldwell wanted to have him explain why he was cut out of the sale. Caldwell tried to act calm, but I would guess that he went over there with a head of steam, and not very happy. Anyway, he said the snow was getting bad and he figured he had better get out of there before he got stuck. I asked him if he saw anyone or anything suspicious, but he said he didn't," Foster concluded.

There was silence. The other three just looked at each other.

Stewart looked around the table, "Proctor was probably dead by then, unless Caldwell killed him."

"Might explain the place setting for two that Duggan claims he saw," said Rob.

"So, Caldwell could've had a motive and was upset with Proctor," said Skip. "I think he just moved up the suspect list."

"So where does the sale stand now?" asked Stewart

"Caldwell says he talked with Attorney Winters, and everything is on hold. By the way, Rob, Caldwell claims that he didn't tell you, because he hadn't talked to the lawyer about the details yet. I knew he'd cover his tracks somehow.

"So, anyway, Winters will be officially appointed the Executor of the Estate. He'll collect rents, pay bills and basically run things on a status-quo basis. No new deals, no properties sold, everything stays as is for now. After that I'm not sure, but Caldwell said that the Lumber Company won't wait that long, so that deal is dead." Foster paused, swallowed half a muffin and took a chug of coffee.

Skip Parker looked over at Rob. "The Chief filled me in a little on the way over; thanks for following up with Frank Joseph. I couldn't talk with him, 'cause the store was closed."

"Sheer luck," laughed Rob. "Never would have heard about it if the Chief wasn't so worried about my personal security."

Don Stewart looked thoughtful. "So, in addition to Caldwell, this opens another avenue, a possible motive for people who would've been negatively affected by the real estate deal."

Rob answered this one. "Frank Joseph and his family knew, the Snows and Jenkins probably knew, and I would guess that most of Bound Brook's teenagers knew from Mary Joseph and Bobby Snow. Of course, that means most of Bound Brook could have known. I talked to Bobby Snow and Junior Proctor. Junior goes steady with Mary and was pretty upset. He said he told his parents, and his Dad, Corey, was really unhappy with Proctor. Chief, interesting that Corey didn't say anything about that when you talked with him before?"

"I thought the same thing," said Foster. "I followed up with him, Mrs. Jenkins and Mr. Snow. Snows and Jenkins are renters. They weren't happy but figured they would find something else in town. Frank Joseph said he didn't like it, but accepted it, and had plans to move to Wareham to work with his brothers in their fish business. The rooming house only has a few tenants in the winter. Proctor made his money renting rooms to college students working summer jobs. Charged them an arm and a leg and jammed in many in as he could. The people in the rooming house are transients, I'll follow up to see if any of them could have been angry with Proctor. Trooper, I'll give you the names, if you could follow up and see if any of them have any records of violence. There's a couple of rough characters I'm not too fond of.

"When I talked with Corey Proctor, he said it was just more of the same with his uncle. He admitted he was upset. Said it was why he didn't go to work for him way back when, and why he got angry when Proctor tried to groom Junior for the business. He said Junior took it hard, thinking Mary Joseph would have to move, but he figured he'd get over it, or next year he could even get a job near Wareham if he wanted. Didn't seem like the *end of the world, to* use his words. He said he didn't bring it up with me before, because it was still a rumor, and with Proctor dead he figured it wasn't an issue anymore."

The four men sat silently, letting the implications of the new direction sink in. Finally, Don Stewart broke the silence. "Well, I have a little to report, but not very helpful, I'm afraid. First, I talked with the FBI about any mob connections to Proctor. I have a contact there I can't reveal, and he said it's possible, but he didn't know anything concrete. He's frustrated because all they do is chase after possible communists. He said Hoover is obsessed with Communism, and with McCarthy fanning the flames, that's all the FBI does. He said he'd try to check it out, but Hoover doesn't believe there is an organized mob syndicate, and he'd have to investigate it on the QT. In fact, he might get in trouble if his bosses found out what he was doing."

"As for the black car, there's Providence mob errand boy and enforcer, Rocco Marini, drives a black Chrysler Imperial. He's a pretty nasty guy, ex-boxer, someone to avoid if you can," Stewart looked directly at Rob.

"This business deal sets up a possibility," he continued. "The mob has so much illegal money that they are always looking for legal ways to invest. To do that, they need cooperative front men, legitimate businessmen willing to go along. We know Proctor had some history with the Providence mob. Could be his connection to this Rocco character. Maybe that's why Proctor was cutting Caldwell out of the deal. Might have been doing him a favor in a way, although Caldwell wouldn't have seen it that way."

"On another note, the state crime lab is really backed up because of the weather. They aren't that fast anyway. I can't get an answer on when to expect news on fingerprints or any forensic evidence. Honestly, I'm not expecting much."

Foster spoke up. "Only the four of us know about the prints, right? I want Rob and Skip to deliberately let some news leak. Work it into the conversation that the State Police might have some fingerprints. Maybe it'll make someone nervous."

"Good idea," chuckled Skip. "I'll mention it to Moose and the highway crew. Think I'll have lunch at Agnes's Restaurant, might just let it slip out. It should be all over town by nightfall."

"I'll tell Phyllis Brown to confirm the report to anyone who calls her," said Rob. "She'll love playing along."

"So, let's go over possible leads and suspects," Stewart offered.

Chief Foster picked up the cue. "We have Reverend Joseph Duggan, fringe-lunatic minister who wanted land that Proctor wouldn't sell him. Then Skip's brother Moose, an avid follower of the Reverend and ready to defend him from others. Caldwell was Proctor's business partner but got cut out of the BCL deal. He admits he went to Proctor's house in the beginning of the storm. If he didn't kill him, and is telling the truth, I think we know why Proctor didn't answer the door."

"Next, we have the people who would have been forced out of their homes by the Lumber Company deal: Frank Joseph, the Snows, Jenkins and rooming house people. None of them seem to have been devastated by the news. Frank Joseph was out of town in Wareham. We have Proctor's nephew Corey, the electrician. He had major issues with his uncle, but it seems to me that as mad as he was, it was just more of the same to him. Then we've got the mob enforcer. Did Proctor cross them somehow?"

"Or someone who hasn't come up yet," Stewart added.

"Good point. Let's keep shaking the bushes. Plant those fingerprint rumors and poke around. We didn't know about the land deal until Rob bought his locks, who knows what might pop up."

"Yes, interesting," Skip chimed in, "how many people probably knew about that sale, but nobody said anything to us until Frank Joseph just happened to mention it to Rob."

Rob had a thought. "With the Proctor deal falling through, I wonder what other pieces of land the Lumber Company might be considering?"

Stewart picked up on this idea. "Interesting, maybe somebody killed Proctor to prevent the sale, but for a different reason. Did somebody want BCL to buy their land instead of Proctor's? Just a thought, but does Caldwell own any prime real estate separate from Proctor?"

"I'll talk to Caldwell again, see what he has to say," said Foster. "Meanwhile, what're you guys doing today?"

"I'm not much help today," said Skip. "Got oil and propane deliveries for Morris Fuel. I'll get to the highway crew and Agnes' though."

"I'll tell Phyllis to spread the fingerprint rumor," said Rob, "and poke my head in several of the usual gossip spots. I'm going to the basketball games in Orleans later on. Never can tell what might come up if I mix in with the Bound Brook fans. A combination of business and pleasure."

"No meeting here tomorrow," said Foster. "Trooper Stewart and Skip can't make it, so Rob, you and I can meet at my office at noon. That OK?"

"Sure."

The meeting broke up and the two cruisers pulled out of the driveway. The sun was bright and, compared to the brutal temperature of the blizzard, it felt relatively warm. The crushed oyster, clam and scallop shells poked through the last of the snow in the driveway. Crushed shells were the Cape Coders answer to gravel, not much crushed stone on the Cape, but lots of shucked shells.

Rob thought about how much his life had changed in a week. Until the blizzard he had been living a quiet, solitary life, hunkered down in his little cottage, re-reading the great literary works, and breaking the monotony with visits to Ben and Phyllis, and stops at the Hooper brothers' Flying A. Now he was at the center of a murder, and investigating a complex puzzle, though the biggest change was his relationship with Rachel.

After returning to Bound Brook four years ago, Rob and Rachel had avoided each other. He had pretended she didn't matter, but now he had to admit to himself that it had been a lie. Of course, she mattered, she was the only one who had ever mattered. Perhaps if he'd returned to town and found Rachel and Jimmy happily married, he could have turned the page. The reality was all too obvious, though, even then: Rachel was unhappy and going through the motions. The young Jimmy had been carefree and fun-loving, but the new version was surly, rude, dour and a pain-in-the-butt. Rob had managed his feelings by pretending they didn't exist, but he couldn't lock the door and throw away the key. The unhappy marriage kept the door ajar, and though he had never acknowledged it, now he knew he'd never given up hope.

He took a deep breath, let it out with a sigh, and went back in the cottage. He dumped the plates and mugs into the sink. Out of the eighteen muffins, only two remained - a blueberry and a corn. He threw out the empty box and put the one with the leftover muffins on the counter beside the breadbox. Tomorrow's breakfast!

Chapter XVI – Spreading Rumors

After Rob cleaned up the dishes, he put on his old Navy pea coat, wool watch cap and gloves, grabbed his new padlock and clasped it through the hasp. He had never locked his cottage before and doubted if many Bound Brook residents ever locked their houses, but if Foster wanted it that way, he'd follow orders. And now with Mr. Broken Nose around, it might be a good idea. He headed over to the Brown's house to talk with Phyllis and get a shower.

On the short drive, he thought about Bound Brook's geography, and its connection to Proctor's murder. There were two business centers and three population centers in the small town of eight hundred residents. Bound Brook center was the largest, and the one with most of the stores and businesses. It extended from the business center down to the harbor and town pier. In normal weather, it was possible to walk to Proctor's house from the general vicinity of the center, especially if you took the short cut over the Bound Brook Creek footbridge. However, in a blizzard, it would be much harder, though not impossible.

The other business center was South Bound Brook. It had a gas station, general store, liquor store, its own post office and was on the state highway. The other population centers were Tyler's Tangle and Proctor's Hollow. Tyler's Tangle straddled the unofficial line between Bound Brook and South Bound Brook. Proctor's Hollow was the largest settlement in the old village of South Bound Brook. Old Man Proctor's home sat on the edge of the Proctor Hollow settlement, on a slight rise set well back from the water, but that had provided a view of the bay from the "widow's walk" atop the house.

In the old days, South Bound Brook had had its own harbor, docks and fishing fleet that rivaled the two piers in Bound Brook Center, but in the 1880s, their harbor had filled with silt. The cod and mackerel had moved further out to sea, and the fishing industry had languished. By the 1900s, the pier near Bound Brook Center was the only working dock servicing the boats that were now, mostly, shellfish draggers.

If you followed the paved highway that circled the shoreline of the little peninsula, it was close to two miles between Tangle and Hollow, but if you cut through the old paths in the woods, it was less than a half mile. From Tyler's Tangle it was an easy walk, even in a blizzard, and the trees would provide some shelter. For anyone living in the sprawling Proctor Hollow settlement, it would be a piece of cake, as little as a few hundred yards, and no more than a quarter mile. It seemed to Rob they needed to focus on finding whoever had started the fire, because that person had to walk or have a plow. It was probably the same person who had murdered Proctor, but even if it was a second person, the fire and murder had to be connected.

He pulled into the Brown yard and knocked on the door before opening it a crack. "Knock, knock, anybody home?"

"I'm in the back," came Phyllis' voice.

He walked through the kitchen and dining area to the living room, where she was sitting on the floor, sorting a huge pile of clothes.

"Three boys and a plumber, sure does make for lots of laundry," she laughed.

"Think I could get a shower?"

Phyllis rolled her eyes. "Of course, you can. By the time you're finished I'll have lunch ready. Chicken stew with dumplings sound good?"

"Sounds great!"

Rob lingered in the spray of the hot shower, enjoying the soothing water. He dried himself with a brisk rubdown and got dressed. Out in the kitchen, Phyllis was stirring a large kettle on the stove. "Heard you gave Benny a basketball lesson yesterday," smiled Phyllis.

"I wouldn't say that. Ben's a pretty good player, especially on defense."

"Well, that was all he could talk about at dinner. Made quite a story. He told us all the teasing he gave you, and how you were holding back your game for the sake of the team practice. Then he described the move you put on him, got up and demonstrated it, and he had the younger boys in awe. You know those kids idolize you. Especially Benny."

Rob blushed. "My filling in at practice was to help the team, not to show off. Of course, that one move I put on Benny sure did feel good. Actually, shut him up for a little while."

She put a bowl, napkin and spoon on the table. "He also told me about that stupid move Junior pulled. Benny tries to be friends with Junior, but honestly, he has a hard time putting up with his temper and ego. He says Junior thinks he's hot stuff and sometimes forgets to play team ball. Since his brother died, his parents have coddled him. Fortunately, Coach Gilmore doesn't let him get away with much."

"Junior's pretty good, but Benny's right, the kid's got a short fuse."

"Ready to eat?" she asked, dishing out a thick creamy stew.

"Got a favor I think you'll enjoy. We're letting the word get out that we may have the fingerprints of the murderer."

Phyllis raised her eyebrows. "You want me to tell folks?"

"Actually, what I'd like you to do is pretend it's a secret you've been keeping. Don't volunteer the information, but when someone calls you, which I am sure they will, act surprised that they know, but then tell them that you heard that too."

"I can do that," said Phyllis with a smile. "Been hearing some other things lately. The word around town is that you and Rachel Gilmore are back together. Ben Sr. filled me in, so it wasn't a surprise, and thank you for the advanced notice. I love it when I'm one step ahead of the gossips in town."

Rob could feel his cheeks turning pink. "Honestly, I don't know where it's going with Rachel. We're back to being close friends, and, this you have to keep a secret for now: Jimmy told her he wants a divorce. Where that leaves us, I'm not sure."

"Wow! I think that's good news for Rachel, and probably for Jimmy too. That marriage was doomed from the start. Those two are miserable with each other. Jimmy runs off to the Army and risks getting killed, so he doesn't have to face the fact that everyone in town knows he took advantage of the situation and stabbed his best friend in the back. So what is Rachel going to do?"

"Well, she's going ahead with the divorce, but she needs to figure out her own life. She says she's been wasting time and wants to go back to school and figure things out for herself."

"Do you think there's room for you in her life?"

"I try not to think about it. I know I'd like that, but I understand she has to sort some things out first." He looked down and attacked his chicken stew, "Any more dumplings?"

Phyllis took it as a sign to change the subject. "Sure, I'll get them. So, what are you up to today?"

"Finishing this delicious stew, and then poking my head into the usual places in town. See if I can pick up some gossip and plant some gossip of my own. Then off to the games in Orleans."

"Ben is picking me up later, and then we're going to see Benny's game."

They made idle chatter about the game and the prospects for the team, while he finished his lunch. Then with a "Thank You!" Rob grabbed his coat and headed out the door. His first stop was South Bound Brook General Store which had a half-dozen cars and two tradesmen's pick-up trucks parked out front. The general store, and South Bound Brook Post Office, were just off the highway on a semi-circle that had been part of the meandering, original old Route 6. He walked through the door to the sight of a half-dozen people gathered in a circle engaged in a conversation, which immediately stopped when they saw him.

"Don't stop discussing the weather just because I'm here!"

That brought a nervous laugh from several in the coffee-sipping crowd.

"I stopped in to announce that we solved the Proctor murder," said Rob with a smirk. "Just kidding," he added.

Jerry Paine took advantage of the opening to ask a question, "Is there anything new?"

"Well, we're hoping we might catch a break with the results from the state crime lab, but I really can't talk about it."

Suddenly all eyes were on him. "What have they got, ah, I bet it's fingerprints, am I right? Is that it?" asked Jerry.

Rob did a good job of looking embarrassed. "Gee, I can't say . . . You know, I said too much already." He made his way to the coffee urn, filled himself a paper cup to go, and dropped some coins on the counter.

The group started to buzz with comments about the Proctor murder. Rob picked up bits and pieces, which included a jumbled version of the sale of property to Barnstable County Lumber, and speculation about where all of Proctor's money and property would go. He felt some satisfaction when someone mentioned that the murderer should be nervous, if the police had his fingerprints. Pleased he'd accomplished his goal, he gave the group a nod and wave, and headed out the door.

"Hey Rob, wait a minute," said Joey Pierce, the store clerk. "Fellow was in here the other day asking where you lived. I didn't tell him, but I think one of the customers gave him directions."

"Big, well dressed, dark hair, broken nose?"

"That's the one. You know him?"

"Think I'm about to."

His next stop was Hooper Brothers' gas station. He pulled up to the gas pumps and Harold came out of the office.

"Might as well top off the tank," said Rob. "Going to the game in Orleans pretty soon."

"Hoopy went home for some lunch," said his brother with a wink. "Personally, I think he might be getting more than a bite to eat, if you know what I mean. Still act like newlyweds."

Rob laughed. "Good for him. Hope you're right."

While Harold filled the tank, he noticed Proctor's Cadillac still parked next to the office, but with the engine running. The black Fleetwood model, with its whitewall tires and rear tailfins, reeked of money. Rob guessed it must have cost three to four thousand dollars. "What's up with the Caddy?"

"Have no idea how long it'll be here, but in this cold weather, I figure it's a good idea to run it now and then to charge the battery. Junior likes to do it, but he won't be here today, what with the game in Orleans. I tell you, that's a nice machine. Think I might take it out for a spin one of these days. You know, make sure everything is working OK." Harold gave another of his winks.

While Harold finished filling the tank, a Bound Brook school bus rolled by, loaded with the basketball teams. Howie Proctor was driving, and he let out a series of blasts on the horn, while the boys and girls opened the windows and waved. Rob knew it was the back-up bus, and Chandler would be filling in for Howie, driving one of the two regular buses on the after-school run.

"Do me a favor," he asked Harold. "Anybody tells you they heard that we've got the murderer's fingerprints, you tell them you heard that too, OK?"

"Sure, want me to tell Hoopy too?" asked Harold with a somewhat puzzled look.

"Yes, in fact, feel free to tell as many people as you'd like." Rob added his own wink.

"Ah, I think I get it."

Rob paid him, then looked at his watch; still a little too early to head to Orleans. Once he got in his car, he decided he'd take a drive to the harbor, but first was a stop at the Public Safety Building. He parked in the lot and started up the stairs to the Police Station.

Across the street, Frank Joseph and his wife, Lucy, were coming out the door of Joseph's Hardware. Frank flipped the sign on the door to *CLOSED* as Lucy looked up at Rob. "Hi, Rob, we're heading to Orleans to see Mary's game. If you need any hardware, you'll have to wait til tomorrow."

"Nope, I'm good, I'll see you at the game. Be heading there soon." He watched the couple get in an older Ford, then continued up the stairs to the office and gave Diane Ellis a smile.

"If you're looking for the Chief, he ain't here," she said. "I think he went to talk to old Mr. Caldwell again."

"That's OK, just driving by and figured I'd stick my head in. Can you give him a message for me? Just tell him I talked to some people and *mission accomplished.* He'll know what I mean."

Diane nodded. "Mission accomplished, got it!"

Rob headed back down the stairs but stopped at the landing. The height gave him a good view of the land that Barnstable County Lumber wanted to buy. The Hardware Store was directly in front of him, with the Snow and Jenkins houses to the left. Across the street from the Jenkins place was the big rambling rooming house, which had been a nice hotel in the old days, around the same time as the Bound Brook Inn. Now it needed new shingles and the trim needed paint.

It was big though. Must have a least a dozen rooms, he thought. It also had a large parking lot, some of which was used to store boats for the winter. Rob counted ten pleasure boats covered in tarps. He figured Proctor had picked up some money charging the owners a storage fee. Overall, it was a sizable piece of land and he could visualize the Lumber Company's potential layout.

As small as Bound Brook Center was, it was pretty densely built, and Rob couldn't think of another parcel as big or conveniently located for a large business like the hardware/lumber company. However, since the highway had been completed last year, there was lots of land located along the new road. If a business wanted easy access and lots of room, it seemed like the natural place to build. *I wonder who owns all the undeveloped parcels along Route 6*, he mused.

He got in the DeSoto and drove slowly down Lower Main Street toward the town pier. When he needed to think the harbor was where he went. Lower Main was a tree-lined, narrow road with a straight shot to the bay. He drove past the old railroad depot, now converted to Morris Fuel and Grain, past some of the oldest homes in town, several converted to summer guest houses. The view opened to the town pier and the few businesses located nearby, half of them summer only. Art's Bar & Grill and Cap't Hallet's were the only establishments that stayed open year-round. Rob tended bar for Art in the summer and had an uneasy relationship with the moody and bossy bar owner. In the winter Art's had a few hard-core regulars, mostly shell fisherman looking for a place to drown their sorrows or avoid heading home to the wife and kids.

Cap't Hallet's, on its own small dock, was the last remaining shellfish shack, and now served as a fish market. Hallet, who must have been in his seventies, still ran the place. More than a fish market, it was where the ancient, old salts hung out, sat around the woodstove, told tall tales, chewed the fat about the good old days, and bemoaned that the world was going to *hell in a hand basket.*

He pulled the car to the edge of the parking lot at the beginning of the L-shaped wooden pier. Giant wood pilings, thicker than he could wrap his arms around, anchored the heavy planks that made the pier. He remembered getting a five-finger boost to the top of a piling and diving into the water at high tide. The boys all did it as a show of bravery, diving as quickly as possible, before Hallet came out yelling threats and sending them scattering.

None of the half-dozen boats of the fishing fleet were tied to the pier, and Rob knew they were out on the water, braving the cold, working to make a hard living. Diving off a piling into warm bay water in the summer was a lot safer than pulling nets out of freezing water on slippery decks in the winter.

He looked at his watch and decided there was time to squeeze in one more stop before the drive to Orleans. He wanted to see the girls' game, mostly to watch Rachel coaching, but he wanted to get there after it started, to avoid talking to her with everyone looking at them. He had a good idea what the crowd at the General Store was discussing when he walked in. The fact they shut up and looked guilty was a dead give-away.

Chapter XVII – Another Look

Rob wanted to take another look at the Proctor fire site. Reading Sherlock Holmes had made him wonder if it would provide any insights. Maybe he could visualize it, and now the snow was melting, maybe something would be revealed.

He turned off the highway on Proctor's Hollow Road and drove past the homes scattered throughout the Hollow. Unlike the houses jammed together in a jumble in Tyler's Tangle, the Proctor houses were spread out on larger pieces of land. He drove past Howie Proctor's nicely maintained Cape, and a little further he saw a truck with "Proctor Electric" printed on the side, parked in Corey's driveway with an old sedan he recognized as Junior's. Corey was probably going to the game a little later. Near the end of the road he turned down Cecil Proctor's driveway.

The fire had cleared much of the snow, and now a week of melting had left the lot of land almost bare. Rob parked on the edge and walked closer to the remains. He knew the state crime lab had gone through the scene with a fine-tooth comb, and it was obvious that the cleanup had started. The yard had been raked and the remaining charred house planks neatly stacked. He doubted there was anything left to find, but he wanted to look while he ran through the timeframe in his mind.

He pictured the stately home before the fire. That morning before the storm, Duggan said he had walked here from the house on Bay View and talked with Proctor about buying land. Soon after, Moose had driven over and tried to talk Proctor into selling, then he had left just before the storm started, to get the truck set up with the plow. If Duggan and Moose were telling the truth, *a big if,* Proctor had still been alive then.

Then there was Caldwell. If he was telling the truth, then Proctor had probably been dead when he got there. Caldwell said he had arrived in the early afternoon, after the first of the snow had started, so there was a gap of time where someone else could have killed Proctor—but if not one of them, then who? In this scenario, sometime between Moose and Caldwell, the murderer had gone to Proctor's, probably argued with him, and then hit Proctor with the poker. Then Caldwell showed up. Moose was probably busy with the plow, but Duggan could have come back again, or Caldwell could be lying, and he had killed Proctor. Where the black car fit in he wasn't sure. The Problem was who, if anyone, was telling the truth.

The fire hadn't started until near the end of the storm. The first people to notice it were Proctor Hollow neighbors, early on the third day. By then, it had been burning a while, roads were closed, snow was deep, and most folks had already lost their power and telephones. There wasn't anything anyone could do except let the fire burn out. The fire trucks and police cruiser didn't get to the fire scene until the storm was winding down, and the plow had cleared the road.

He wasn't sure who had noticed it first, or how the fire department and police had gotten notified, but he was sure the Chief knew, and if it were important he would have filled Rob and Skip in on the details. Still, maybe he should ask.

Rob walked to the back of the yard where a path led into the scrub pine and brush. It connected to the main trails that wove their way to the rest of Proctor's Hollow, Tyler's Tangle and over to Bay View. When he was a kid the Tyler cousins would sneak to the edge of Old Man Proctor's house and try to snoop. The stately old manor was intriguing and somewhat spooky to the young boys, but Proctor rarely left the house, and if he spotted them, he came out yelling threats, and they ran as fast as they could. He could be scary when he was angry.

The sound of tires crunching on the driveway caught his attention. He peered through the charred house remains and saw a shiny black car parked next to the DeSoto. He waited, but nobody got out, so he walked around the burned house and approached the car. He stopped a free-throw length away from the front bumper of a

Chrysler Imperial with a Rhode Island plate, and saw one man in the driver's seat. Another minute passed before the door opened.

A large figure emerged, dressed in a black wool, three-quarter-length topcoat, hatless in the cold air. The man gave Rob a lopsided smile. He was shorter than Rob, but still close to six foot, with thick, black hair, and a crooked nose.

"Were you a heavyweight?" Rob asked.

"Started light-heavy, but ended up heavy-weight," said a raspy voice.

"You really from Rhode Island?"

"I'm from a lot of places, but mostly Jersey."

"Think I saw you fight in Providence back around '41. Went by Rocky, right?"

"Could be, but enough with twenty questions," said Broken-nose. "Did you get LaVache's letter?"

"First, I've got some questions for you, answer mine and I'll see what I can do."

"Ok, deal. I'll answer what I can," replied Rocco.

"Did you see Proctor, and if so why?"

"The people I work for had me deliver a package, and they wanted it delivered in person."

"Did you talk to him?"

"Nope, just gave him the package. Most people get my message, know what I mean?"

"So, I assume you're the personal contact LaVache mentioned. What are you doing working for him?"

The man laughed, "You'se could call me the personal contact. The Frenchman has a few friends that I work for, simple as that. It's a favor. Now your turn, only a few questions, answer 'em right, I'll be on my way. Understood what the letter meant, right?"

Rob nodded.

"You'se heard from Marie?"

Rob shrugged.

Broken-nose pulled a business card from his coat pocket, "If you do, call this number, right?" He tossed the card on the ground.

Rob shrugged again.

"I didn't hear your answer."

Another shrug.

"Didn't think that was our deal. I need an answer, or do you gonna get cute with me?"

Shrug.

"OK, pretty boy, want to get a nose like mine?"

Silence, and just a shrug.

"If you'se seen me fight, you know you don't want to get me started."

No answer.

Broken-nose came at him low and fast. For a big man he was light on his feet. Rob was ready, but broken nose feinted left and came in with a quick right, to Rob's left side. His arm partly blocked the blow and his thick coat helped, but it slipped past and landed on his ribs. The arm immediately went numb. A fast combination, left to the stomach, another right to the ribs, left to the kidney, and Rob's breath escaped. Instinctively, he used his height, reached over the boxer's back, grabbed the bottom hem of Broken-nose's topcoat, and gave it an upward yank. His left arm tried to help, but it wasn't working too great. The bottom of the coat pulled up over Broken-nose's head, and momentarily immobilized his arms. It was a move Rob had used in the Shore Patrol, grabbing the back flap of a sailor's white blouse and yanking it over his head, tying up his arms, rendering him helpless. Of course, they were usually drunk!

Rob hung on for dear life, trying to regain his breath. Head covered by the coat, his assailant mumbled curses while he struggled to get free. Broken-nose jerked backward, black buttons popping off, leaving Rob with an empty topcoat, staring into the face of a very angry man.

Broken-nose went back into his crouch, danced forward, and threw a left-right-left combination that would've really hurt, but the boxer pulled his punches just short of their mark.

"They said you wasn't no push-over, but I hope you'se get the message, 'cause what you got was only a small taste."

"No promises, but I got the message. I'm well aware of Mr. LaVache's methods."

"I'll be checking, don't make me come back! Stayed with the body punches this time, but next time your red-headed lady friend won't be looking at such a pretty face."

Rob tossed the coat toward the thug, who grabbed it out of the air. Something flew out of the coat pocket and landed on the driveway. Broken-nose scooped it up, but not before Rob recognized the shape of a .38 revolver. The man looked at Rob, gave his own exaggerated shrug, got in his car and backed down the driveway.

Rob picked up the business card, just a plain cardboard rectangle, with nothing on it except the exchange for a Providence, Rhode Island telephone number.

Chapter XVIII – The Game

Despite the heavy coating of snow that reflected the glare of the afternoon sun, February 26th was starting to feel like the end of winter. The sun was higher in the sky, and the days were gradually getting longer. His ribs ached and his left arm wasn't going to be able to dribble a basketball for a while, but he was sure he'd been lucky. Broken-nose looked familiar. If he was who he thought he was, Rocco had been a contender and Rob didn't want a second sparring session.

He didn't know what he'd do if Marie found him. He didn't know how or where to contact her, so he had no choice but to wait. Her father was not a man to mess with, but despite the threat, Rob didn't think he'd force his daughter to return to France. Maybe she still cared for him, but he had moved on, and perhaps he had never really loved her at all. He started to understand that it was a little like Rachel with Jimmy. At that time of his life he'd been lonely, still nursing his feelings for Rachel and looking for someone. Marie was beautiful, younger than Rob, and she had idolized him. It was hard to resist. What timing: just when Rachel and he had found each other again, Marie might be back in the picture. *What to tell Rachel? Nothing for now. In fact, he wasn't planning on telling anyone about Marie or his personal involvement with Rocco.*

He cruised along Route 6 to the Orleans Rotary and turned onto Route 28. Just before the slight hill to Orleans High School was the brick façade of the Snow Library. Parking spaces in front of the main entrance were full, but the lot on the side was mostly empty. He parked next to the Gilmore Chevy and the Joseph Ford.

He walked up the steps of the stately brick building and through the door. Directly across the main hallway was the entrance to the combination auditorium/ gymnasium, where a woman, probably a faculty member judging by her prim dress, sold tickets. Rob paid a quarter and took a program from a high school girl, waiting just inside the double doors. He stood at the top of twenty rows of built-in arena seating that looked down on the basketball court. On the opposite side of the gym floor was a stage, where a half-dozen people sat at the official scorer's table and ran the controls for the new electric scoreboard, one of the first on the Cape. He took a seat in a back row to get a clear view of both the court and the stands.

Orleans parents clustered in the center section of the lower rows that overlooked the sunken level of the gym/auditorium court, while they watched the game closely. In the section to Rob's right were Orleans students, seated in three groups: the boys, the girls and the couples. Three couples sat halfway up the rows, the boys casually draping their arms over the back of the girls' seats, as close as they dared to make actual physical contact under faculty supervision. In other groupings, eight or ten boys joked with each other, and a dozen girls chatted and giggled, while one or two "messengers" shuttled between the groups. None of them seemed to be paying the least bit of attention to the game. Bound Brook fans and the boys' basketball team sat in two separate groups, in the section to Rob's left.

Coach Gilmore sat at the end of the row of Bound Brook boys. Rob remembered the coach's routine. During the first half of the girls' game, he would call one player at a time to come sit next to him while he reviewed their role in the upcoming game, all the while giving them positive encouragement. He also welcomed questions and listened to their problems and concerns. It was at those moments when Gilmore cemented his bond with his players.

He looked around the Orleans gym, and remembered the games he had played there. Orleans was a tough rival and always fielded at least a good team, sometimes a very good one. The Orleans gym was one of the better courts on the Cape, bigger than those at Bound Brook, Chatham, Harwich, Yarmouth, Wellfleet and Sandwich, and more comfortable than the one in Provincetown. Only the larger, Upper-Cape schools—Barnstable, Bourne and Lawrence High in Falmouth—had gyms that were bigger. Provincetown had a unique court, a sunken level like Orleans, but made entirely of concrete, with concrete walls and bleacher seats. It had been nicknamed the "swimming pool" by some, and less flattering names by others.

After taking his seat, Rob checked the score: Orleans 18, Bound Brook 9. Girls' Basketball always puzzled him; he had never understood why it had different rules. In the girls' game, there were six players, three forwards and three defenders, who had to stay on their own end of the court, and nobody could cross the center line. Defenders only touched the ball if they got a rebound or stole a pass, and they never got to shoot. Girls were allowed just three dribbles, and then they had to stop, and either pass or shoot. When a girl finished her dribbles, she was often stuck with nowhere to go, which led to lots of jump balls and fouls, and slowed the pace of the game.

The Orleans team was leading the Cape Cod League, but Rob had always been impressed with Mary Joseph, playing forward for Bound Brook. She was quick and agile, not tall, but with springs in her legs. She had good instincts, and unlike the other Bound Brook girls, she knew where she was going with the ball, and never got stuck without an option. Mary reminded him a little of Rachel when she had played. Both would have benefited from boys' rules that allowed full-court play.

While he watched, Orleans stole the ball, crisply moved it down court and fed a pass to their tall center, who faked one way and then turned and shot over the hapless, shorter Bound Brook defender; 20–9 now. Rachel stood up and called a play for the team. Bound Brook passed the ball inbounds and the player took three dribbles, then made a nice pass to Mary Joseph, who had run to the center line. Mary pivoted toward the basket, made three quick dribbles and passed to the right forward, who made a return pass to her as she broke to the basket, made two dribbles and scooped the ball off the backboard for a pretty layup. *A give and go, nice play!* he thought.

The Bound Brook fans jumped to their feet, clapping and cheering. Rob noticed Mary's parents, Frank and Lucy, along with

Maggie Gilmore, leading the cheers. The boys' team yelled encouragement, but one player, Junior Proctor, stayed seated with his head down. Orleans called time-out.

The teams huddled around the coaches. Rachel was dressed in a teacher outfit: grey wool skirt, white cable-knit sweater and penny loafers. Her luxurious auburn hair framed her pretty face and china-doll complexion. Her trim figure made her look like a model in a magazine commercial for the girl next door. In short, she looked stunning! Rob noticed several of the Orleans boys whispering to each other, pointing toward the huddle, checking out the Bound Brook girls and particularly their coach. Rachel was an adolescent boy's dream.

After the time out, Orleans changed their defensive strategy, putting one player on Mary Joseph at all times. With Mary closely guarded, the Bound Brook offense struggled, and the defense had no answer for Orleans' tall center. At half-time the score was 34-14.

The Bound Brook boys, still in street clothes but wearing sneakers, took to the court for some warm up shots. George Gilmore looked up, spotted Rob, and gave him a little head nod that indicated he wanted to talk, so Rob headed down the aisle.

"Hey Coach, what's going on?"

"Sometimes I wish we could just keep the boys and girls apart—you know, separate buses, or games on different days." Gilmore was shaking his head.

"What happened?"

"Halfway here, Junior and Mary had some sort of spat! Junior moved to a separate seat and pouted, Mary broke into tears and the other girls consoled her. Rachel checked on her, but she said she'd be OK. I talked to Junior, but he wouldn't say anything. Rachel and I decided to let it be, not make a bigger scene, and hope it worked itself out. As if we needed another distraction!"

Rob looked down on the court where Junior was standing by himself, half-heartedly taking a few shots that clanked off the rim. "Looks like Junior won't be much use today."

Gilmore nodded. "Wish he reacted more like Mary. I think she's even more motivated than usual. With Snowy hurt and Junior pouting, not sure we'll have much of a chance, but we'll see. That's why we play the games, right?"

A horn sounded as the girls' teams returned to the court, and the boys left for the locker room. "See you after the game?" asked George.

"Probably, I'll play it by ear."

The coach followed the boys to the locker room, and Rob made his way over to the section of Bound Brook fans.

Maggie Gilmore smiled at him. "I think we're a little out-classed, but the girls are playing a pretty good game."

"Yes, but Orleans has too much height, and you can't teach that."

He gestured Maggie to step aside, "Heard there was a problem on the bus, did you hear about that?"

"Just a little. I guess Junior and Mary broke up."

"Do Mary's parents know anything about it?"

"I saw them talking with Mary before the game, so I would guess they do. When the kids get home, and start making phone calls, I'd guess the whole high school will know."

"Any clue what happened?"

"Who knows? High school romances break up, I think you can relate to that. You might see what Frank and Lucy know." She moved back to her seat as the players returned to the court to start the second half.

Rob slid into the row behind Mary's parents. "Mary's playing a good game."

"Thanks," replied Frank. "She's a little spitfire. Wish we had some more good players, but she likes the game, and I guess that's what matters."

Lucy Joseph turned and gave Rob a meaningful look. "Yes, and she loves playing for Rachel, worships the ground she walks on. That woman is something special, don't you think?"

Rob flushed. "She sure is, I think everyone agrees with that."

The second half started, and Mary's parents turned to watch the game. "Everything OK with Mary and Junior?" asked Rob. "I heard there was a problem."

Frank half-turned and spoke over his shoulder. "That's Lucy's department, I try not to get involved."

Lucy sighed. "Junior and Mary have been going out for a year, and sometimes it's a bit stormy. Junior's moody, and it isn't the first time they've broken up. So far, they always get back together. Time will tell."

"Sorry to be so nosy, but any particular reason?"

Mary's mother turned and gave him a look. "Not sure why you're interested, but Mary says Junior's been worse lately, angry and moody. She also said he's been pressuring her about making a bigger commitment."

Frank turned. "OK, if Junior's bothering her, then that's my department. Nobody bothers my little girl!"

"No Frank, not like that!" Lucy rolled her eyes at her husband and turned back to Rob. "They're already going steady, but Mary's got another year of school, and Junior's graduating. I think he's worried that once he graduates, she'll go out with someone else. They care for each other, but they're just kids."

She turned back to the game and Rob gathered the conversation was over. Meanwhile, Orleans was making it hard for Bound Brook to get the ball over half court, and Mary Joseph rarely got the ball. With two minutes left, and a big lead, the Orleans coach called time out, and put in the second team. Mary Joseph immediately scored three quick baskets, but by the time the horn blew, Orleans had won 56-32.

The Orleans and Bound Brook boys' teams took the court for warmups and some of the girls' parents got ready to leave. Lucy now turned to Rob. "I talked with Rachel before the game. She suggested we take Mary home, so she doesn't have to go on the bus. Might minimize problems. Nice to talk with you. Good luck with everything." Her voice had an edge to it, like she and Rob shared a secret. He had a feeling she wasn't referring to the murder investigation.

"Thank you, would you mind if I talk with Mary for a minute before you go?"

Lucy gave her a husband a concerned look. "Sure, I guess so."

"It'll just be a minute, just curious if she's heard any rumors going around the school. Why don't you meet me out in the hall?"

From the doorway, Rob watched the boys run through their warm-up drills while he waited for Mary to join her parents. As he watched, five Bound Brook cheerleaders took the floor to do a cheer for the team. Halfway through their routine, three girls joined them. Rob recognized them from the basketball team. At tiny Bound Brook High, it was common for a few girls to do double duty, playing basketball and being cheerleaders.

Mary Joseph came out of the locker room. Rob saw her parents talking with her and pointing in his direction. The Joseph family came up the stairs and met him in the main hall.

"Lucy and I will get the car," said Frank. "Mary, when you're done just meet us outside."

Rob turned to the pretty teenager. "Nice game, Mary, Orleans was just too tall and too good."

"Thank you, we don't win very often, only two this year, Sandwich and Wellfleet. What did you want to talk to me about?"

"First, is everything OK with you and Junior?"

She started to lose her composure, her eyes turning misty. "I broke up with him. I didn't want to, but I don't know, he's been getting even moodier lately. Ever since he thought I was going to move, he's been, I don't know, I guess you call it possessive. He just pressures me about the future, like we'll always be together. I guess I love him, but I'm only sixteen, how do I know what's going to happen to us?"

Rob waited for her to continue. "On the bus, he was nagging me, talking about how we could go away somewhere. I mean, why do I want to go away? I just couldn't take it anymore. He got mad and said I didn't really love him, if I did, I'd run away with him. I told him I don't want to run away, not with anybody. I love it here with my friends and family, why do we have to leave? So, he got mad, and I told him if he felt that way, then it was over!"

"Why does he want to run away?"

"I don't know, it didn't make any sense. He said something about his father, and how it'll never be the same now that Old Man Proctor is dead. I'd like to help him, but he's driving me crazy. Maybe we'll get back together, it's not the first time we've broken up, but I'm not leaving Bound Brook, at least, not if I can help it."

"Junior said something about Old Man Proctor. Any of the kids talking about what happened to him? Any rumors or theories?"

The change of topic seemed to help Mary gather her composure. "No, it's pretty old news now, at least as far as the kids are concerned."

Rob put his hand on her shoulder. "Mary, I'm sorry if I upset you. You going to be OK?"

She nodded, gave him a smile, and headed out the door to join her parents.

He went back into the gym, nodding to the woman who had sold him the ticket. The game had started, and two minutes had ticked off the game clock. The scoreboard told the story, Orleans 8, Bound Brook 2. Not a good start. He watched as Bound Brook struggled to get the ball up the floor, Orleans intercepted a pass and drove in for a layup, 10 to 2. Coach Gilmore called time out.

Rob saw Junior Proctor heading to the scorer's table to report into the game. Johnny Webster inbounded the ball to Junior, who quickly dribbled it up the floor and passed to Vinnie Costa. Bound Brook went into an outside weave, just like they'd practiced. After five or six quick passes, Junior got open for a layup and it was 10-4. With Junior in the lineup the team settled down, traded baskets with Orleans, and at half time trailed 28 – 16. Benny and Tony were doing a fairly good job sharing the center position, but the team really missed their tallest player, Bobby Snow. Benny was working hard on defense against the much taller Orleans center, but he already had four fouls. One more and he'd foul out.

Rob had been so intent on the game that he was surprised to see how many parents and fans had arrived. Corey Proctor sat alone in the front row, focused on the court. Behind him sat Ben and Phyllis with some other Bound Brook parents: Websters, Snows, Costas, and Olivers.

Ben gave him a wave and headed over to Rob. "Heard the girls lost. And I guess something happened on the bus ride?"

Rob nodded. "What are the parents saying about things?"

"The Snows are still mad at Bobby for crashing the car and hurting his arm. Generally, they're all pretty disappointed, not very optimistic about how the season's going to end."

"Any talk about Proctor's murder?"

"Yes, as a matter of fact. Mostly they talked about the State Police having fingerprints, but nothing else new." He gave Rob a look, "Maybe what's most interesting, is what they aren't talking about."

"What do you mean?"

"I get the feeling that they're dying to ask Phyllis and me about you and Rachel. You ever heard the saying about *the elephant in the room*? Well, it's a little awkward, you can almost see it on the tip of their tongues. I think Phyllis is really enjoying it."

Rob just shook his head. "Want to watch the game with me for a while?"

"Sure."

The teams finished their warmups and the horn sounded to start the second half. The Orleans center won the jump, but his teammate bobbled the ball, and he and Junior both dove for it. The two players knocked the ball out of bounds and fell to the court in a tangle of arms and legs, with Junior on the bottom. When he moved to get up, he grabbed the Orleans player and shoved him off, then gave him an extra shove while he was still on the ground. The Orleans boy jumped up, and before he could do anything, Junior punched him in the face. Then all hell broke loose.

The referees blew their whistles, Orleans players rushed at Junior, and Bound Brook players tried to hold them back. The Orleans coach and George Gilmore ran on the court, pulling players away from the rapidly growing scrum. Benny grabbed Junior in a bear hug and dragged him over to the bench. Some Orleans faculty jumped on the court and separated players. Gradually order was restored.

The referees huddled, then ejected Junior from the game. On the sideline, Corey Proctor had come out of the stands and was restraining his out-of-control son. George Gilmore conferred with the referees, and then they all headed over to talk with the Orleans coach. After a brief conversation, the referees went to the scorer's table and had another conference. The official scorer grabbed the PA microphone and announced, "Game is over. Bound Brook has forfeited, Orleans wins the game."

The next five minutes were a blur. Rob and Ben made their way to the court, where Ben headed over to Benny. Several fathers, Webster, Oliver, and Costa were on the court trying to keep their own sons out of trouble. Coach rounded up the team and steered them toward the locker room.

Corey Proctor grabbed Rob's arm. "I'm taking Junior home, can you tell Coach, and have someone get his stuff? Glad Delores didn't come, she gets nervous enough at his games."

Rob went to the locker room and found Ben and Benny, "Can you get Junior's clothes for him?"

Benny nodded. "Sure, what a way to finish a season."

Rob spotted Coach Gilmore. "Corey Proctor asked me to tell you he's driving Junior home."

Gilmore shook his head slowly. "Most of the boys are getting rides, and a lot of girls left already. It'll be a pretty empty bus, although that's probably a good thing."

He saw Maggie and Rachel waiting near the entrance, and Rachel gave a small wave to beckon him over.

"Tough way to end the game," said Rob.

"It sure was," replied Maggie. "I wonder what George will do about the final game. At least it's against Sandwich, so might be a decent game, even with us so shorthanded. Pretty sure Junior will be suspended."

Rachel looked at Rob. "Dad and I have to ride the bus back to chaperone, but can I come over after dinner? I'd like to talk to you about my plans."

Rob smiled. "That would be nice!"

George Gilmore now joined them. "I only got three boys riding the bus, what've you got, Rachel?"

"Only four."

Maggie gave George a kiss on the check and patted his shoulder. "I'm going to head home. We can talk tonight."

Gilmore gave his wife a forced smile and turned to Rob. "Junior's done for the season; I'll call him tonight. I guess we'll play Sandwich Friday night. Can I pick your brain tomorrow after school? I'm cancelling practice, I think we need time to calm down and regroup."

"Oh course." Rob walked to the door with the Gilmores, then stood and watched father and daughter get on the bus. Maggie said good-bye to them and walked over to her car in the side lot. Rob stepped aside as some Orleans parents and their sons passed through the doorway. He considered his options: drive home, open something in a can for supper, and wait for Rachel? He decided to stop at The Fair Wind for a hamburger instead.

Chapter XIX – Developments

Tuesday night at the end of February was not a busy time for The Fair Wind. Less than half the booths were filled, and there were only a few people at the counter. Rob recognized two Orleans families from the game and gave them a casual nod when they glanced his way. He sat on a stool at the Formica counter and glanced at the menu. On the blackboard the daily special was shepherd's pie. Sounded good, some winter comfort food.

"The special and a coke," he told the middle-aged waitress.

A large mirror facing the counter gave a panoramic view of the row of booths behind him. In addition to the Orleans families there was a familiar pair, engaged in a deep conversation, sitting in the far corner booth. The waitress delivered his coke with a napkin and silverware. He stood up and took a sip.

"I'll be back when the food's ready," he told the woman.

With his coke in hand, Rob walked to the far booth, where Reverend Duggan looked up in surprise. Seeing Duggan's expression, Moose Parker turned, and frowned when he saw who it was. Rob took another sip.

After an awkward pause, Duggan recovered his composure, "Hello, Officer Caldwell, what a surprise. Didn't expect to see you here."

"Came for the basketball games, but they ended early."

Moose turned from Rob and looked at Duggan, then down at his empty plate. "Hi, Rob," he mumbled without looking his way.

"We were just finishing, but would you care to join us?" asked Duggan.

"Sure, just until my food's ready," replied Rob. "What brings you two here?"

Duggan slid over and Rob slipped into the booth. "Arnold gave me a ride to Harwich to visit a sick parishioner. Thought we'd grab a bite before heading home."

Moose looked across at Rob. "So how'd the games go?"

"The girls lost, not a surprise, and the boys had to forfeit. They were down twelve at half-time anyway, but Junior Proctor lost his cool, punched an Orleans kid and got ejected. Everything went crazy, and Coach decided to forfeit to let things calm down. It was pretty wild for a while."

"Wow, I got tossed from a few games, but I never actually punched anybody. What's Coach gonna to do now?"

"They have Sandwich at home Friday night, but Junior's suspended and Snowy is hurt. Coach said they'll probably play, Sandwich is bad, but without those two I don't like our chances. At least it'd give some of the younger kids an opportunity to play. I guess we can forget about making the playoffs though."

Duggan turned to Rob. "Anything new on Proctor? Arnold told me they have fingerprints."

"We think so, other than that, nothing much new. What about you, anything happening with finding a church location?"

Duggan glanced at Moose before responding. "Well, the other reason we were in Harwich was to look at properties. Mr. Armstrong got a legal order. He's taken over control of his mother's finances, so I have thirty days to leave the property in Bound Brook. Not a big deal really, I would've left before summer anyway. The widow and her family plan to use the house then. I'm looking at land in the Harwich/Orleans area to build a church. Actually, it might be good for the church, give us more access to the mid- and upper-Cape areas. With the Armstrong situation, I may have to set my sights a bit smaller."

"Where are you going to live in the meantime?"

"Well, Arnold has been kind enough to offer to put me up temporarily. If we find a location in the Harwich area, I'll need to move there permanently."

"Shepherd's pie," called the voice of the waitress.

"Guess my food's ready," said Rob, getting up from the table. "Make sure we have an address and number where we can reach you. Might have to ask some more questions."

Duggan glared at him, then softened his look. "Of course. Always glad to help the authorities with any *legitimate* questions."

Rob nodded. "Moose, Reverend, nice to talk with you. See you around."

He dug into his meal. Duggan and Moose left soon after and gave him a nod of their heads on the way out the door. *Interesting developments* thought Rob. *Not sure it's connected with the murder, but sometime in the near future, the Reverend will be leaving Bound Brook.* He knew it would make a number of residents happy, but you had to wonder at the timing.

His dinner finished, he made the short ride home, and thought about Rachel's upcoming visit. Hard to imagine that just a week ago they'd hardly spoken to each other. Now things were changing rapidly, almost too fast. Back at the cottage he had to keep his headlights on, aimed at the door, so he could dial his combination to open the padlock. He hadn't thought about that disadvantage, but at least there were no crayon notes on his kitchen table.

He lit two lanterns and started the woodstove, then settled into the rocking chair. *The Hound of the Baskervilles* rested on the side table. *If only I had the deductive powers of Sherlock Holmes.* He wondered if Sir Arthur Conan Doyle could have crafted an ending to the Proctor mystery. He was dozing in the chair when he heard the sound of tires on the crushed-shell driveway.

Rachel opened the door before he got up from the rocker.

"Hi there," she said with a shy smile. "Did I wake you?"

"Just resting my eyes." He got up and gave her a hug.

She gave him a little squeeze back, and then pulled up a kitchen chair, leaving her coat on. "I need to keep a little separation," she laughed, "or else this conversation won't go very far."

"What's up?"

"I've been busy." The words came out in a rush. "Talked with my parents about everything and talked to a lawyer in Orleans about filing for divorce. The divorce is Jimmy's idea, so it should move fairly quickly. We don't have any property or children, and I don't want any alimony, so it shouldn't be too complicated. He's due to be rotated stateside, so I think we can get the paperwork done."

She paused and caught her breath. "So even though the word is all over town about the two of us, I think we need to keep it cool. At least until the divorce is filed. I don't think what happened the other night should happen again, at least any time soon."

"But if we don't have sex, wouldn't that make us just like a married couple?" joked Rob.

"Very funny, wise guy, but I'm serious."

"I know you are. You're the only woman I've ever truly loved, and if I have to wait, it's worth it."

She blushed. "Well, that may make the next part harder. I've been thinking about this for a long time. I'm signing up for summer courses at Boston University, and applying for full-time admission in the fall. It means I'll be living up there. My uncle, one of Dad's brothers, lives in Winchester, and I can live with them and take the commuter train into Boston while I go to school."

"So you won't be around here?"

"I can take the bus home on weekends this summer, if *someone* will meet me in Hyannis. The courses I'm taking don't meet on Fridays, so I can be in Bound Brook for long weekends."

Rob smiled. "A week ago we barely spoke. I had no hope of really talking with you, let alone being friends again, or having a deeper relationship, so spending time with you Friday through Sunday this summer sounds pretty good."

"Really? I mean, it could be a long time before I'm free or even ready to make a commitment. I don't want to tie you down when I can't make any promises."

"You may have noticed that my social calendar isn't exactly full these days," he laughed.

"I know, but I don't want to lead you on, you know what I mean. I don't know what'll happen when I go to college, or even what I want to do afterwards, of course, that assumes I finish . . ."

"Whoa! Why don't we take it one step at a time? You've been waiting twelve years to go to college, and get your life started. I don't think you need to rush it now."

She leaped out of her chair and gave him a big hug. "This is so new to me! For you to encourage me is great. Jimmy just wanted me to be home when he got there, but then he barely talked to me. I could never tell him about my hopes, or he would've gotten mad."

She backed away with a huge smile. "I need to leave right now or something else will happen. But, before I forget, my Dad asked if you could substitute tomorrow for Tom Keane. He fell on some ice and wrenched his back."

"Sure, I'm supposed to meet with the Chief at noon, but we can probably do it later. Can you call the night dispatcher and pass the message to Foster for me?"

"I'll call as soon as I get home." Rachel headed for the door. "I've got to go, I'm flying high as a kite." She turned back quickly to Rob, gave him a quick kiss on the cheek and then ducked outside.

He waited for the sound of her car leaving, but then the door opened, and she stuck her head back in, "You know, you might want to do something about getting a phone. If I'm in Boston for the summer, I can't drive over and talk with you whenever I want. Know what I mean?" Then she was gone, her engine started, and tires crunched down the driveway.

He went to the doorway and watched the headlights fade down the road. Rob felt like a whirlwind had just blown through the cottage. He guessed twelve years of suppressed emotions and ambitions could do that.

He stayed at the door, making sure there wasn't another car, but he had a feeling that Broken-nose was finished with his mission for now, although he knew he'd be back.

Chapter XX – Confessions

Rob put aside the *Hound of the Baskervilles* and pulled out the thick tome of *The Complete Works of Shakespeare.* He had subbed a few times in the winter when George Gilmore was really desperate, and Rob wasn't working some construction job. Gilmore would've liked him to sub more, but Rob was reluctant, and told George to only use him when he was really stuck. Rob's lack of a phone also meant George couldn't call him in the morning.

He had subbed once or twice for Mr. Keane, who'd also been Rob's teacher in high school. Tom Keane taught History, French, English and sometimes Latin and Biology. At the little high school most teachers taught more than one subject, and Mr. Keane, a true renaissance man, could teach anything and everything. Rob knew the English class was finishing *Macbeth,* so he scanned the pages of Shakespeare's famous tragedy. When he'd had Keane in high school, the witty teacher had commented that Shakespeare had written comedies and tragedies; the difference was the comedies ended with everyone getting married, and in the tragedies, everyone died.

He turned to Act 5, Scene 1, the famous passage of the sleepwalking Lady Macbeth trying to wash the blood from her hands:

Come out, damned spot! Out, I command you! One, two…, it's time to do it now.—Hell is murky!—Nonsense, my lord, nonsense! You are a soldier, and yet you are afraid? Why should we be scared, when no one can lay the guilt upon us?—But who would have thought the old man would have had so much blood in him?

Was there someone in Bound Brook feeling that same guilt? Were they trying to remove the stain of "blood on their hands" from Proctor's murder? Trying to forget the Proctor riddle, he thought about his studies with Mr. Keane. Four years of French with Tom and three semesters at Brown had been a great help when Rob was stationed in Marseille. Then a year with Marie and her father had improved his French until he became fluent. Of course, other than the occasional French-Canadian tourist, he was pretty rusty now, but certainly more than capable of teaching Bound Brook students.

That night, his left arm and ribs throbbed, and he had to sleep on his right side, but there were no dreams, at least none that he remembered. The alarm woke him early. He went through his morning routine and dressed in slacks, white shirt, tweed jacket and tie. He didn't have a dressy topcoat, so the mackinaw would have to do. He arrived at school early, so he'd have time to prepare, and look over the materials. George's car was already in the parking lot as Rob headed to the Principal's office.

Gilmore was seated at his desk, jotting notes on a legal pad. "Hi Rob, thanks for filling in, you know I wouldn't ask if I had anyone else. I was just filling out your schedule, and here are the plans Tom gave me over the phone."

He tore the top sheet from the pad, put it with two other pages and handed them to Rob. "Tom thinks he'll be back tomorrow, but if he isn't, and you can't sub, I can get it covered."

"Merci beaucoup," replied Rob.

George laughed. "You know that's wasted on me. Terrible ear for languages, I just barely manage English. I'll drop in on you when first period gets started, see how you're doing. By the way, Rachel called the Chief and let him know you couldn't meet at noon, but you'd stop in later. I can get someone to cover your last period history class if you need to leave early."

Rob took the pages and headed for Tom Keane's room on the basement level. Mr. Keane had a freshman and sophomore homeroom of about 24 students. He reviewed the lesson plans and grabbed the books he'd need. Two girls wandered in while he worked at his desk. Surprised to see him, they gave him timid smiles, and ran back out the door, no doubt to inform the rest of Bound Brook High they had a substitute. Gradually the homeroom students drifted in, whispering to themselves. Rob noticed Vinnie Costa from the basketball team. Paula and Susan, the two girls who'd spread the word, approached his desk.

"Mr. Caldwell, would you like us to take attendance for you?" asked Paula.

"Thank you, girls that would be very helpful."

The girls giggled and Susan blushed. Rob tried to ignore their flirtatious glances while they called the names and marked off the attendance.

"Mr. Caldwell." Rob looked up at Vinnie Costa. "Have you heard what's gonna happen with the basketball season?"

"No Vinnie, I'm sure Coach Gilmore will let you know."

The girls handed him the attendance sheet. "Everyone's here," said Paula.

Rob thanked the girls, and asked Vinnie to lead them in the Pledge of Allegiance and Lord's Prayer. Paula offered to take the attendance to the office, and the bell rang to start first period. About half the sophomores and a few freshmen left and were replaced by the arrival of three juniors. The group was a combined French I & II class for potentially college-bound students. It was common in the small school to have classes that combined grades or levels. Teachers divided the work; it was liking running two classes at the same time, but sometimes they matched the older or more advanced students with younger ones.

The students all knew Rob and looked at him with eager faces. "Mr. Caldwell is it true you were in France during the war?" asked Paula.

"Yes," Rob walked to the world map on the wall and pointed, "I was in the port of Marseille."

"Mr. Keane always uses you as an example," she continued. "He says you never know when you might need to know French."

Rob laughed. "Leave it to Mr. Keane to bring that up. Would you like to know a little about Marseille, France?"

"Yes," replied a dozen voices. So Rob spent five or ten minutes telling the class about Marseille, its importance as a port, why he had been there, and the French people. He left out Marie, her father and Broken-nose. When he finished, Paula raised her hand.

"Mr. Caldwell, you went to college, were in the Navy and lived in France. Why'd you come back to Bound Brook?"

"Well Paula, that's a good question. I'm not sure I know the answer exactly. I guess when it comes down to it, Bound Brook is my home. It's as pretty as anywhere I've ever seen, and mostly, I guess, it's the only place I care about. Maybe it's easier to come back because I've seen some of the world. If I'd never been anywhere, maybe I'd always wonder, have an urge to travel, but right now, this is where I want to be."

The class sat silently, absorbing the words. Rob wasn't sure they understood. He doubted he would have when he was fourteen, but they seemed to be thinking about it, perhaps each one coming to their own conclusion.

The quiet was broken by the entrance of George Gilmore. The class glanced at each other, and some giggled, then on cue they greeted the principal in unison. "Bonjour, Monsieur Gilmore, comment allez-vous?"

"As usual, I have no idea what you're asking, but if it's *can we get out of school early,* the answer is no," joked Gilmore.

Rob remembered the silly retorts Gilmore used with the foreign language classes. It was always fun to see what response he came up with to their French or Latin greetings. It was an established routine, almost a tradition, dating back to Rob's own high school days.

"OK class, get started on your exercises while I talk with the Mr. Gilmore."

George motioned Rob to the door and the two stepped outside, with George holding the door open. "Listen, a few updates I don't want the class to hear. I called Junior's house last night several times and didn't get an answer. He's not in school today, which may not be a surprise, but unusual for him. I think they know he's suspended for the remainder of the season, and maybe he didn't want to face his classmates today, but still a bit peculiar. Anyway, you all set with the classes?"

Rob replied he was all set, and the two agreed to talk again at lunch. The morning moved quickly, with a freshman English class studying grammar, then the sophomore group reading *Macbeth,* followed by world history studying the Roman Empire, and finally time for lunch.

At the cafeteria door, George Gilmore tapped his shoulder, "Go to my office. Chief Foster needs to speak with you. I'll bring you some lunch."

Rob turned and went up the stairs to Gilmore's office, where he found Foster examining a portrait of a distinguished-looking man on the office wall.

"Any idea who this gentleman is?" the Chief asked.

"No idea," replied Rob, "but he's been up there forever. I think he came with the building."

"Probably a Proctor, be my guess. Let's sit down."

Rob sensed even more urgency than usual from Foster. "I just got back from Provincetown, delivered Corey Proctor to the jail there. Got to the office this morning about eight and Corey was there. He confessed to murdering his Uncle Cecil."

Rob was stunned. "Wow, I didn't see that. Did he explain?"

"Sure did. He said Junior was furious when he heard that Mary was moving, and felt it was all Cecil's fault. He went to Proctor's house and they had an argument. Junior screamed at him, and the Old Man smacked him hard across the face and gave him a bruise."

"That explains his black eye," said Rob. "I wondered how he'd gotten that, guess it wasn't basketball."

"Junior took off for home," The Chief continued, "and ran into Corey coming back from a job. He said the kid was crying and incoherent, but he finally got the story out of him. Corey says he lost it. He was still mad at Proctor from before, and when he saw Corey's eye, he charged over to the house. He said Proctor saw him coming, and was holding the fireplace poker, ready to defend himself. They yelled at each other and Corey demanded an apology, but Proctor said he'd never apologized for anything in his life and wouldn't start now."

"He claims Proctor shoved him, and when Corey shoved him back, Proctor swung and missed with the poker. Corey yanked it away and hit him with it. He claims he didn't mean to kill him, and at first didn't even realize he was dead, kept expecting him to get up, but when he didn't, he panicked and ran home."

Foster paused to catch his breath. "When he got home, Junior asked what had happened. When he told the kid, he realized he needed to go back and check on Proctor. Said he hoped he was alive and maybe he could call Doc Carter. When he got back it was obvious Proctor was dead. So he went home again. He made Junior promise not to tell anyone, even his mother. He said the two just went around in a daze until his wife got home from the neighbor's house. By then the storm was already bad."

"What about the fire?" Rob interrupted.

"Corey says for another day he didn't know what to do, just hoped it would all turn out to be a bad dream. But before dawn the next morning, he told his wife that he and Junior needed to go out and shovel. Then he woke up Junior, and the two went over to Proctor's house, a real short walk even in the blizzard. He said he'd already decided to burn the place, and had Junior get the jerry jug from the shed. They stayed outside, he said he didn't want Junior to see Proctor, then splashed the kerosene all over the side of the house and used his cigarette lighter to start it."

"So Junior was involved?"

"Corey was adamant it wasn't the kid's fault. He said he didn't tell him what they were going to do, and all the kid did was get the kerosene for him. He was really afraid we were going to arrest Junior for being an accomplice. We may have to, but that'll be for the D.A. to decide."

"So, you took him to jail in Ptown?"

"I got the full statement from him, and Ptown's the closest jail, so yes, they booked him and put him in a cell. He called that lawyer, Winters. He'll probably end up with some other lawyer eventually, one that's got more criminal experience. Anyway, I just got back."

The two just sat there looking at each other. There was a knock on the door and George Gilmore came in with two lunch trays. "Looks like I'm interrupting something important, so I'll just leave the trays for you two."

Foster held up his hand. "No George, stay a minute. I want to give you a head's up, because this will be all around town soon, and the kids will be upset. Corey Proctor just confessed to killing Proctor. He's in jail in Provincetown, and the State Police are on their way to talk with him."

Gilmore's shoulders slumped and he shook his head. "Corey Proctor? That family has been through so much, first losing the older boy in the war, and now this."

"George, don't say anything to anybody yet, but I wanted to get you prepared for dealing with the reactions from students and parents."

"Thanks for letting me know," replied Gilmore. "I better get back to the cafeteria. Rob, do you need to leave? I can make do somehow if you need to."

Rob looked at Foster, who shook his head. "No, I think I'll be fine."

Gilmore left the office and Rob turned to Foster. "Where are Junior and his mother now?"

Foster was digging into his sloppy joe, mashed potatoes and green beans, "Corey said something about them going to his wife's family in Hyannis, but they're probably still in town. We'll need to talk with Junior, get a statement and see if the D.A. wants to bring any charges against him. I think he's still a minor, so that'll be a consideration, no hurry right now."

"Did Corey say anything about writing the note to me?"

"You know, I never asked him," said the Chief, "he covered everything so fully, I just let him talk, and took his statement. Writing a note isn't a crime, so that's the least of his problems."

"Will he be staying in the Provincetown jail or will the State Police move him?"

"Eventually they'll move him, but I gathered Trooper Stewart is tied up with something in Plymouth, so probably later or even tomorrow. His lawyer in Ptown needs to talk to him. Probably take him to court in Hyannis and jail him there."

Rob wiped tomato sauce from his chin. "Would it be OK if I talked to him after school gets out?"

"Sure, why don't we go together? I want to make sure we don't do anything to mess up the D.A.'s case. Don't think you've interviewed too many murder suspects, at least not ones that weren't in the Navy. I'll pick you up at 2:30, OK?"

They both wolfed down the remnants of the lunch. Rob grabbed the trays and headed to the cafeteria, while Foster exited the building. Dropping the trays off, Rob noticed all eyes watching him. Of course, people must have seen the Bound Brook police cruiser, and he was sure the rumors were flying.

His next class was American History, and then last period, a small advanced French class with only eight students. He was distracted, so limited his classes to reading and written exercises. Clearly the students knew something was going on. He ignored the whispers and notes that were passed, but at least no one asked him any questions.

About 2:20, George Gilmore appeared at his door. "I can cover the end of class. Why don't you head out and meet the Chief ahead of the buses? He called and said he'd be here."

Rob grabbed his coat and hat and headed up the stairs to the main exit. He walked across the traffic circle to the edge of the school grounds, where Foster could pick him up without parking. A minute later the cruiser came up the hill and pulled over next to him. He hopped in the passenger side for the ride to Provincetown.

Chapter XXI – Tragedy

The ride took less than twenty minutes, cruising along at the 45-mile-per-hour speed limit, despite a light snow that had started to fall. On the way they said little. Finally, Rob turned to the Chief. "If Corey did it the way he said, you think he has a chance at a self-defense plea?"

Foster never looked away from the road. "You know, after all my years with the State Police, I've finally learned never to get into it, that's for the lawyers. My job is to find out what happened and who did it. However, the problem for Corey is that he's the only witness, and then he acted very guilty, didn't call anybody, and burned the house. Not good for a self-defense plea."

Rob didn't reply. They took the exit for Provincetown Center, pulled up at the Town Hall, and parked in one of the spaces in the back reserved for police business. Provincetown was deserted compared to the throngs of tourists who crowded the streets in the summer. He followed the Chief to the Police Station. They nodded to the desk sergeant, who grabbed a ring of keys and gestured for them to follow. "I'll bring him to the interrogation cell." He pointed to an empty room.

They went in the room and sat at the table. A few minutes later, Corey Proctor entered in handcuffs. The electrician seemed to have shrunk and aged ten years. He shuffled to the table. The sergeant pulled out a chair, nodded to the Chief, and left the three of them alone.

"Corey, we want to go over your statement again if that's OK with you. Can you tell Rob what you told me?"

Corey nodded, and proceeded to give the same account he had told the Chief in his confession. Rob listened carefully, to see if there were any inconsistencies or changes, but the story was almost exactly the same.

"Did you tell your wife?" asked Rob.

"She didn't know anything until late last night. I finally told her. Said I was going to the Chief in the morning to confess."

"Why did you decide to confess now?" asked Foster.

"I heard you had fingerprints from the jerry jug. Any prints you have will belong to Junior. He took his gloves off when he got the kerosene and opened it for me. But that's all he did, just what I told him. I didn't want him blamed or have him arrested, 'cause it wasn't his fault."

Corey gave the Chief a pleading look. "He won't get in trouble, will he?"

"Not for me to say," answered the Chief.

"That was the other reason I came forward. The whole thing has been eating at Junior, driving him nuts. He's got a temper, but what he did in basketball the last couple of days, that's not him. I couldn't let it keep going on any longer, not fair to him, I don't think he can take it."

"What did you tell Junior and your wife to do?" asked Rob.

"Delores was, I guess what you'd call distraught. I told them to wait at the house. I figured you might need to talk with them. I want them to go to Delores's family in Hyannis. Don't want them around Bound Brook with all this going on."

"Corey," asked Rob, "Why did you write that note to me?"

Corey looked surprised. "Note?"

Rob glanced at Foster. "Yes, I got a note telling me to back off."

"Oh, right, the note. Sure, I forgot about it."

"Corey, you remember when you wrote it, and what it said?"

A look came over him. His eyes shifted side to side, and he opened his mouth, but nothing came out. Foster and Rob waited.

"Corey, what did the note say, and when did you give it to me?"

"Just like you said, it said for you to back off."

"What were the words?"

"I don't remember the exact words. There was a lot going on, I can't remember everything."

"Corey, what time and what day did you give me the note?"

Proctor looked down at the table.

"Come on, Corey, you can remember that, can't you? What about where you left it, how can you forget that?"

"I don't want to talk about it. You got my confession. I did it, what more do you want? Sergeant, I want to go back, I'm not talking anymore!"

The desk sergeant came in and took an agitated Corey Proctor back to his cell. Rob and Foster sat at the table too shocked to speak. Finally, Rob spoke. "He didn't do it!"

"Well, we know he didn't write the note, but that doesn't mean he didn't do the rest," said Foster.

"I don't think so. If somebody else wrote the note, like Junior maybe, why did he get so shook? He could've just said he did the murder and fire but didn't do the note. Instead, he tried to *pretend* he wrote it, and then he fell apart. It's all a lie!"

"You're right," said Foster, after pausing for a moment. "It was like he had his story all set, and then it all unraveled when he got caught trying to fake it."

The Provincetown sergeant came back. "Chief, your dispatcher is calling you, said it's important. You want to take the call?"

"Be right there." Foster headed for the office and picked up the phone handset lying on the desk.

"Yes, Diane, what's going on?" He listened intently for a few seconds. "We're on our way, keep me posted."

He hung up, gestured to Rob and headed for the door. Picking up his pace even more, with Rob following, the two jumped in the cruiser. The snow had gotten a little heavier and was just starting to stick to the pavement. Foster started the car, backed out of the space, put on his flashing lights and accelerated through town and along the shore road in North Truro until it connected to the highway, where he pushed the cruiser to sixty despite the increasingly slick surface.

"Diane got a call from Delores Proctor. She's panicky, said Junior's been unstable, acting crazy about his father being arrested. She was worried, so she hid his car keys, but he snuck out of the house and . . . she doesn't know where he is. Maybe left a half hour ago."

"Kid's upset, probably wants to be alone, seems natural," said Rob.

"That's not all of it. Delores just got a call from Mary Joseph, who said Junior had called her from somewhere. She said he was sobbing, and she could hardly understand him, but he said something about *it was all his fault*. Mary was really scared by the way he was talking."

Foster was interrupted by the radio. "Dispatch to Chief." He grabbed the microphone and acknowledged the call.

"Chief, I just got a call from Harold at Flying A. He said Junior was at the station and used the phone. Harold was pumping gas and didn't really notice him, but all of a sudden Junior came out, started Proctor's Cadillac and took off, burning rubber and driving crazy! Last he saw him; he'd turned towards town."

"We're ten minutes away, see if you can reach Skip on the other line. Have him meet us if he can."

Foster added the siren and accelerated. Fortunately, the road was empty. Rob held his breathe as the Chief navigated the heavy cruiser on the straightaway of the highway. The Chief flew past the first turn-off for the center. "Want to avoid the center. Too slow, too many people."

At seventy miles per hour, they were at the next exit in less than a minute. The Chief slowed carefully on the snowy road as the cruiser took the corner and turned onto the narrow road. He headed up the hill past Olde Creek Inn, took the left turn on Lower Main, and screeched to a stop at the police station with the cruiser slipping sideways into the parking lot. They both leaped from the cruiser, took the snowy stairs two at a time and burst into the office.

Diane looked up from the phone, "Yes, OK, where is he, Mary? OK, keep him talking if you can." She looked wide-eyed at Foster, pointing and gesturing outside. Rob moved to the front window that over-looked Joseph's Hardware and the family's second floor apartment. He noticed the shiny, small, black tailfin of an auto, just visible in the parking space behind the store.

"Damn, he's at Mary's!"

"Where'd he go, Mary?" asked Diane, then turned to the Chief. "He's running."

Rob ran out the door with the Chief close on his heels. The Cadillac backed out fast, slammed on the brakes and shifted to first, just as they got to the cruiser. Rob saw Junior behind the wheel. The Fleetwood's tires squealed and burned rubber, accelerating toward the harbor.

Foster pulled out with flashers and siren sounding. The Cadillac already had a fifty-yard lead. He floored the gas pedal and shifted quickly through the gears. Rob saw the needle climb as the powerful Chevy Cruiser's engine roared, but the Caddy had the lead, a reckless driver and an equally powerful engine.

"Jeez, that kid's gonna kill somebody!"

Rob saw the Cadillac streak past Morris Fuel and down the narrow tree-lined Lower Main, headed to the Marina. At the pier the road took a sharp right along the Bay. He better slow down or he'd never make the turn, especially in the snowy conditions. Where the hell was he headed anyway?

The police car was gaining slightly as the inexperienced driver had trouble keeping the Caddy headed straight. Junior swerved and wobbled over both sides of the road, and Rob was sure he was going to lose control. At the intersection with Holcomb, the Cadillac never slowed; in fact, it seemed to gain speed. The Chief followed and Rob prayed nobody was in the intersection. The cruiser's needle was hitting eighty and still the Caddy showed no signs of slowing.

They were only a few hundred yards from the 90-degree turn toward the bay, and Junior kept accelerating. The next few moments seemed like a dream. The Cadillac sped toward the pier and made no effort to slow. It flew past the turn, through the marina parking lot and onto the wooden pier. Foster followed to the marina, then jammed on the brakes; the cruiser skidded and spun to a stop just before the pier.

Rob kept his eyes on the Caddy. The sleek Fleetwood flew down the length of the pier. Just short of the end, the car hit the bump of a raised plank and took to the air. Three feet off the ground, white-wall tires spinning, the setting sun shining off the polished surface, the Cadillac hit a three-foot diameter piling. In slow motion, the car flipped, its grill and hood collapsing, as giant splinters flew into the air, and with an unworldly *CRACK!* the giant piling snapped.

Rob jumped out of the cruiser and sprinted down the pier. The Cadillac was upside down, twenty feet out, sinking rapidly, with only the spinning tires and exhaust system above the surface. He ripped off his mackinaw and suit jacket, yanked off his shoes and jumped feet first into the freezing harbor. He tried to keep his head above water, his eyes on his target, as he broke into a strong overhand crawl. The front end of the car was now underwater with the rear tires and tailpipe still exposed. A gas slick rose to the surface.

Rob surface-dived toward the driver's side door. Despite the stinging salt and cold, he kept his eyes open, conditioned by years of diving in the Bay's seawater. The door wouldn't budge, but it didn't matter, because there was nobody inside. On the last of his air, he pulled himself to the windshield. Most of it was gone with only jagged glass clinging to the outer edges. There seemed to be an air bubble trapped in the upside-down, submerged car, but Rob, running out of air, pushed off from the car and surfaced.

A rope landed near him. "Grab hold, we're getting a boat!" yelled Foster. "Don't need two of you drowning."

Rob wrapped the rope around his sore left arm and used his right arm to paddle. The rope pulled him to the pier's wooden ladder. Foster leaned over and grabbed his shirt while Rob climbed. He already felt his strength leaving as the effects of the freezing water took their toll. Foster wrapped Rob's mackinaw around him and added his own coat as well.

"You need to get in the car. I'll get the heater running; you'll be hypothermic if you don't."

Rob was starting to shiver. "A minute. I've got to see if they find him."

Tricky Tyler pushed a dory from the side of his trawler and started rowing toward the car. Men were running from Art's Bar & Grill, and Cap't Hallet and some old-timers were moving from the shellfish shack as fast as old age would let them. The siren of the fire engine moved down the road. Someone yanked the outboard on the harbormaster's boat and got it started. The fire truck arrived at the same time that Tricky rowed up to a sodden bulge that rose to the surface.

"I see him!" yelled Tricky.

The harbormaster's launch sped toward his location. Tricky reached Junior first, dropped the oars and struggled to turn him over. A life on the water and strong arms from hefting shellfish made Tricky amazingly strong for his size and wiry frame. Still, it was all he could do to flip the body on its back.

"I got him," yelled Tricky. "Don't look so good, he's real blue."

The launch pulled to the other side of Junior's body. Rob recognized the harbormaster, Bing Tyler and his assistant Davey Sousa. Bing grabbed the boy under his arms, Davey pulled him by his coat, and Tricky pushed his legs. Together they managed to roll him into the launch. Bing spun the boat around and headed toward the floating dock near the harbormaster's shack.

"Diane called it in when we took off after him," said the Chief.

Rob saw the fire engine pulled up next to the shack, with Skip Parker and Buddy Barrows running to the floating dock to help. Behind the engine, Doc Carter's car skidded to a stop. Bing and Davey lifted Junior onto the dock and Skip, a summer lifeguard, started pumping his chest. Doc Carter arrived with his medical bag and knelt beside the body.

By now a crowd had gathered. People leaned over the edges of the pier, and everyone held their breath. Buddy stopped pumping and Doc Carter moved his hands around Junior's body. Even from a distance, Rob could see that Junior's face was a pale blue. Sadly, he had seen that look before. More time passed, before Doc Carter rose to his feet and shook his head. Buddy took off his fire-chief coat and covered the body.

More cars pulled into the parking lot, and Rob recognized the Josephs' Ford. Frank reached out to stop Mary, but she eluded his grasp and ran toward the dock. Skip Parker grabbed her, and hugged her until her mother and father wrapped her in their arms.

"NO! NOT AGAIN!" screamed a female voice!

Rob saw Delores Proctor. One look at the shocked expressions of the crowd, and Mary Joseph sobbing hysterically, and she knew. She fell to her knees and let out a keening wail.

"NOOOO! I ALREADY LOST ONE BOY. I CAN'T LOSE ANOTHER!"

Cap't Hallett did his best to comfort her, but she flailed her arms and ripped at her hair. Doc Carter ran to the distraught mother, removed something from his medicine bag and yelled for some men to help. Moose Parker and Honk from the highway crew ran over, and the two burly men managed to get Delores to the ground and hold her arm down, while Doc gave her a shot.

"Come with me, or Doc will be working on you next," said Foster, as he led Rob to the police car and started the engine.

"Here, get your wet clothes off and wrap up in these. Stay here with the heater. That's an order!" He ripped off Rob's outer clothes and covered him up with the coats.

Rob nodded. He was already feeling numb. The snow was falling hard now and visibility was obscured. Getting confused, he thought he saw a crying Rachel running to the cruiser. In his dream he saw her open the door, climb inside, and hug him hard. She opened her coat and enveloped him in her embrace, her warmth and words providing comfort. Through the blur he heard, "I love you . . . I love you . . . I won't lose you again." He drifted into a daze.

Chapter XXII – Aftermath

It was hard to believe that the Cape was being hit with another crippling storm, but the snow intensified and dumped even more of a white coating on the region. In Orleans, the town library, ironically named the Snow Library, burned to the ground, with all but one fire engine unable to reach it because of the deep, wet snow. The one engine that reached the blaze lost its water when the town plow cut the hose as it tried to clear the road for the other equipment. Eventually, fire hoses pumped salt water from the Town Cove, but by then the library was a total loss. Once again, the weather and competing news caused the tragedy in little Bound Brook to be largely overlooked.

March roared in like a lion, but the salt air and constant winds off Cape Cod Bay made quick work of even the deepest snow, although the shaded deep woods still had patches. Rob walked to the Harbor, taking the short cut over Bound Brook footbridge. It was sunny with temperatures in the upper forties, with the typical early morning calm that would likely give way to a stiff breeze in the afternoon.

It had been two weeks since the fatal crash, and Rob had suffered from a letdown, a lethargic depression he couldn't shake. A week ago, he had started taking long walks, hoping for a break from the combination of cabin fever and the need to digest the events of the past month. Physically he was fine, but he felt emotionally drained. His moods bounced from excitement about his renewed relationship with Rachel, to despair over the tragic loss of Junior and its resulting devastation to Corey and Delores, as well as the Bound Brook community in general.

Doc Carter had determined that Junior had died from multiple causes: a fractured skull, broken neck and a crushed chest, any one of which could have killed him by itself. Doc figured that Junior had gone through the windshield, his head hitting the frame, causing the fracture and breaking his neck. The Cadillac's steering wheel was the likely cause of the chest and internal injuries. Doc said Junior had never had a chance, and probably died instantly.

Delores Proctor had been taken to Cape Cod Hospital and then transferred to a facility south of Boston. She was being treated for shock and severe depression, and Rob gathered that she was medicated and constantly watched. She had never fully recovered from the loss of her older boy in the war, and the death of Junior, her baby, seemed more than she could take. Rob heard she had retreated into a shell and was rarely responsive, even to visits from her husband. There were rumors that they might try electro-shock treatments.

Corey had been released from jail and found a temporary place to stay near Delores' facility. Technically the D.A. could have brought obstruction and other charges against him but given the circumstances no one wanted to pursue it any further. Before charges were dropped, Chief Foster and Trooper Stewart had interviewed Corey to put the pieces together. Rob had sat in on the conversation.

"Please tell us what really happened, to the best of your knowledge," Stewart had asked.

"It happened almost exactly like I told you, but it was Junior, not me. He was furious when he heard that Mary Joseph was moving because of Cecil selling the store. He went to the house and they had an argument; that's when Cecil smacked him in the face and gave him the black eye. Junior said he shoved Cecil to the floor. When he got up, Cecil grabbed the fireplace poker and swung it at him, but he ducked, and it missed. That's when Junior wrestled it away and hit Cecil. He panicked when he realized Cecil wasn't breathing, and he ran home. With the storm coming, we were busy and distracted. I noticed the bruise, but Junior said it was from basketball."

"You know," he continued, "he kept it all bottled up until after the game in Orleans. When I drove him home after the game was forfeited, it all came pouring out. He told me that during the storm he got up at dawn, while we were still sleeping, went back to the house and started the fire. I never suspected anything, never put things together, but he was acting so different. He flew off the handle at everything. I guess the pressure of holding it all in was too much. Then Mary broke up with him on the bus ride to the game and he punched the Orleans kid. He just snapped, and on the ride home it was like the dam burst."

"At first, I didn't know what to do, but there was no way I was going to put him or Delores through all that. Junior was all Delores and I had left. So I took over his story and made Junior promise not to tell anyone, including his mother. I wasn't thinking straight, but it seemed like the only thing to do, I'd do anything to protect that boy." Corey paused and choked back tears.

Stewart waited before asking, "Corey, what happened when you told your wife that you did it?"

"It was awful! She lost it, couldn't believe I could do something like that. Then she didn't want me to go to the police; she wanted us to move, run away somewhere. I told her I had to confess because even though I did it, Junior's prints would be on the jerry jug and I didn't want him dragged into it. When she realized that something could happen to Junior, she finally agreed. Now that I look back, I think she might've suspected, maybe something about the way Junior had reacted. There was a look between them, just for a second. Anyway, I told her I needed her to be strong for Junior, and I'd try to explain that Cecil had swung the poker at me first."

"The one thing Junior never told me was about the note he must have written to Rob. When Rob asked me about it, I got thrown off. If Junior'd told me, I would have been ready for the question, but I fell apart. I guess it doesn't matter anyway . . . wouldn't have stopped what Junior did."

At that point, Corey put his head down and cried. The three policemen sat quietly and let the grief come out. "I thought I was protecting him. I thought if I took the blame, he and Delores would be OK. But I made it worse. Maybe if I had brought him to the Chief, and he'd explained what had happened, he'd still be alive. Maybe Delores could've handled it, but I didn't know. I thought I was helping, but it's all my fault. I don't think I can live with myself. If it wasn't for Delores, I'd take the same route Junior did." Corey had completely broken down and the interview was over.

When Rob got to the little footbridge over Bound Brook, he realized he had been so lost in his thoughts that he didn't even remember walking the back paths through the Tyler Tangle and South Bound Brook. He crossed the bridge to Lower Main and walked past the Public Safety Building. He thought about checking in, but since the case was closed, he wasn't an active policeman now. Besides, he'd had enough.

Across the street, Joseph's Hardware still had a closed sign in the window. Also, victims of the tragedy, the Joseph family had gone to Wareham to stay with one of Frank's brothers. They were still undecided about returning to Bound Brook or moving permanently. According to Rachel, Junior's death had shaken Mary to the point where her parents felt she might need a fresh start.

He walked Lower Main past the Snows, the Jenkins and Proctor's boarding house. None of them would be sold now. In fact, the rumor was that Barnstable Lumber was looking at some property on Route 6 in South Bound Brook, owned by Richard Caldwell. Thinking about it made Rob sick. Two people dead, others suffering . . . and his SOB grandfather got richer. He tried to push his anger aside. Richard Caldwell had lots of money, but what good had it done him? He had no family, no one he loved, and no one who loved him. He'd have a lonely old age, and nobody would mourn his death, least of all his grandson.

He walked past Morris Fuel and down the tree-lined section that led to the pier. The wild ride in the cruiser, chasing Junior at eighty miles per hour, was still vivid in his memory. He realized now the whole chase had happened in a matter of minutes, though at the time it had seemed like slow motion. Bound Brook High School was still in a state of mourning. George had forfeited the final basketball game against Sandwich and said that students and teachers were just going through the motions, everyone in a stupor, bewildered and constantly reminded by the absence of Junior and Mary Joseph. Rob's cousin Benny was struggling with the loss, and he wasn't the only one. The teenagers were too young to remember the War, and for most of them this was the first death of someone their own age.

There should have been a funeral, but Delores was in the institution and Corey was out of town. So Junior had been buried in the South Bound Brook Cemetery next to his brother. Corey arranged it to be done in secret—no fanfare, no mourners, just one evening he was buried, and the next day a small white cross was the only sign he was there. However, Rob stopped at the grave site almost every day, and the white cross was now covered in flowers from unseen family and friends.

With the case closed, Cecil Proctor's body was released by the state lab, and a few days after Junior's internment, he was buried in the Proctor section of the same cemetery, only a few yards away. Cecil's burial was no secret, but despite the knowledge, only the minister, grave-diggers and Howie Proctor attended. Afterward, Howie said he'd only gone to represent the Proctor family, and to make sure Cecil was really dead. No flowers graced his grave.

Rob now walked through the marina parking lot and out to the end of pier. The jagged edges of the massive piling were a stark reminder of the power of the Cadillac's crash. In the doorway of Hallet's shack the Cap't nodded and gave Rob a small wave. Tricky Tyler, on the deck of the Mary Mae, was pulling out into the channel for a day of fishing.

He went back down the pier and onto the sandy beach. He walked all the way to the end, to the remnants of the old Bound Brook Inn, the stubby spikes of its wharf pilings just poking through the ebbing tide. Rob felt everything coming full circle. Here was the property that had cemented the Proctor fortune, now just a relic. What would become of Proctor's vast properties? Where would the wealth go? Then he realized; he didn't care.

Instinctively, he knew where he was going. He walked up the backside of a sandy dune that led to Tyler Hill and took a narrow path through scrub pines and a bramble thicket. The path came out in a backyard, covered in bear berries, or what the natives called "hog cranberries." He walked around the house, up the shell driveway, and knocked on the door. Maggie Gilmore opened and led him into the kitchen.

One look and she knew what he needed. She opened her arms and wrapped him in a mother's hug. Rob cried like he had never cried before. He cried for Junior, Corey and Delores. He cried for Mary Joseph and her family. He cried for the twelve years lost from Rachel. He cried for Jimmy's messed-up life. He cried for the grandmother who had longed for his love. He cried for the father he would never know, and the grandfather he barely did. He cried for Bound Brook, which would never be the same. Mostly he cried for his mother, Roberta Caldwell. He cried more than he had when she had died. The secret place opened, and all the bottled feeling escaped. The crying felt good.

Chapter XXIII – A Fresh Start

It was June on Cape Cod and you could feel the pulse of summer in the air. A few early tourists were enjoying the lack of hustle and bustle that would start after the Fourth of July. Bound Brook handymen were busily employed repairing summer cottages before the arrival of the long-term summer residents. Shutters were removed, screens repaired, water turned back on, yards spruced up, a myriad of chores that kept the local economy humming. It was the time of year that natives both loved and hated. They loved the business that would give them enough money to make it through another tough winter, but they hated sharing their quiet village with outsiders who often thought they were superior to the dimwitted locals.

Rob had decided to take the summer off from bartending at Art's on the pier. He'd never cared much for the pushy Art anyway, and now that Rachel would only be home on weekends, he didn't want to miss spending time with her. Her summer classes at BU had just started, and she was flushed with enthusiasm, though perhaps a bit apprehensive as well. As a 31-year-old freshman, she felt like a fish out of water. She told Rob she was happy though, and for the first time in twelve years she felt she had a purpose and direction.

Chief Foster had hired a couple of Bound Brook college kids to direct traffic downtown and handle the simpler details for the summer. Skip was willing to take the weekend shifts and Rob did part-time Monday through Thursday, which left him Fridays to pick up Rachel in Hyannis from the Boston bus. He wasn't worried about the decreased income and knew he could dip into his still-ample savings if he needed more cash.

It would be a relief to most people when the school year ended in another week. Seniors had already graduated with a mixture of celebration and melancholy, making an effort to put thoughts of the winter events out of mind. Once again, there hadn't been enough players for Bound Brook to field a baseball team and so the school year had just rolled by. Some of the older boys' attendance got spotty as they helped their fathers and relatives on the fishing draggers.

Rob had made arrangements for the electric and phone lines to be run out to his isolated cottage by the shore, and had plans to make some more overdue improvements, including indoor plumbing and a septic system. Finally, he was rejoining the modern world.

Rachel had heard from Jimmy. He had been wounded, losing two fingers, and would be returning from Korea soon. Although the injury was not serious, it sounded like it would put an end to his plans to make a career of the Army. There was still no sign of Marie, and Rob had started to doubt she would actually come to see him. As for Broken nose, Rob had been taking the shutters off his cottage in May when the black sedan pulled into the driveway.

Rocco had gotten out and stood by the car door. "Gotta leave for a while, got other things to do."

"Don't hurry back on my account."

"Oh, I got a feeling I'll be back. You know she's gonna show up eventually, and when she does, I'll be there." With that, the ex-boxer had gotten back in his car and driven away.

Author's Notes

This is a work of fiction. The town of Bound Brook does not exist, and neither do any of the local characters. However, there is a Bound Brook Island in Wellfleet, an area of land near the Truro line that was once its own village but is now deserted and part of the Cape Cod National Seashore. Those familiar with the geography of Wellfleet may find some similarity to the layout and landmarks of the town of my youth.

Two actual events spurred the plot of this novel. Once, in my on-going Cape Cod/Wellfleet research, I read about a fire during a blizzard in 1938 that killed the elderly Mr. Paine of South Wellfleet. My writer's conspiratorial mind thought, *Ah, but what if it wasn't an accident?*

The second event happened when I was about eleven or twelve years old. After breaking up with his girlfriend, followed by a night of drinking, a young man drove *his convertible* off the end of the Wellfleet pier, at close to one hundred miles per hour. *Amazingly, he lived!* The fact that the top was down, he had no seat belt and it was low tide combined to save his life. When I started this project, I knew I was going to work it into the plot.

There was never a Bound Brook Inn, but there was a Chequesset Inn built over the water in Wellfleet. In 1934 it was destroyed, not by fire but in a blizzard. There was a Wellfleet Consolidated school until 1959 when Wellfleet merged into the Nauset Regional School System. For Wellfleet aficionados, I leave it to you to try to figure out some of the landmarks whose names I changed.

The closest to a real character in my novel is Mr. Gilmore, the Principal/Coach. My father, Dick Cochran was the teaching-principal of the Wellfleet Consolidated School from 1938-1943, and then again 1952-1959. He came from Medford, Massachusetts, had been a basketball star at Tufts University, and had later coached Tufts into the NCAA basketball tournament in 1945, where they lost to Kentucky.

There are also a few cameos. Mr. Keane (my wife's family name) is similar to the amazing Tommy Kane, teacher, musician, Truro Town Father and writer of an award-winning newspaper column for 43 years. Chief Foster is a morphing of Wellfleet Police Chiefs Bill Fleming and Frank Davenport. Chief Davenport bore a resemblance to a skinnier John Wayne. To family, friends, fellow writers and long-time Wellfleetians . . . see if you can spot some of your names embedded in the story.

This book has been fun! The story continues in Bound Brook Pond: Cape Cod Mystery II. Check the next pages for a preview.

Bound Brook Pond

Cape Cod Mystery II

By

Rick Cochran

Chapter 1 - Elaine

Saturday Night, July 5, 1952

Elaine Samuels grabbed the cold bottle of Narragansett beer that dripped with condensation, slapped a dollar on the bar and took a long swig. The bartender gave her a look and pushed the bill back.

"Thanks, Franky."

He winked. "Professional courtesy."

"I can really use it tonight. I owe you one."

"Forget it." He smiled. "Tough night?"

Elaine nodded and took a sip. "Sometimes I get sick of smiling and wiggling my hips, but men give the tips and they like to look."

She had just finished her shift waitressing at the Mayflower Café, a restaurant and bar in Provincetown. The Mayflower was a town institution. It was her first summer working there and she loved the Janoplis family business that had been around since 1929. On the left wall were funny caricature drawings of famous people and local characters, drawn by Jake Spencer, a bar regular. Rumor had it that sometimes Mike Janoplis accepted the drawings to cover Jake's large bar tab.

It was a busy Saturday night on the steamy holiday weekend and Elaine was beat. With the windows and doors open, the salty smell of the harbor permeated the air. The night was so still you could hear the chatter of pedestrians and the sounds from the fish pier across the street. The Fourth of July was the official start of the Cape's summer season, and good news from an economic standpoint. Most Cape residents made the bulk of their income in the busy season, but it came with a price. It meant putting up with traffic, crowds and pushy city folks who wanted a vacation, but had not adjusted to a slower, more relaxing pace.

"One guy says to me what is that odor? Smells like rotten eggs," laughed Elaine. "I told him, welcome to fish guts and low tide at Provincetown Harbor."

Franky grinned, "I know, I think they want the movie version without the smell of fish processing and mud flats. Like a Hollywood film starring Spencer Tracy or Jimmy Stewart."

"Well, I ain't no Doris Day. They want America's Sweetheart; they should go to the cinema. My cheeks are so tired from faking a smile that I've got a headache."

To be fair, most of the tourists were nice, curious about the Cape, and full of questions for a native. However, some wanted the local residents to know how important they were and seemed to feel the natives were one-step above domesticated animals. One table of New York/New Jersey accents had given Elaine a particularly hard time. The women were whiny and asked a million questions about how the seafood was prepared. The men made rude suggestive comments as their leering eyes stared at her chest.

"I had one table, man, if they weren't customers, I would've punched them."

The oppressive heat of the day had seeped into the building, and she took a seat at the far end of the bar, close to one of the establishment's fans. Now she wanted to relax and have a few drinks before heading home to Bound Brook.

Provincetown was once a struggling Portuguese fishing community, but artists, writers and tourists had adopted the town. Its unique atmosphere, a blend of old-world charm and rugged seashore beauty, drew people from all corners of the earth. Elaine hadn't traveled far from the Cape, but she believed the people who said there was no other place quite like "P'town."

She knew most of the men in the bar. Fishermen and workmen, their clothes carried the odor of fish and sweat. They were regulars; some gave her a nod or a wink, but all of them gave her a long look through the smoky haze. No surprise, her tight black t-shirt and white shorts accentuated her curves. She pulled the bow from her ponytail, so the long, black hair framed her striking Mediterranean features. At thirty-one Elaine was still a male magnet, although her face was just starting to show the signs of a hard life: too much booze and too many men.

She was used to the attention, part of life when you are pretty and have a good shape. In her younger years, it had been her treasure— the only thing that got her noticed and made her feel worth something. Now, it seemed a burden. Mostly it got her the wrong kind of attention and combined with her own recklessness often caused trouble.

"Hey, Elaine, you still need a lift home?"

She looked up at Arnold "Moose" Parker, the bar's custodian, doorman, bouncer and general handyman. Moose had been her classmate at Bound Brook High.

"Sure, Moose, that would be great."

He gave her a shy smile and went back to his station by the door. She shook her head. Moose was an imposing figure and had been the class bully, but around women, he was meek and tongue-tied. Maybe she should have latched on to him instead of the string of low-life losers that dotted her life.

She pulled a crushed pack of Pall Malls out of her back pocket and shook out a cigarette.

The small flame from a lighter appeared. "Allow me."

On her left was a handsome man. He seemed to be around her age, maybe a little younger, with classic, chiseled features, short haircut and dressed in a polo shirt, tan slacks and shiny shoes.

"This seat taken?"

"Nope! Free country, free seat."

"Well, it's my lucky night, an open seat at the bar next to the prettiest girl on the Cape."

Elaine rolled her eyes and gave him a smirk. "Boy, that's original. So what's your rank?"

"It's that obvious?"

"Buzz cut hair, neat clean civvies, and I've never seen you before
. . . adds up to Camp Wellfleet. Also, the United States Army logo on
your cigarette lighter was a pretty good clue."

He threw his head back and laughed. "Ok, you nailed it. I'm Ted,
Ted Bowers, or Sergeant Bowers when I'm on the base. And you are?"

"Elaine Samuels, technically Elaine Stevens, but nobody,
including me, calls me that."

"I sense that there's a longer story there."

"Actually, a very short story. Army guy, like you, near the end of
the war, back from Germany. Another bar, another pick-up line, too
much to drink and it was love at first sight. A week later, we were
married and three days later he shipped out to God-knows-where.
Never seen him since and haven't missed him a bit." She took a long
pull from her beer.

"Well, I feel it's my responsibility to compensate for the U.S.
Army's dereliction of duty. Let me buy you something stronger than
that Gansett."

Elaine waved to Franky. "Rum and Coke, please."

"Gin and tonic," said Ted. "Put them on my tab."

Franky nodded, but gave Bowers a frown.

"So, you got my story, what's yours, Sergeant Ted Bowers? Why
did you join the army?"

"My father was army and he came from Mt. Carmel, Illinois. He
named me for a Union Civil War hero who came from that town and
had the same name. The combination sealed my fate; it was just
assumed I'd join the army."

"Following in Daddy's footsteps?"

"I hope not. He was a jerk, drank too much and beat my mother.
When I enlisted, it was either stay home and probably kill him or
answer the call of Uncle Sam."

"Well, that gives us one thing in common: my parents were
drunks."

"So, we probably should change the subject. Tell me about Cape Cod, and I'll tell you about some of the places I've been stationed that weren't in war zones."

*****

After the rum and Coke, Elaine switched to shots of bourbon while Ted nursed two more gin and tonics. Moose remembered Ted from the previous weekend. He'd been in Friday night, and walked around chatting with some of the guys. Then he'd gotten into a whispered conversation with Brian Francis, and the two of them had ducked out of the bar for ten minutes. Brian was not a nice guy, and not exactly the most law abiding. When they got back, Ted had chatted with Liz Santos and then later she had left with him. The next night Liz's father, Sal, had come in with murder in his eyes, looking for "that army guy." Fortunately, he wasn't there.

Moose gave Franky a look, then moved his eyes to the couple at the bar. Franky cocked his head and nodded, indicating that Moose should come over.

"You know that guy, Franky?"

"Not really, but I don't trust him. I know Elaine can take care of herself, but I wish she'd ditch him."

Moose nodded, "I get this feeling about him, like I know something, but I can't put my finger on it."

Franky leaned close and whispered, "Something happened with Liz Santos that made her old man mad as hell. Liz is a nice girl; I don't think she knows how to handle a guy like him. I wish Sal Santos had found him. I wouldn't want to mess with Sal when he's mad. If that guy did something to Liz, I'd give Sal a hand with the job."

"Wish I could remember where I've seen him before." Moose shook his head, but the memory didn't click. He went back to the door, where he focused his attention on Elaine and Ted.

The bar had started to empty. "Last call!" yelled Franky.

Part of Elaine was kicking herself: *Here we go again, another pick-up. When am I ever gonna learn?* However, Ted seemed intelligent and he certainly was good looking. He had striking eyes, grey or light blue maybe; she couldn't tell in the dim light. He had a trim, athletic build and well-toned muscles stretched his short sleeve shirt.

"This muggy heat is brutal. I'm new here, is there some place we could go to cool off? You must know all the beaches."

Elaine paused. "Sure, what the hell. I know a spot: a nice, cool pond. Let's go."

Ted threw a bunch of bills on the bar and gave Franky a nod.

Heading to the door, Elaine smiled at Moose. "I'm all set for a ride; thanks anyway. I'm gonna cool off my new friend in Bound Brook Pond."

"I can pick you up on my way home if you want."

Elaine gave him a tipsy giggle. "Maybe next time, old buddy."

"Alright." Moose glared at Ted. "Be careful ... both of you."

Ted winked. "Will do, big guy."

Out on Commercial Street, Elaine wobbled as they started down the sidewalk.

"Careful, kid." Ted took her arm. "Let me help; we've got to walk around the corner. It was so crowded I had to park on the backstreet."

They took a left on Standish to Bradford Street, where Ted had parked his army Jeep.

"I'm impressed; you get your own Jeep? Thought you were just a Sergeant."

"The Lieutenant is the only officer until tomorrow, and he is so green he needs me to tell him what to do. So, basically that leaves me in charge." He laughed. "Rank has its privileges, and you know Sergeants really run the army."

Bowers drove the road along the bay past rows of tourist cottages. A full moon reflected off the still water. In ten minutes, the road connected to the newly completed double-lane highway. A few minutes later, Elaine pointed to a road off the highway to the left. A bit over a mile down the twisty back road, she pointed left again and the Jeep turned down a rutted, dirt road with over-hanging branches that ended in a small parking lot overlooking a circular body of water twinkling in the moonlight. The outline of a small raft broke the mirror glass reflection.

Elaine leaped out of the open Jeep and ran down the slope. "Last one in's a rotten egg!"

Ted followed a trail of sneakers, shorts, and t-shirt as he heard a splash and then a screech. "Wow, that's cold."

He smiled as he removed his loafers, slacks and polo shirt. He waded up to his knees, took a deep breath and dove forward.

*****

Moose nodded to the last customer and locked the door. He looked at Franky, who was washing the last of the glasses.

"Franky, it just dawned on me, I think I know who that guy is, and if I'm right Elaine could be in trouble. Would you mind if I split out of here? I'm gonna take a ride to Bound Brook Pond."

"Think that might be a good idea. I'll sweep up for you."

"Thanks."

"Moose, you think you need to take that with you?" Franky pointed toward the baseball bat he kept behind the bar for protection.

"No, I'm sure I can handle things myself."

Moose hurried out the door, climbed in the old Chevy pick-up he had parked in the alley, cut through a driveway and came out on Bradford. The P'town police cruiser was parked in the gas station on the corner, and he waved to Tony Oliver who was waiting to pull over any drunks. Once he got past Tony, he picked up speed. Probably no other cops were out this late, and he had a sense of urgency.

Moose made good time on the empty highway, turned left on the paved back road and pulled the old pick-up onto the dirt road to the pond. He slowed down to try to minimize the truck's noisy bouncing, then put in the clutch and coasted alongside an army Jeep. With the engine off, he could hear splashing, voices and laughter. Then the laughter changed to anger.

"I told you NO, not here, not NOW!"

More muffled voices, then a deep voice, "DAMN, that hurt. I'll get you for that, bitch!"

Moose jumped out of the truck, ran down the slope and bumped into Elaine. The shadow of Ted was splashing out of the water with mumbled curses.

"Get in my truck."

"I'll just grab my clothes."

Ted squinted at the large form moving toward the water's edge. "She bit my hand. I'll probably need a tetanus shot. Look." Bowers stepped closer, holding out his hand as evidence.

Moose lunged, at the same time thrusting both arms forward. The heels of his hands hit Bowers in the solar plexus, the force driving him backward, where he sprawled in the shallow water.

"Stay away from Elaine! And I better not see you in the Mayflower again. You hear me?"

The only sound was Bowers gasping for breath.

Moose climbed the slope and found Elaine in the truck, dripping wet, but dressed in her shorts and t-shirt. "You alright?"

"Yeah, I'm fine. That jerk started getting rough."

"I'm taking you home."

"Thank God you got here, Moose."

He could feel himself blushing, as he mumbled, "No sweat."

Then the two were quiet as the pick-up bumped down the road and out to the highway. They only passed two other sets of headlights on the ride back to Bound Brook.

"Moose, would you mind staying with me tonight? I don't want to be alone. I just need to know someone is there."

"Sure, Elaine, I'll take care of you."

*****

Bowers stretched back in the shallow water and tried to stay calm. He'd had the wind knocked out of him before, and his brain told him he would be all right, while his body panicked without any air. Then a breath, a big intake of air, rushed to fill his lungs. In a few minutes, his breathing became steady.

Between the drinks and his lack of oxygen, Ted felt drained. He let the cool water lap over his body. His right hand now started to throb. With his left-hand fingers, he felt a ridge where Elaine's teeth had found their target. The fresh liquid was soothing, and he let himself relax. It would be easy to stay in the comforting pond. Despite the pain, he felt at peace. Maybe he could stay here floating in the calming fluid. Time slipped by.

His brain started to clear, and he realized his night was done. He might as well head back to the Camp. He had pressured the Lieutenant into giving him the night off. The poor kid was so new he needed Bowers to tell him what to do. So he had headed into Provincetown for the night: part business with Brian Francis and, he had hoped, part pleasure. With the new base commander and supporting team of officers due tomorrow afternoon, it might be his last chance for the rest of the summer.

Ted pulled himself up, stood calf deep in the pond and took a deep breath. A noise caught his attention. "Someone there?" A shadow came down the slope.

"Not you again? Okay, you made your point; I'll leave her alone, nothing happened anyway."

The shadow moved closer and he saw a slim figure, not Moose's bulky form. Then came recognition.

"Oh, I know you. What are you doing here?"

The figure stepped closer, one foot in the pond, a long arm raised high above its head. Bewildered, Ted couldn't comprehend how the arm could be so long. Too late he understood. The arm swung down, and some kind of club smashed into his shoulder. He screamed in pain as he heard a bone crack.

"What the hell are you doing?"

The long arm pulled back in a circular arc that ended with the club crashing down on Ted's skull. The last thing he heard was, "You shall reap what you sow."

Made in the USA
Middletown, DE
04 August 2021